THE IVORY DAGGER

Titles by Patricia Wentworth

THE IVORY
DAGGER

PATRICIA WENTWORTH

PERENNIAL LIBRARY

HARPER & ROW PUBLISHERS, New York
Grand Rapids, Philadelphia, St. Louis, San Francisco
London, Singapore, Sydney, Tokyo, Toronto

A hardcover edition of this book was originally published in 1951 by J. B. Lippincott Company.

THE IVORY DAGGER. Copyright © 1950 by Patricia Wentworth Turnbull. All rights reserved. Printed in the United States of America. No part of this book may be used or reproduced in any manner whatsoever without written permission except in the case of brief quotations embodied in critical articles and reviews. For information address Harper & Row, Publishers, Inc., 10 East 53rd Street, New York, N.Y. 10022.

First PERENNIAL LIBRARY edition published 1990.

ISBN 0-06-081027-0

90 91 92 93 94   OPM   10 9 8 7 6 5 4 3 2 1

THE IVORY DAGGER

CHAPTER 1

The young man in the hospital bed threw out an arm and turned over. His first conscious thought was that he must have called out, because the sound of his own voice was ringing in his ears, but he didn't know why he had called out or what he had said. He blinked at the light and got up on his elbow. There was a screen round his bed. The light came in over the screen. He blinked at it, and a nurse came round the edge of the screen and looked at him. She had a good plain face and nice eyes. She said, "Oh!" and then, "So you've waked up."

He said, "Where have I got to?"

She came right up to him and took hold of his wrist.

"Now don't you worry. The doctor will be along to see you in a minute."

"What do I want a doctor for? I'm all right."

She said, "That's fine. You were in a train smash. You just had a bump on the head."

He said, "Oh—" and then, "It feels all right."

She went away after that, and presently she came back again with some sort of milky cereal that tasted like baby food.

By the time this happened he had made sure

1

that he was all there and in one piece. Actually when she came round the screen he was out of bed seeing if he could stand on one leg. The leg felt shaky, so he wasn't too sorry to get back and take his scolding. It was part of a nurse's job to scold when you broke the rules.

She went away when he had finished the cereal, and he lay there wondering how long he had been in hospital. He had lost muscle, and his hands were a horrid sickly white. You don't lose a good strong tan in a day or two. He wondered just how much time he had lost, and how he had come to be in a train smash, and where he was now. The last thing he remembered was going to see Jackson in San Francisco. After that, "nix," as they said over here.

It was about twenty minutes before the doctor came—youngish, darkish, efficient. He led off just like the nurse.

"So you've waked up?"

This time he was ready to come back with a question of his own.

"How long have I been out?"

"Quite a while."

"How long?"

"A month."

"Nonsense!"

"Have it your own way."

He took a long breath and said,

"A month—"

The doctor nodded.

"Quite an interesting case."

2

"Do you mean to say I've been asleep for a month?"

"Well, no, not asleep—though you managed to put in a good bit of that too. Just no sense—didn't know who you were. Do you know now?"

"Of course. I'm Bill Waring. I came over about patents for my firm, Rumbolds, London. Electrical apparatus—all that sort of thing."

The doctor nodded.

"Well, you came in here as Gus G. Strohberger and it took us the best part of ten days to find out you weren't. We had to wait for the Strohberger family to get back from a trip and identify you, and when they said you weren't Gus we had to start all over again."

Bill stared.

"What happened to my papers?"

"The train caught fire. You're lucky to be here, you know. Gus didn't make it, but a grip with his name on it was only partly burned, and the guys who dug you out seemed to think it belonged to you. They got you just before the fire did. I'll say you're lucky."

Bill Waring grinned.

"Born to be hanged," he said cheerfully.

They didn't let him have his mail till next day. There was a very decent letter from old Rumbold dated ten days back. Very sorry to hear about the accident. Hoped he was making a good recovery. A pat on the back for having fixed everything up before he let a train smash get him. And he wasn't to hurry back till he was perfectly fit. There were other letters, but they didn't matter.

There was only one from Lila. Not airmail, and dated six weeks ago. It must have been waiting for him in New York when the train went to glory. He read it three times with a frowning intensity which would certainly have made Nurse Anderson adjure him to relax. She wasn't there, so he read the letter for the fourth time and continued to frown. There wasn't really anything very much to frown over. The letter wasn't very long or very informative. Lila Dryden was twenty-two. It might have been written by someone a good deal younger than that.

He read it a fifth time.

"Dear Bill,
    We have been very busy. It has been rather hot, and it would have been nicer in the country. I get tired in London. We dined with Sir Herbert Whitall and went to the theatre. His house has some wonderful things in it. He collects ivories, but I think most of them are rather ugly. There is a figure which he says is like me, but I hope it isn't. He is a friend of Aunt Sybil's and quite old. We are lunching with him tomorrow and going down to his place for the week-end. Aunt Sybil says it is a show place. She seems very fond of him, but I hope she isn't going to marry him, because I don't really like him very much. I thought I could go and stay with Ray Fortescue

4

whilst she did the week-end, but she says I must come too, and it isn't ever any good saying you won't if Aunt Sybil wants you to. She is calling me, so I must go.

Lila"

He folded the letter up and put it away in its envelope.

CHAPTER 2

"It was a very foolish affair," said Lady Dryden. "Cake, Corinna?"

Mrs. Longley looked, and fell. She said, "I oughtn't to," and helped herself to the larger of the two slices already cut from the dark rich cake.

Lady Dryden acquiesced grimly. They had been at school together, and in any case she never minced her words.

"You are putting on."

"Oh, Sybil!"

"Definitely," said Lady Dryden. "Cake at tea is absolutely fatal."

"Oh, well—"

"Of course, if you don't mind—"

Corinna Longley wanted to change the subject. She had been one of those slim, rather colourless fair girls with a lot of hair, wide sky-blue eyes, and pretty little hands and feet. At fifty the hands and feet were as small as ever. The hair now hovered between a mousy brown and grey, and the slim figure had spread. She minded, but not enough to do without cake at tea. It was all very well for Sybil, who would never put on an ounce or allow anything else to happen which was not exactly planned and provided for. She had always known just what she wanted, and she had always managed to get it. And the thing of all others which she had wanted and managed to get was her own way. It wasn't just luck. Some people got what they wanted, and Sybil Dryden was one of them. Look at the way she had managed this business of Lila's. She came back to it partly to get away from the subject of cake, and partly because it was going to be one of the marriages of the autumn and it would be nice to be in the know.

"You were telling me about Lila," she said. "Of course she is a very lucky girl. He is quite enormously rich, isn't he?"

Lady Dryden looked down her handsome nose and said in a repressive voice,

"Really, Corinna!" Then, after a slight pause, "Herbert Whitall is a man whom any girl might be proud to marry. He has money of course. Lila is not at all suited to be a poor man's wife. She is not very robust, you know, and a girl has a hard time now if she marries a professional man—all the work of the house to do, all the care of the children, and practically no help to be got. I agree that Lila is extremely lucky."

Mrs. Longley helped herself to the second piece of cake. She always did feel hungry at tea-time, and perhaps Sybil wouldn't notice.

The hope was vain. Lady Dryden's eyebrows rose. The pale, formidable eyes glanced at her with a momentary contempt. Very curious eyes, neither blue nor grey, but oddly bright between very dark lashes. People used to say she darkened them artificially, but it wasn't true. Sybil's eyes had always been just like that, pale and rather frightening, and the lashes really almost black. Corinna Longley said in a hurry,

"I expect you are right. My poor Anne has a dreadful time—three babies, and a doctor's house, which means meals at all sorts of hours, and not even daily help as often as not. I can't think how she does it. I'm sure I couldn't. But she takes after her father—so practical. Now Lila isn't practical, is she? But I did like Bill Waring."

Lady Dryden repeated a previous remark.

"A very stupid affair. More tea, Corinna?"

"Oh, thank you. Is he still in America?"

"I imagine so."

"Did he—did he—how did he take it?"

Lady Dryden set down the teapot.

"My dear Corinna, you really mustn't talk as if Lila had thrown him over. The whole stupid affair just faded out."

Mrs. Longley took her cup, and said, "Oh, no, thank you" to sugar, in the hope that this would be accounted to her for righteousness. Buoyed up with a feeling of virtue, she ventured to say,

7

"It faded out?"

Lady Dryden nodded.

"A few months' separation gives young people a chance of finding out whether they really care for each other. Very few of these boy-and-girl affairs stand the test."

Mrs. Longley reflected that an engagement between a girl of twenty-two and a man of twenty-eight hardly came into this category, but she knew better than to say so. She made one of those murmuring sounds which encourage the person who is talking to proceed, and was duly rewarded.

Lady Dryden went on.

"I don't mind telling you that I said a word to Edward Rumbold—he's the head of young Waring's firm and a very old friend. So when he told me they were sending someone out to America—something to do with patents—I said, 'What about giving Bill Waring the chance?' I don't know if it made any difference. I believe there was someone else they were going to send, but he was ill. Anyhow Bill went, and the whole thing just faded out."

"You mean he didn't write?"

Lady Dryden gave a short laugh.

"Oh, reams by every post at first. Too unrestrained. And then—well, just nothing at all."

Mrs. Longley's eyes widened to their fullest extent.

"Sybil—you *didn't!*"

Lady Dryden laughed again.

"My dear Corinna! You've been reading Victorian novels—*Hearts Divided*, or *The Intercepted Let-*

ters. Nothing so sensational, I'm afraid. Americans are very hospitable. Bill Waring found himself in a rush of business by day and amusement by night. He was very well entertained, and he didn't find or make time to write to Lila. She didn't like being left flat, and Herbert Whitall made the running. That's the whole story, and no melodrama about it. She is a very lucky girl, and they are being married next week. You got your card?"

"Oh, yes—I'm looking forward to it. I expect her dress is lovely. He has given her pearls, hasn't he?"

"Yes. Fortunately they suit her."

Mrs. Longley leaned forward to put down her cup. She began to collect a bag, gloves, a handkerchief, talking as she did so.

"Well, I must go. Allan likes me to be in when he comes home. Of course pearls are lovely, but my mother wouldn't let me wear the little string Aunt Mabel left me—not on my wedding day. She said pearls were tears, and she took them away and locked them up. And of course I've been very happy, though I don't suppose it had anything to do with the pearls."

At this point she dropped her bag. It opened, her purse fell out and a compact rolled. When she had retrieved it from under the tea-table she felt suddenly brave enough to say,

"He *is* a lot older than she is, isn't he?"

Lady Dryden said coldly,

"Herbert Whitall is forty-seven. Lila is an extremely lucky girl."

Afterwards Corinna Longley was surprised at

her own courage. She told Allan all about it when she got home.

"I just felt I must say something. Of course he's got all that money, and she'll have a lovely house, and a proper staff of servants, and everything like that. But he *is* a lot older, and I *don't* like his face, and she *was* in love with Bill Waring."

At the time, she fixed swimming blue eyes on Lady Dryden's face and said with a choke in her voice,

"Is she happy, Sybil?"

CHAPTER 3

Lila Dryden stood looking at herself in the glass which not only gave back the slim perfection of her figure but repeated it in the great wall-mirror behind her. She could see how beautifully her wedding dress was cut. She had wanted something softer and whiter, but that was when she was planning to marry Bill Waring. She didn't really like the deep, heavy satin which Aunt Sybil had chosen. It reminded her of the ivory figure in Herbert Whitall's collection. He had brought it out and set it on the mantelpiece for everyone to see and said that it was like her. She hated it. It was very old. She hated being told that she was like something which was thousands of years old. It made her feel as if—no, she didn't know what it made her feel, but she didn't like it.

She looked into the mirror and saw her own slim ivory figure repeated endlessly. She didn't like that either. It was like a rather horrid dream. Hundreds of Lila Drydens going away down an endless shadowy vista—hundreds of them, all with her pale gold hair and the ivory satin dress which Aunt Sybil had chosen.

The ivory figure had once had golden hair. The gold had worn away because the figure was so very old, but Herbert Whitall had held it under the light for her to see how the gilding still clung to it here and there. She heard him say in the voice which frightened her most, "Gold and ivory—like you, my beautiful Lila."

These thoughts didn't take any time. They were there, just as the carpet was there under her feet. The carpet was there, and the floor was solid under it. It was silly to feel as if she was floating away to join all those gold and ivory Lilas in that queer looking-glass world. She heard Sybil Dryden say,

"Do you think it would bear to come in the least possible shade at the waist?" And Madame Mirabelle's instant and emotional reaction, "Oh, but non, non, non, non, non! It is *perfect*—absolutely *perfect*. I will not take the responsibility to touch it. Mademoiselle will be the most beautiful bride, and she will have the most beautiful dress—of a perfection, of a simplicity! One would say a statue of the antique!" Her short, stout figure came into the mirror—a hundred Mirabelles going away to a van-

11

ishing point, all black, all wonderfully corseted, with waving hands and a torrent of words.

Sybil Dryden nodded.

"Yes, it's good," she said, in her calm, unhurried way.

She stood up and came into the picture too, another black figure, but a slim one. She carried herself with distinction. Everything about her was just as it should be, from the faultless waves just touched with grey at the temples to the slender arch of foot. The black coat and skirt conveyed no suggestion of mourning. There was a flash of diamonds in the lace at the throat. The small hat achieved just the right note of restrained elegance, endlessly repeated by the mirrors.

Hundreds of Aunt Sybils . . . Lila saw them in a swirling mist. She heard Mirabelle exclaim, and the mist broke into a shower of sparks.

Lady Dryden was nothing if not efficient. She caught the swaying figure as it fell, and since a white sheet had been spread on the floor of the fitting-room, the wedding dress took no harm.

CHAPTER 4

Ray Fortescue got off her bus and walked up the street. She was wearing her new autumn suit, because nothing gives you so much confidence as to feel that you are looking your best. The suit was a success, and so was the little off-the-face hat that went with it. They were perfectly matched, and they were just two shades lighter than her dark brown hair. There was a spray of autumn leaves and berries on the hat, repeating the gay lipstick which went so well with the clear brown of her skin. She wasn't a beauty, but she had her points, and she knew how to make the most of them. Her eyes were a clear amber with very dark lashes, and they were widely set. Her face showed balance, character, control, and she had the figure which most girls long for. It looked very well in the brown suit.

She rang the bell at the small house where the window-boxes were gay with asters against very bright green paint. Whatever Lady Dryden said and whatever Lady Dryden did, she was going to see Lila. Lila might call Lady Dryden Aunt Sybil and be well down under her thumb, but when all was said and done they weren't really relations at all. Old John Dryden had adopted Lila, and then five years later Sybil had married him and more or less bullied him into his grave. She remembered his giving them sweets behind Sybil's back, a nice woolly old thing and always finishing up with "Better not let your aunt know. She thinks they're bad for you. But—" chuckling—"we know better, don't we?" Not an awfully good way to bring up a child, but that was the sort of thing that happened under a totalitarian regime.

Lady Dryden's elderly parlourmaid opened the door.

"Good afternoon, Palmer. I've come to see Miss Lila."

Palmer looked down her long thin nose. Imitation is the sincerest form of flattery, but with the best will in the world it didn't really come off. Lady Dryden had the nose for it and Palmer hadn't, but she went on trying.

"Well, I don't know, I'm sure, Miss Ray. She fainted this morning after her last fitting, and her ladyship was very particular she should be kept quiet."

Ray's spirits soared. Lady Dryden had obviously gone out. A nice colour came up in her cheeks. She smiled her wide, warm smile and walked into the hall.

"Oh, yes—she is doing far too much. Get a big stick and keep out everyone but me! I don't count, but everyone else can just go home again. Where is she—in her room?"

She was half way up the narrow stair before Palmer could finish a "Well, her ladyship said—"

and round the turn before she gave up with a sniff and went back down the basement stairs. Her ladyship wouldn't be pleased—she knew that well enough—but how was she going to stop Miss Ray? First cousins are not much different to sisters. And Miss Ray a bridesmaid too. She sniffed again and prepared to be aggrieved.

Lila was on the sofa. She looked lovely and fragile. She had a make-up box on her lap with samples of lipstick, rouge, and nail-polish. She had just been trying a sample called apple-blossom and was contemplating the result in the ivory handglass which belonged to her new dressing-case. She was sorry about its being ivory, but Herbert wouldn't hear of anything else. All the things were inlaid with a delicately traced initial in pale gold, and everyone admired them very much. She looked up when Ray came in, and said in a languid voice,

"I'm trying all my samples. Do you like this apple-blossom thing?"

Ray sat down and gave the matter her critical attention.

"Yes, it's very good. You'd better stick to it. The lipstick is a marvellous match."

"They all go together. I've just done one nail with the polish. I thought it was good. I look frightful in most of the shades—they're too bright."

"You can't stand those bright things. I've told you so again and again."

"You wear them." Lila's voice had a fretful tone.

Ray laughed.

"Well, if I didn't decorate the face a bit, no one

15

would look at it. Anyhow it's not your style. You stick to your apple-blossom, and you can hand me over all those nice barbaric shades."

Lila pushed the box away.

"I look frightful anyway," she said. "I fainted this morning whilst I was having that horrible wedding dress tried on."

There was just the least trace of satisfaction in the mournful tone.

Ray took a good deep breath.

"If it's horrible, why wear it?"

Lila laid down the ivory glass. Her hand shook. Her voice shook too.

"Aunt Sybil chose it."

"Can't you choose anything for yourself?"

"You know I can't."

"Not even the man?"

Lila began to cry in a gentle, childish manner. The tears welled up in her lovely eyes and trickled down over her lovely cheeks. Her lips quivered.

"You know I can't."

Ray fished a clean handkerchief out of the pocket of her brown suit and tossed it over.

"Stop it!" she said briskly. "What's the good of going on spilling the milk and then crying because it's spilt? I've come here to tell you something, and you've got to dry your eyes and listen."

Lila dabbed with the handkerchief.

"Wh-what is it?"

"I met Mr. Rumbold this morning."

"D-did you?"

"He said Bill was coming home."

16

Lila stopped dabbing and said, "Oh—"

"Tomorrow."

Lila said, "Oh—" again.

"Boat train from Southampton."

Lila dropped her handkerchief. Her fingers twined helplessly.

"What is the good?"

"Well, there's really nothing to stop you meeting the train, is there?"

"I couldn't!"

"Oh, yes, you could. You could meet the train. You could tell Bill that Lady Dryden has bullied you into saying you'll marry Herbert Whitall but you don't want to, and what about it? I gather Bill's due for a rise, and it only takes three days to get married. *What about it?*"

Lila sat bolt upright. She looked terrified.

"I couldn't—I couldn't—*I couldn't!* He didn't write—he hasn't written for ages. Aunt Sybil always did say it wouldn't come to anything, and that just showed. And it wasn't a real engagement—Aunt Sybil always said it wasn't."

Ray's brows made a stern dark line above eyes that were bright with anger.

"And what Aunt Sybil says goes? For God's sake, Lila, wake up! It's you and Bill who know whether you were engaged to each other, not Lady Dryden. If you were happy, I wouldn't say a word. If you wanted to marry Herbert Whitall, I wouldn't say a word. But you're not happy. And you don't want to marry him. And you're of age. You're perfectly free to walk out of this house and meet Bill

Waring's train. You're like a rabbit in a trap. Well, the door is open and you can walk out. Are you going to be mesmerized into staying in the trap until the door isn't open any more and you *can't* get out?"

Lila went on looking terrified.

"He didn't write," she said.

"He didn't write because he couldn't. He was in an accident—he's been in hospital. Mr. Rumbold told me. But he's all right again now, and he's coming home tomorrow. What are you going to do about it?"

Two big tears ran down over the apple-blossom. Lila said faintly,

"I can't—I can't do anything—"

"You can—if you want to."

She shook her head.

"It's too late. All the invitations have gone out—there are three hundred wedding presents. I can't do anything now."

On the last word the door was briskly opened and Lady Dryden came in.

CHAPTER 5

Bill Waring jumped down on to the platform. He hailed a porter and directed him briefly, but all the time his eyes were on the barrier, looking for Lila. There was a bit of a crowd there—people waiting to get through for the next train. He would see her in a moment. He had sent off his cable and followed it up by a telegram from Southampton, so she was simply bound to be there. The trouble was he couldn't see her. He hurried the porter, picked out his luggage, and went striding away to give up his ticket.

But when he had passed the barrier it wasn't Lila who came up to him with both hands out, but Ray—Ray Fortescue with her shining eyes and her wide, warm smile. She said, "Oh, Bill!" and before he knew what he was going to do he had kissed her. It happened just like that. Her mouth smiled, her eyes shone, and he kissed her. And why not? They had known each other long enough. She was Lila's cousin and the best friend in the world.

He kept his hold of her, a hand on either side of her shoulders, and said,

"Where's Lila?"

"She couldn't come."

A first premonitory fear made him say quickly,

"She's not ill?"

"No."

"She's not in town? But I wired to Holmbury as well—"

Ray Fortescue said,

"She couldn't come. Lady Dryden. . . . Look here, I'll tell you all about it—there's been rather a hoo-ha. But we must get away from here. You're coming back with me. Cousin Rhoda will be out. We'll have the flat to ourselves, and I'll tell you all about everything. Lila isn't ill—she just couldn't come. Look—that's your porter, isn't it? We'll have to go and queue for a taxi."

He gave her a long look before he let go. There was something up, but she wasn't going to tell him what it was—not here. The deep antagonism which had always been between him and Sybil Dryden rose up in him. Lila was a great deal too much under her thumb. Just because your husband adopts a distant relation it doesn't mean you've a right to own her body and soul. When they were married Lady Dryden was going to be put in her place. It was nice of Ray to come and meet him. He felt warmly towards her.

She walked beside him and made pleasant talk. Underneath she stiffened herself. If you've got to run knives into the person you love best in the world, well, you've got to. No good sickening and shrinking. It was better for her to do it than anyone else, because she loved him. She never made any bones about that. She loved Bill, and Bill loved Lila. As a matter of fact she loved Lila too. You couldn't help it. Lila was the sort of fragile, helpless creature who needed to be loved. But loving her wasn't enough. Neither she, nor Bill, nor anyone else could speak with her voice and say no to Herbert Whitall and Sybil Dryden. Between them they gave her about as much chance as a gossamer thread would have in a roaring gale.

She looked at Bill and saw him grave, with a waiting look. He was thinner. His hair wanted brushing—the rough fair hair which never would lie down for very long. In his blunt-featured way he was as fair as Lila. He oughtn't to have fallen in love with her, but of course he had. Those large men always did fall for something lovely and helpless.

Their eyes met.

"What is it? Ray, what is it?"

Not here—not now. She said quickly as the taxi turned a corner,

"You're thinner."

"I was in a train smash. It knocked me out for a month."

Ray felt her heart miss a beat. That was what could happen when seas divided you. He could be in a train smash—in hospital. He could have been dead and buried, and she wouldn't have known—not till she met Mr. Rumbold, as she had met him yesterday, by chance. He had said, "Waring's back home tomorrow—Bill Waring." But if Bill had died out there in America, she would have had to hear him say, "I suppose you've heard about Bill Waring. A train smash—shocking affair. . . . Yes, he's dead."

She said, "Oh, Bill!" and put her hand on his arm. She didn't know that her colour was all gone, and that fear had brimmed up in her eyes.

He laughed and said,

"Don't look like that—I'm all here. I cabled as soon as I came round, so I hope no one worried."

She took her hand away.

"I didn't know—I don't think anyone knew."

He was frowning.

"It's the best part of the three weeks since I cabled Lila. Haven't you been seeing her?"

"Not very often."

"Ray—what *is* all this? Why haven't you seen her? Has she been ill? Have you quarrelled?"

"No, of course not. She just hasn't had time. Lady Dryden's been rushing her off her feet—and you know what she's like. Lila just can't stand up to her."

He turned away with an abrupt movement and sat staring out of the window for the rest of the way. But when they had paid off the taxi, and left the luggage in the hall, and gone up in the small automatic lift to the flat where Ray boarded with a middle-aged cousin, he turned round from shutting the sitting-room door and said bluntly,

"What's wrong? You'd better let me have it."

Ray said, "Yes."

She went over to the piano and stood there looking down at the polished rosewood top and stripping off her gloves. Cousin Rhoda always would keep flowers on the piano. The red and bronze chrysanthemums were reflected in the polished wood, their colours dimmed and withdrawn. She said slowly,

"Yes, there's something wrong."

"What is it?"

"Haven't you heard from Lila?"

"No."

She said, "Oh!" It was an involuntary sound of pain. She came a step nearer. "She ought to have written—somebody ought to have written."

"What is it?"

After all, you can't break bad news, you can only tell it. She made her voice steady and told him.

"She is going to marry Sir Herbert Whitall."

There was a frightful silence. Herbert Whitall's name seemed to hang in it. It went on and on.

In the end Ray made herself move—look at him. He had the thick pale skin which sometimes goes with great physical strength. Now, with all the blood drained from it, he had a ghastly air. He said in a horrid strained voice,

"It's not true."

Well, she had to convince him, push the knife right home and kill the thing which wouldn't let go of its belief in Lila. It was quite horrible, but it had got to be done. She said, "Bill—" and in a moment he had her by the shoulders.

"It's a lie! I say it's a lie!"

She was held in a bruising grip. His eyes blazed, his voice came thick with stumbling words.

"It's a lie! She couldn't—you're making it up! Say it isn't true!"

She said nothing at all, only let her eyes meet the fury in his with a long sorrowful look.

They stayed like that until suddenly he took his hands away and stood back.

"I'm sorry." He looked at his hands in an odd bewildered manner, and then at her. "I didn't mean to hurt you."

Her bruised shoulders were rather a relief than otherwise, but she couldn't tell him that. She said,

"It doesn't matter."

"What's been going on?"

"You didn't write. Lady Dryden made the most of that. Herbert Whitall made the running."

He said in that stumbling voice,

"I sent her a cable—three weeks ago. And one the day I sailed. I wrote five letters—after I came round—in the hospital."

"She hasn't had them—I'm sure she hasn't had them."

"Someone is going to pay for that."

His voice had cleared and steadied. There was a frightening edge to it. She wanted to cry out. Instead she rushed into speech.

"Bill—you mustn't—it's no good. I've done my best—I really have. I'd do anything—you know I would."

"Yes. It's not your fault. I must see Lila."

Ray looked at him. In her own mind something said, "You can't help people who won't help themselves. Lila won't help herself." She stood silent

24

because she had nothing to say.

And then Bill had himself in hand. Something closed down over the naked anger which had dominated him. She knew that it was there, but a door had been shut on it and a guard set. He began to fire questions at her.

"Are they engaged?"

"Yes."

"It's given out?"

"Yes."

"Rather fast work, wasn't it? But they couldn't afford to let the grass grow under their feet. I might have come home. I have come home. They've not been quite clever enough. Anything fixed about the wedding?"

"Yes."

"When?"

She wanted to look away, but she couldn't. She said,

"Next week."

There was no change in his face.

"I've got to see her."

"Lady Dryden won't let you in."

He laughed.

"Let her try and keep me out!"

Her colour rose. She came a step nearer.

"Bill, that's no good. If you crash your way in, there'll be a scene."

"Do you think I care?"

"No, but Lila will. If there's a scene, she'll be frightened, and if she's frightened she'll go to bits."

He said with a sort of deadly calm,

"I'm going to see her."

"It's no good crashing in."

He walked across to the window and came back again.

"No—you're right. I'll see her here. Ring up and tell her to come round. Don't say anything about me. Just get her to come."

"She'll know you're here."

"How?"

"I told her. I tried to get her to come and meet the train."

"What did she say?"

"She said it was too late."

Lila's voice came to her with its plaintive note— "All the invitations . . . three hundred presents. . . . " You couldn't say that to Bill.

He said sharply,

"It wouldn't be too late if she was walking up the aisle! If I don't see her anywhere else I'll see her there. You'll ring her up, and you'll tell her I'm here. If she wants a scene, I'll come round and make one. If she doesn't want a scene she'll come here. Tell her that!"

The telephone stood on one of Cousin Rhoda's gimcrack tables, its utilitarian outline disguised by a simpering doll with spreading green and lavender skirts which were rather the worse for the London grime. As Ray dialled she had the feeling that the numbers which she was releasing one by one were like birds flying—like the birds which had been released from the Ark, floating in turmoil and tempest. The fantastic image passed through her mind and was gone. It left her with a sense of inevitability. Bill had told her to ring up and she had rung, and now everything that was going to happen would happen.

The click of the receiver being lifted, and Palmer saying "Hullo!" Her own voice quite smooth and steady.

"Good evening, Palmer. It's Ray Fortescue. Can I speak to Miss Lila?"

The line was very clear. Bill, standing behind her, could hear Palmer sniff. They could both hear her say,

"They've gone down into the country, Miss Lila and her ladyship. A week-end party at Vineyards."

She hung up. Bill said,

"What's Vineyards? Whitall's place?"

"Yes."

"Where?"

She told him.

He said, "Thanks," and went out of the room without another word. The door of the flat fell to behind him.

Ray stood there and was afraid.

CHAPTER 6

Vineyards lay in the lap of the Downs. There was woodland to the right and to the left, with the house in a clear space between and the ground falling from terrace to terrace full in the eye of the sun. The site was much older than the house. There had been a Roman villa there. It was a Roman who had planted the first vines on those sunny slopes. The bomb which struck the third terrace had brought to light a tessellated pavement deep down under the soil. There was no sign of war damage now, but the painted tiles were displayed in the County museum. After the Romans had gone and the Normans had come in, there had been a religious foundation, and monks had worked on the vines with sleeves rolled up and gowns hitched out of the way. Their house had gone as the Roman villa had gone, swept away by fire after the dissolution of the monasteries under Henry VIII. Elizabeth gave the demesne to Humphrey de Lisle, and he built on it a simple, beautiful house with which he and five generations of de Lisles were vastly content. The vines languished and were done away with, all except the famous one on the house, and, sole survivor of the lower vineyards, another giant which hung all one side of the bottom terrace with graceful leaves and clusters of pale green grapes. The de Lisles petered out like the vines. The last daughter of the house took the property into the Wootton family, who added a pillared front and ruined the Elizabethan hall with a marble staircase in the Italian style, complete with caryatids holding lamps. They also built on right and left, and presently ruined themselves. Vineyards was sold, and sold again. During the nineteenth century it changed hands four times. In 1940 it was requisitioned by the Air Ministry.

Six years later Herbert Whitall bought it and began to set it in order. Adrian Grey, who was neither secretary, architect nor steward, but an informal blend of all three, considered that they had made a pretty good job of it. The terraces went down in beauty, and the house had lost some of its excrescences. Only in the matter of the marble staircase had Herbert Whitall been quite intractable. He actually liked the beastly thing.

Discerning this unpalatable fact, Adrian, a peaceful soul, had sighed and put away his beautifully drawn reconstruction of the original oak stair going up nobly to the gallery which ran round three sides of the hall and served the bedroom wings. He was a tall, thin man with the scholar's stoop which five years of military service had failed to correct. He had been wounded, a long time in hospital with a leg injury which would not heal, and finally relegated to light duty. For the rest, he was forty years old, of a kindly and gentle disposition, and inclined towards peace with all men—even with Herbert

Whitall, who sometimes tried him to the limit. Just lately it had once or twice occurred to him that the limit might be past. If this were to happen, he would find other interests, and he was fortunate in possessing a modest private income, but he would miss Vineyards very much.

He stood on the upper terrace and looked away to a distant glimpse of the sea. The evenings were beginning to draw in. There was still sunlight, but it had a golden autumn look like the leaves which gilded the dark mass of woodland on either side. This terrace was a suntrap. He set a knee on the low marble balustrade and found it warm to the touch. There was no wind stirring. The night would be clear, and tomorrow would be fine again. This autumn weather was the best of all the year.

He went on looking away towards the sea and finding it good to be alone. House-parties were not much in his line, and he would have to entertain Lady Dryden, who always made him feel as if he had nothing to say. It did not matter of course, because she could, and did, do all the talking herself—which ought to be a relief, but in fact gave him the feeling of being out in a very high wind.

He had got as far as this in his thoughts, when a very faint sound made him turn his head. Lila Dryden had come through one of the long windows which still stood wide to the terrace. She wore a grey flannel coat and skirt and a white jumper, and she was bare-headed. Her pale gold hair was the only colour about her until the gold lashes lifted and he saw the forget-me-not blue of her eyes.

She came over and sat down on the balustrade.

"They're talking," she said.

"Yes?"

"About me. I wish they wouldn't."

She had known Adrian Grey for almost as long as she could remember. He had planned and built a marvellous doll's house for her when she was seven years old. Grown-up people generally tried to make you do something you didn't want to do. But not Adrian. He always tried to find out what you did want to do, then he helped you to do it. It gave you a very safe, restful kind of feeling. She was twenty-two now, but she had never had cause to change that seven-year-old opinion. People wanted things, and they pushed until they got them. They said it was for your good, or that you owed it to them, or that they were in love with you, but it all came to the same in the end—they pushed, and you had to give way. Only Adrian didn't push. He listened, and he was kind.

He was being kind now. He said,

"Never mind, my dear."

The blue eyes were lifted. They had a wincing look.

"It's Aunt Sybil—why does she want to make me?"

He said very gently indeed,

"What is she making you do?"

"Why does she want me to marry Herbert?"

"Don't you want to?"

31

Her eyes were bright with tears. She shook her head.

"I don't want to marry anyone. I'm frightened."

He sat down beside her on the parapet.

"Look here, my dear, don't you think you've just got the wind up? You know my sister Marian—the one with the jolly husband and four boys. Well, two days before her wedding she came to me and said she couldn't go through with it, and I must tell Jack. She said she knew she was a wretch and her name would be mud, but she couldn't marry him, and that was that. So at last I went and told him. He burst out laughing and said, 'We'll soon see about that!' Well, as soon as she saw him she flung her arms round his neck and began to cry, and said she thought she wasn't ever going to see him again. I went away and left them to it. Afterwards, when I asked her what she meant by making a fool of herself and me, she just laughed and said it was stage fright and I oughtn't to have taken any notice. Now don't you think—?"

"No—" she shook her head mournfully—"I'm not like that."

"Are you sure?"

She nodded.

"You don't understand."

"Suppose you try and tell me—that is, if you want to."

She nodded again. It was always easy to tell Adrian. He didn't push, and he didn't fuss, and he didn't try to make you say what you didn't mean. A momentary colour came into her face. Her eyes fell.

"I don't like being touched—"

"My dear child!"

He was too deeply disturbed and concerned to keep the sound of it out of his voice.

She took his hand in both of hers and held it with a kind of quivering intensity.

"I can't bear it—with almost anyone. Even with Bill I didn't like it when he really kissed me—and I'm fond of Bill—I really am."

"Bill Waring?"

She nodded. Her eyes were brimming over.

"Aunt Sybil said we weren't engaged. It wasn't given out—because he was going to America. And she said, 'Wait till he comes back.' Only he didn't write. Ray says he was in hospital—he'd had an accident. And she wanted me to meet his train—but I couldn't, could I? Only afterwards I thought if I had, perhaps I wouldn't have had to marry Herbert."

"Don't you want to marry him?"

Her clasp became agonized. Her "Oh, no—" came on a long sighing breath.

"But, my dear child, why did you ever say you would?"

"She made me—Aunt Sybil."

"But, Lila—"

"She can make you do anything. It's not only me. She pushes and pushes until you just can't go on saying no." She looked up at him very piteously. "Why does she want me to marry him?"

"I don't know, Lila. But no one can make you do it if you don't want to."

She let go of his hand as suddenly as she had caught at it.

"You don't understand."

The tired, hopeless tone wrung his heart. He had to wait a moment before he said,

"Lila—listen! Tell Lady Dryden, and tell Whitall, that you want a little more time. It isn't usual for an engagement and a wedding to be run together in a few weeks. I don't think they would like any talk about it, and if you said you felt you were being rushed, I don't see how they could refuse to give you more time."

She made a slight helpless movement.

"It's no good. I've tried—last night. She wouldn't listen. The invitations are out."

"She could say you had measles or something. My cousin Elizabeth Baillie did that."

"Aunt Sybil wouldn't."

It was impossible to make himself believe that she would. Feeling like that about it, there really wasn't much chance of convincing Lila. His thoughts recurred to Bill Waring. There had been something about meeting a train. If it was a case of meeting trains, Bill must be back. He gazed at her in an unhappy way and put the question.

"Is Bill Waring back?"

"Yes, he *is*."

"Have you seen him?"

"Oh, *no*."

An unaccustomed frown drew his brows together.

"You said something about meeting a train. When did he get back?"

She caught her breath.

"It was yesterday. Ray wanted me to go and meet him. Adrian, I couldn't—could I?"

Instead of saying, "Not if you didn't want to," which was what she expected, he took her by surprise.

"Why couldn't you?" •

A faint flush tinged her cheeks. Her eyes widened.

"The invitations—Aunt Sybil—"

"That wouldn't have stopped you if you had really wanted to go." He waited a moment, and then said, "Would it?"

She looked at him like a pleading child.

"He didn't write. Aunt Sybil said he'd forgotten all about me. I didn't know he'd had an accident."

"Did he have an accident?"

"Ray said he did. She said he was in hospital and he didn't even know who he was. So he couldn't write, could he? But he's all right again now—she met Mr. Rumbold, and he told her."

"And you still didn't want to go and meet him?"

She hung her head.

"I thought he'd be angry—about my marrying Herbert."

"My dear child! You wouldn't expect him to be pleased—would you?"

Her hand came out and slipped into his.

"I *can't* bear it when people are angry. Bill gets dreadfully angry."

"With you?"

She said in a doubtful voice,

"No—not really. But if he did, I couldn't bear it. There was a man throwing stones at a dog—its leg was broken—I thought Bill was going to kill him. He frightened me *dreadfully*."

If Adrian felt an inclination to smile, he subdued it. He could imagine Bill Waring dealing out summary justice. With a genuine desire for knowledge, he enquired,

"What did he do?"

Lila shuddered.

"He knocked him down, and when he got up he knocked him down again. The poor man's nose was bleeding dreadfully. And he looked as if he liked it—"

"The man?"

This time there was no doubt about the smile.

Lila gazed reproachfully.

"No—Bill. And he did the dog's leg up in a splint and took it to the vet. So you see I do know what he's like when he's angry. And it's no use Ray saying go and meet the train, because I couldn't. And anyhow it was yesterday."

There was relief in the conclusion, but in a moment it gave way to fear.

"Adrian, it's dreadful—Ray says he's coming down. That's why I had to find you."

"Bill is coming down here?"

"Oh, *yes*. And he *mustn't*. She says he wants to

36

see me. And it isn't any good, Adrian, is it? She rang me up and told me—just now, while Aunt Sybil and Herbert were talking. She said he had to stay in town today and see Mr. Rumbold, and then he was coming down. And I said it wasn't any good, and please not to let him come, and she said, 'You can't put a cyclone in your pocket.' Ray says things like that. And I didn't know what she meant, but I thought it sounded as if he might be quite dreadfully angry. Don't you think so?"

He said very moderately,

"If he loves you, you couldn't expect him not to be angry when he heard you were going to marry someone else—especially if he thought you and he were still engaged."

She said, "Oh—" Then, in a wavering voice, "It wasn't given out."

"I don't think he would feel that made any difference."

She pulled her hand away.

"But he mustn't come. You won't let him, will you? Aunt Sybil would be quite dreadfully angry—and—and Herbert. You'll stop him, won't you?"

Adrian Grey had been blessed, or cursed, with a good deal of imagination. It provided him with a vivid picture of Bill Waring determined on an interview with Lila and quite unlikely to stick at trifles in order to get what he wanted. With Lady Dryden and Herbert Whitall participating, there were all the ingredients of a really first-class row. What he could not see was what he could possibly do to prevent it. He had never felt any urge to ride the whirlwind and control the storm. At the best he could only hope to hold a humble umbrella over Lila's cherished head.

She said, "You *won't* let him come!" And all he could say was, "I'll do what I can."

They seemed to have reached an impasse. What he wanted to do was to pick her up and take her away. He had a car in the garage, and enough petrol to take her to Marian. She was of age, and nobody could stop them. It was a perfectly possible thing to do, and he could no more have done it than he could have done any of the other things which were against his code. Afterwards he was to reproach himself very bitterly. At the time he could only look at her.

Just what he would have said, he didn't know, because Miss Whitaker came out on to the terrace in her neat clerical grey with its high-necked shirt and severe black tie. She was the real secretary, and it was stamped all over her. Not badlooking in a rigid way—dark hair impeccably waved, hands carefully tended, eyes quite good if a little closely set, eyebrows shaped to an arch. She came briskly up to them and addressed Lila.

"Lady Dryden is asking for you."

CHAPTER 7

Herbert Whitall was in his study, which was so exactly like what a study ought to be that there was very little more to be said about it. The only thing it lacked was that indefinable something which suggests that a room has been lived and worked in for many generations. So far as the actual structure was concerned, this was true enough. It was one of the eighteenth-century rooms, well proportioned and well lighted, and it had had time to mellow. Adrian Grey, who had had a hand in assembling the furniture, came to the conclusion that everything was a little too much of one period, with none of those treasured shabby survivals which are generally to be found in a room where a man expects to take his ease. The handsome curtains were as new as yesterday. There wasn't so much as a rubbed place on arm or seat of any of the leather-covered chairs. It was a good room, a perfectly suitable room, but it missed the touch of familiar comfort.

But then no one would have called Herbert Whitall a comfortable person. His grandfather, shrewd and coarse, had made one of the large mid-Victorian fortunes. Railways, iron, steel—whatever he touched just turned to gold. His son achieved a baronetcy. Herbert Whitall, a competent business man, confirmed the family fortunes, and was understood to have political ambitions. The best tailor in Savile Row had conferred elegance upon a tall, spare frame. He had the high, thin nose and the straight, thin lips of the FitzAscelins. His mother was Adela FitzAscelin, in direct descent from the Ascelin of Ghent who had come over with the Conqueror. If it was this strain which gave him his taste for curious ivories, the stubborn Whitall stock declared itself in the ruthless zest with which the taste was pursued. To lose to another collector was unimaginable. What he fancied, he must have, no matter what the effort or the cost. He had a cold acquisitive eye, and the long, thin hands of his mother's family. But whereas the FitzAscelins had for many generations been letting everything slip, Herbert Whitall could pride himself on the fact that he got what he wanted and knew how to keep it.

He stood in front of the hearth and spread those long fingers to the fire which had just been lighted—a wood fire, as befitted a country house. It gave out a pleasant smell, and he savoured it. They had been cutting down some old apple trees, and Adrian had given orders for the wood to be kept for this room and the drawing-room. Very knowledgeable fellow Adrian—useful.

He turned round as Miss Whitaker came in, and spoke to her, his tone easy and familiar.

"Sybil Dryden says we had better have some people in tonight. The less of the tête-a-tête business the better. Lila has nerves, it appears. You had better do some ringing up."

She moved to the writing-table.

"Who do you want asked?"

"Well, Eric Haile was coming anyhow. You don't like him—do you?"

Her carefully arched eyebrows rose a little.

"It isn't my business to like—or dislike—either your guests or your relations."

"Oh, he's not such a near relation. My great-aunt Emily's grandson—what does that make him?"

"Second cousin, I believe."

"You know everything! What a treasure you are, Milly! Why don't you like Eric Haile?"

"I don't either like or dislike him."

Herbert Whitall laughed.

"He is considered charming—the life and soul of every party. That is why I chose him to be my best man. Also he's about the only relation I've got, thank God. Let us hope he will add to the gaiety of tonight's proceedings. At the moment the prospects are a trifle on the gloomy side."

She took all this without any sign—any secretary waiting for her employer to come to the point. When he had finished she repeated her former question with the slightest possible variation.

"Who do you want me to ask?"

"The Considines—they are friends of Sybil's. Old Richardson—I'd like to show him that ivory-handled dagger and see if it doesn't make his mouth water. How is that for numbers?"

"Five men and three women."

"You'd better come in. It's the best we can do. Richardson has no social feelings, and Sybil will be an excuse for the Considines, but the notice is too short for anyone else. Just say we came down here on the spur of the moment. Say Lila was being overdone in town."

She lifted the receiver of the table instrument. He turned back to the fire and to his thoughts. The thin lips smiled. He spread his hands to what was now a cheerful blaze.

Millicent Whitaker was being quiet and competent at the telephone. Presently she hung up and said,

"That's all right—they'll come. I said a quarter to eight."

"Good. Richardson will be late—he always is."

She had been sitting at the table. Now she got up.

"I had better let Marsham know."

"If you will."

She had taken her way towards the door. She stopped now and said,

"Have you done anything about filling my place?"

He was leaning against the mantelshelf, looking at her without appearing to give very much attention to what she said. There was no grey in his dark hair, but it was beginning to recede from the temples, and he looked his age. When she repeated her question a little sharply he smiled and said,

"Certainly not."

She came nearer.

"Herbert, I will not stay here once you are married. I told you that a month ago."

"Forget it, my dear."

"I meant what I said. Whether you've got anyone else or not, I shall go."

"Oh, I think not. It would be so very foolish, and you are a sensible person."

She shook her head.

"I won't stay."

All at once his expression changed. The hard eyes, the fine nose, the forward thrust of the head, gave him a predatory air.

"My dear Millicent, you are being not only foolish but tiresome. You are an excellent secretary, and I propose to retain your services. If you want a rise you can have it."

She shook her head.

"I won't stay."

He laughed.

"Consider your salary doubled!"

The colour blazed in her cheeks.

"Take care, Herbert—you may go too far!"

"And so may you, my dear. There is such a thing as knowing which side your bread is buttered. I shall be signing a new will next week. Under the old one you benefit—quite substantially. Long and faithful service—ten years, isn't it? Well, it depends entirely on yourself whether that legacy goes into the new will or not. I have always told you that I would make provision for you and the child, and I am prepared to carry out my promise. But if you leave my service, the legacy comes out."

She stood for a moment, mastering herself. At last she said in a quiet voice,

"Why do you want me to stay?"

"I don't like changes. I should never get a more efficient secretary."

"I can't do it. You mustn't ask me."

He said, "Come here, Milly! I don't want to hear any more of this nonsense. You'll stay! If I have any more trouble I'm afraid I shall have to do something you wouldn't like—I'm really afraid you wouldn't like it at all. You see, I kept that cheque."

All the colour drained out of her face.

"It's not true. I saw you burn it."

"You saw me burn a blank cheque which cost me twopence—a little comedy, just to set your mind at rest. The cheque you, shall we say, altered, is—you'd like to know where it is, wouldn't you? But you just go on guessing. It won't do you any harm so long as you behave yourself and don't let me have any more of this nonsense."

There was only a matter of six feet between them. Neither of them moved to make the distance less. She stood looking at him until every shade of the angry colour had slowly drained away, leaving her dreadfully pale. She seemed as if she were going to speak, but though her lips moved, there were no words. Words wouldn't butter her bread or keep her child.

He said in that easy, familiar tone, "Run along and tell Marsham." And then, just as she had reached the door and was going out, he called after her, "Tell him who is coming, and then send him along here to me. There was something I meant to have drawn his attention to."

She stood there, her hand on the door, a little surprised.

"And you forgot?"

"My dear Milly, I never forget anything—you ought to know that. Let us say I—saved it up."

She gave him a long, hard look before she turned and went.

CHAPTER 8

It was between half past six and seven o'clock when Bill Waring drove his old rattletrap of a car under the pillared portico of Vineyards. He jumped out and rang the bell with a good deal of vigour. He had, as a matter of fact, run well out of any stock of patience which he may originally have possessed. Rumbold had kept him and kept him, breaking off in the middle of their session to go and see somebody else, and only coming back to insist that they lunch together before going on with their talk. By the time he finally got away it wasn't going to be possible to make Vineyards by daylight. Since he neither knew nor wished to know Herbert Whitall, and could hardly expect a welcome from him or from Lady Dryden, not only the conventions but common prudence might have suggested that he would be well advised to find somewhere to put up for the night and defer any attempt to see Lila until the morning. Prudence had never been his strongest point, and he was far beyond caring for the conventions.

He flung up the drive of Vineyards as if it belonged to him, rang the bell with a will, and stood champing on the top step. Marsham being busy with his silver, the door was opened by the lad Frederick, a tall, well-grown boy who was putting in time and saving money between leaving school and being called up for his military service. He knew that it was pretty late for a visitor, but he didn't feel equal to saying so. The impatient gentleman who was asking for Miss Dryden might be a relation, or he might have been invited and Mr. Marsham hadn't happened to mention it. When Bill Waring stepped past him into the hall he therefore showed him into the small room immediately to the left of the front door, turned on the ceiling light, and having enquired what name he should say, departed in search of Miss Lila. Having ascertained that she was not in the drawing-room, he was about to look elsewhere, when he encountered Lady Dryden.

"If you please, my lady, there's a gentleman asking for Miss Dryden."

Her eyebrows rose.

"A gentleman? What name did he give?"

"Mr. Waring, my lady."

Lady Dryden did not permit her feelings to appear. If it became borne in upon Frederick that she was displeased, and that her displeasure might be formidable, it was not because of anything in her look or in her voice. She said smoothly,

"Miss Dryden is in her room. There is no need to trouble her. I will see Mr. Waring. Where is he?"

When the door began to open Bill Waring had a moment of sickening apprehension, because as soon as he saw Lila he would know what he had come here to find out. If she ran to him, if she wanted him to get her out of this mess she had somehow been pushed into, he was prepared to walk her out of the house here and now and carry her off in his old rattletrap. Ray would take her in, and they would be married as soon as it could be fixed. He thought it took three days—one clear day's notice—at a register office. He had read that somewhere, he couldn't remember where, but it wasn't the sort of thing you invented. If she didn't want him, if she was happy—

The door opened and Lady Dryden came in. Well, it was war to the knife, he could see that. No vulgar brawling—that wasn't her line. Just a voice and manner straight off the ice and straight to the point. There weren't going to be any social greetings.

She stopped a yard inside the door, surveying him as if he were a solecism, and said,

"Why have you come here, Mr. Waring?"

What you might call a rhetorical question, but he didn't mind answering it. Do him good to put it into words, and do her good to hear it.

"I've come to see Lila."

"I'm afraid you can't do that."

"I'm afraid you can't stop me."

"Really, Mr. Waring? I think you will find that you are mistaken. There is a footman and a butler in the house, as well as Mr. Grey and Sir Herbert Whitall. I think you will admit that between them they could put you out. There would be a painful and humiliating scene, and Lila would be very much upset. I prefer to believe that you will behave like a gentleman and go away quietly. I will ask her if she wishes to see you, and if she does, I will let you know in the morning. If you wish to do so you can ring up, and if she is willing to take the call she will be perfectly free to do so."

If he had been at all inclined to undervalue his opponent, he would certainly never do so again. With an almost casual ease of manner she disclosed the strength of her position. If he wished, he could court a degrading ejection from a house to which he had not been invited—he could figure as a common gatecrasher in a common brawl. He did not need Lady Dryden to tell him what would be the effect on Lila.

Having revolved these things in a stubborn silence, he stared her straight in the face and said,

"I will ring up in the morning. I didn't intend to be so late. I was delayed, or I would have been here earlier. I don't want to upset Lila, but she will have to see me."

She met his hostile stare with unruffled calm.

"That is for her to say."

He went on as if she had not spoken.

"When I left England we were engaged to be married. As far as I am concerned that is still the case. If she wishes to break off our engagement she must do it herself. I'm not taking it from anyone else."

"I have never admitted that there was an engagement, Mr. Waring."

He looked, and felt, as obstinate as a mule. Lady Dryden derived some pleasure from the fact. She had always disliked him. He was now a definite menace, and the game was in her hand. To win against that stubbornness, to score against that obstinate strength, gave her an agreeable sense of power. She had Lila under her thumb, and there was nothing he could do about it. She moved aside from the door and said,

"Good-night, Mr. Waring."

He went because there really was nothing else that he could do—not there, not at that time.

She didn't ring for Frederick to show him out, but stood there in the hall herself to see him go. As he went down the steps under the pillared portico he heard the key turn in the lock of the door behind him.

Well, that was that. The next move lay with him. He gave her ten minutes to get away upstairs or into the drawing-room. During this time he drove his car round the first turn of the drive. Sitting there, he took pencil and paper, wrote briefly, and addressed an envelope to Miss Lila Dryden. Then he walked back to the portico and rang the front door bell.

Again he had the good fortune to encounter Frederick. He said,

"Sorry to bother you, but I'm afraid I left my cap."

Even Lady Dryden could hardly marshal the chuckers-out to deal with a polite request for one's own property. Bill was rather pleased with himself for having thought about leaving his cap. Lady Dryden had made him so angry that he might easily have forgotten everything else. Being in a rage was rather like being out in a thunderstorm—you couldn't hear yourself think.

Frederick produced the cap, and Bill produced two pound notes.

"Look here, I want Miss Lila Dryden to have this letter, if you can manage it."

Frederick said, "Oh, yes, sir."

All the notes changed hands. Bill nodded and stepped back. The front door shut.

Frederick, full of romantic zeal, ran up the back stairs and tapped on Miss Lila Dryden's door. The whole thing didn't take a minute. Nobody saw him come or go.

Lila took the note with a shaking hand. She locked the door before she dared to read it, and when she had read it she sat down on the bed, a thing Sybil Dryden never allowed, and began to cry.

CHAPTER 9

At a quarter past seven Lady Dryden tried the door
and found it locked. Ridiculous nonsense. She
didn't approve of people locking themselves in.
Particularly she didn't approve of Lila locking herself in. It was a measure of defense, and she was
inclined to suspect it of being a measure of defi-
ance. She knocked in a peremptory manner and
said,

"Let me in at once, Lila!"

There was a little delay, but not much. Lila stood
back from the door and received an astonished
stare. She was still wearing the grey skirt and white
jumper, only the coat had been removed and
thrown down carelessly across the foot of the bed.
She had stopped crying some time ago, but the
marks of it showed on her face.

Lady Dryden was brisk.

"You haven't left yourself much time to dress.
You'll have to hurry."

"I don't think I can."

"You don't think you can what?"

Lila said, "*Anything*—" in an exhausted voice.
She didn't feel as if she could do any of the things
that confronted her—dress herself in one of the
new trousseau frocks she hated, go down to dinner

and talk or be talked to through an endless evening; endure Herbert Whitall's good-night kiss; creep down in the dark after everyone was asleep and tell Bill she wasn't engaged to him any more; and in no more than six days' time—six dreadful hurrying days—put on that ivory satin wedding dress and be married to Herbert Whitall, with Aunt Sybil giving her away. She was past having any sense of proportion about these things. They all felt equally dreadful—difficult—impossible.

She gazed at Lady Dryden in a bewildered manner.

"My dear Lila, you look half asleep! For goodness' sake wash your face! First hot water and then plenty of cold! It will wake you up. You will wear your new crepe—it is just the thing for a small dinner. You know there are some people coming in, and you certainly look your best in those ivory shades. And you had better put on a little colour. You are too pale. High time you were out of town."

Lila stepped out of her grey skirt, took off the jumper, stood at the washstand, poured hot water and then cold. The hot water was soothing, the cold gave her a tingling shock. With her face hidden in the towel, she answered Lady Dryden's "What has been upsetting you?" with the one word, "Bill."

Lady Dryden felt as if some of the cold water had splashed up in her face.

"How did he upset you? You haven't seen him."

"He wrote—" The words were only just audible from behind the towel.

Lady Dryden was so much relieved that her laugh sounded quite good-tempered.

"Is that all? Naturally he feels sore. But he will get over it. You don't suppose you are his first love, do you, and you certainly won't be his last. What have you done with his letter?"

Lila had turned away. She was folding the towel.

"I burned it."

"Where?"

"After I got it."

Sybil Dryden's voice was very decided indeed.

"I said *where*. You haven't been burning anything here."

"It was downstairs—after I got it."

"And when did you get it?"

Frederick's job hung in the balance. Other things too. More important things.

Then Lila did what was perhaps the best thing she could have done. She burst into tears.

Lady Dryden could have slapped her with the best will in the world. She restrained herself, picked up the wet face-cloth and the towel, and spoke with cold authority.

"That's quite enough of this nonsense! Wash your face again and dry it! And see that it stays dry this time!"

Lila said in a quivering whisper,

"I can't marry him."

"You are not being asked to marry Mr. Waring."

There was a piteous shake of the head.

"I can't marry Herbert—I can't."

Lady Dryden said in a bracing voice,

"You are not being asked to marry anyone. You are being asked to behave like a civilized person and dress for dinner, and that is what you will do!" She stepped to the wardrobe, took out the long, straight ivory dress, put the grey coat and skirt on a hanger, folded away the jumper in a drawer, and went over to the door.

"You'll have to hurry," she said. "The Considines are asked for a quarter to eight."

CHAPTER 10

Lady Dryden took her way to the study. If Eric Haile had arrived, she would not be able to see Herbert Whitall alone, but there was a good chance of being able to plant a few well chosen hints.

She said, "May I come in?" and was gratified to find him alone and already dressed.

His "Of course" was all that it should have been from a well bred host, and yet a sensitive person might have been aware of a faint sarcastic undercurrent. If Sybil Dryden was aware of it, she could dismiss it as immaterial. What she had to say would be said, and unless Herbert Whitall was a complete fool, it should have a beneficial effect.

With a slight gracious smile she crossed the room to stand beside him and remark that a fire was really very pleasant now that the evenings were drawing in.

He received this highly original sentiment with amusement.

"My dear Sybil, did you really seek me out to say that? If you didn't—Eric Haile will be here at any moment. He also has an urge to see me. I imagine he hopes to touch me for a loan. So if there is anything you want to say—"

She showed no resentment.

"Only this, Herbert. I have just found Lila in tears. Eleventh hour nerves—the sort of thing every girl goes through, but it wants handling with care. Don't be too affectionate."

He gave a short laugh.

"I don't get much chance, do I? I practically never see her alone."

"It is just as well. Believe me, you really cannot be too careful. That is all I came to say, so I will leave you to your interview with Mr. Haile. I hope it will be a pleasanter one than you seem to expect."

He laughed again.

"I assure you it won't disturb me. Keep your good wishes for Eric—he is going to need them."

"That sounds—" She paused for a word, and then said, "Vindictive."

"But that is just what I am. Didn't you know it? I expect my uttermost farthing. If I don't get it—if I don't get it, Sybil, I can be extremely—vindictive. You will remember that, won't you?"

He had been walking beside her to the door. He opened it now and stood aside for her to pass. She went out with her head high.

She came into the drawing-room, and found her-self alone there. Rather a formal room, with its four windows hidden by curtains where pale brocaded flowers bloomed on an ivory ground. Couches and chairs had loose covers repeating the same shades. An Empire mirror between two of the windows showed her her own image, a very handsome one in the close-fitting black which did full justice to her tall and upright figure. There was a double row of pearls and a diamond flower to relieve what was otherwise the extreme of severity. Very few women of her age could show such a faultless turn of neck and shoulder—no blurring of the line, no sagging of the flesh, no wrinkling of the skin. She was a beautiful woman, in a maturity as yet untouched by the least hint of decline.

At the sound of voices in the hall she turned and went to meet the Considines. She was very well aware that her effect would be a little daunting.

Mabel Considine had been a dowdy girl, and was now a dowdy elderly woman. Like Corinna Long-ley, she was an old schoolfellow. Even in those far-off days, and with the help of a school uniform, she had never managed to achieve tidiness. At fifty her hair broke into ends and stuck out in unex-pected places. She had a good deal of it, of an unbecoming pepper-and-salt colour, and she did her best with hairpins and a net, but without any marked success. She had been a thin, poking schoolgirl. She was still thin, and she still poked. As for her clothes, they were lamentable. She had a passion for picking up remnants and handing them over to the village dressmaker to be contrived into some horrid shapeless garment. The one she was wearing tonight had been pieced together from a length of over-bright artificial silk eked out with crimson satin. A long coral chain had been passed three times about a distressing neck.

She came in beaming, voice and manner much younger than her face.

"Sybil—how nice! You look as if you had stepped straight off the cover of *Vogue!* How do you do it? Doesn't she look marvellous, George! No one would think we were the same age, would they?"

George, large and florid, covered his embarrassment with a hearty greeting. He detested smart women, and especially smart elderly women. Sybil Dryden made him feel that his dinner-jacket was twenty-five years old, and that his hands were rough. And why not? He did things with them. He had just finished a new hen-house, and he had been digging potatoes. Of course his hands were rough, and he hadn't quite got the creosote off his right thumb. Well, he had done his best, hadn't he? And he liked his old clothes. He had had some good times in them, and they were comfortable. He liked a woman to be comfortable. Thank the Lord, no one could say Mabel was smart. Comfortable—that's what she was. And kind. Always doing things for people. Did too much. He had to put his foot down, or she would be everybody's slave. Too unselfish. But when his foot was down it was down.

With all this in his mind, he shook hands, and was presently saying, "Not at all—not at all," to Herbert Whitall, who strolled in with a casual apology for being late.

There was one of those aimless arguments as to whether the quarter had struck or not. The village church had its chime, but if the wind was not just right, the sound did not carry as far as Vineyards. Anyhow nobody had heard it. Mrs. Considine consulted a wrist-watch on a leather strap and made it five minutes to eight, at the same time admitting that it gained five minutes a day, and that she had no idea when she had set it last.

In the middle of all this Mr. Eric Haile walked in. If he had just had a disagreeable interview with his host, he showed no sign of it. His handsome ruddy face was all smiles as he greeted Lady Dryden and the Considines, his manner affable to the point of familiarity.

"My dear lady, I needn't ask how you are—so very, very easy on the eye. . . . Mrs. Considine—wearing yourself out with good works as usual! . . . Ah, Considine—how are the hens?"

If Lady Dryden stiffened a little, it did not trouble him. He had dark dancing eyes that went from one to the other, and an air of being quite certain of his reception. He could not have appeared more perfectly at home if Vineyards and his cousin's great fortune had been his own by right of birth. He was just saying, "I hear you acquired some new treasures at the Harrington sale, Herbert," when Professor Richardson was announced, a little round man with a bald head and a face like a cross baby. He rolled into the room, protesting that he wasn't late. He never was. People didn't look after their watches, and then went out of their way to put the blame on other people who did.

"As for Whitall—" he was shaking hands with Lady Dryden—"he'd put anything on to anyone. Don't trust him a yard. Never did. Never shall. Get the better of a blind orphan starving in a snow-storm—ha, ha!" He gave a short explosive laugh. "Well, Whitall, isn't that so? Isn't it?"

He got an affable smile and a touch on the shoulder.

"My dear Richardson, I fly for higher game than blind orphans. You for instance, or Mangay. And I rather think I brought it off at the Harrington sale. Mangay would have liked that dagger."

The professor stared.

"Daresay he would. He hasn't got a bottomless purse—nor have I. Not that I wanted the thing myself. Probably spurious. Didn't trouble to go to the sale."

Herbert Whitall smiled with those thin lips of his.

"No—you had Bernstein bidding for you, hadn't you?"

Professor Richardson's bald head glowed. The red frill which stood up all round the back of it like an Elizabethan ruff appeared to quiver as if every individual hair was angry. His eyebrows, a shade more sandy, bristled. He glared, and burst out laughing.

"Me? Not at all! Who told you that? Lot of damn lies flying round! Very doubtful origin, that dagger.

A fake, likely as not. Mrs. Considine, my house-keeper told me to tell you those pullets she had from you have started to lay. She is as pleased as Punch."

"Isn't that nice!" said Mabel Considine in her warmest voice.

Miss Whitaker came in, and made her unobtrusive greetings. She had done the conventional things to her face, but there was an underlying pallor. Like Lady Dryden she wore black, but with a difference—high neck and long sleeves, skirt to the ankles. At the throat the kind of brooch that a humble dependant may wear. But she didn't look humble. Outwardly perhaps, but not to the discerning eye. Herbert Whitall was pleasantly aware of a seething pride. Eric Haile was intrigued. Mabel Considine, moving to speak with gentle kindness to the least considered member of the party, was thinking, "Dear me, I'm afraid that girl isn't happy. I do hope she hasn't become too much attached. Secretaries so often do."

Herbert Whitall looked at his watch.

He said, "Lila is late," and turned to Lady Dryden. "Is she all right?"

And then the door opened and Lila came in with Adrian Grey. She wore the ivory crepe dictated by Lady Dryden. There was a Greek simplicity in its graceful lines. She looked lovely, pale, and dreadfully tired. Adrian was speaking to her as they came in. She had a faint smile for him.

Marsham sounded the gong, and they went in to dinner.

60

CHAPTER 11

Considering all things, dinner might have been a great deal worse. Herbert Whitall could be an agreeable host when he chose. Tonight he laid himself out to play the part. Lady Dryden's social tact was equal to any situation however strained. Eric Haile could be relied upon for the newest scandal and the latest *bon mot*. And Mabel Considine could, and did, produce an unfailing stream of village small talk. Lila, placed tactfully between Mr. Considine and Adrian Grey, had only to look lovely and contribute an occasional yes or no. There were long periods when she did not even have to do this, because Adrian and Mr. Considine had got into a long argument about the new surface cultivation versus deep trenching, and there really wasn't anything she could find to say.

The table was an oval one, and since she was as far from Herbert Whitall as it was possible for her to be, she felt able to relax. On one side of her there was Adrian, the Professor, and Mrs. Considine. On the other George Considine, with Miss Whitaker on his left and Eric Haile between her and Lady Dryden.

Eric was finding it amusing to speculate as to Milly Whitaker's reactions. Would she stay, or would she go? And if she stayed, what sort of a fist would Herbert make of running a three-in-hand? He wondered how much Lady Dryden knew, and decided she would certainly see to it that she did not know too much. All this whilst he told quite a new story about a Bishop, a Bright Young Thing, and a Raid on a Night-club. He didn't expect anyone to believe it, but he hoped it might shock Mrs. Considine. She was, however, so deeply involved in telling Professor Richardson all about Jimmy Grove, who was his daily's nephew and coming on so very nicely under George in the garden, that she merely looked round in amiable surprise at the general laughter.

Food and service were both excellent. By the time dinner was over there was certainly less tension and a more favourable atmosphere. Coffee was served in the drawing-room, and the men adjourned there after the briefest interval. The room was comfortably warm, and the scent of apple-wood hung pleasantly on the air. Conversation was light and desultory until Herbert Whitall put down his cup and got up.

"Well, Richardson," he said with a flavour of malice in his tone, "you'll be wanting to see the dagger."

"I don't know why you should think I'm interested." The Professor's voice was a growl.

"Oh, but you must be. You're going to prove it's a fake, aren't you? If you haven't got a magnifying glass, I can lend you one. It is going to be very interesting to watch the struggle between your obstinacy and your antiquarian conscience. Of course you may have knocked it on the head, but I am giving you the benefit of the doubt. So come along!"

He crossed to the far end of the room and drew back a wide curtain. It screened a steel shutter cutting off the alcove in which he housed his ivories. The shutter slid back when a key had been inserted and turned, disclosing a deep semicircular recess, windowless and furnished with shelves covered in velvet of a very deep blue. On these shelves and against this background the ivory plaques, figures, and other triumphs of craftsmanship were displayed. In the place of honour there was the figure which Lila disliked so much. Of an archaic simplicity, the head a little bent, the hands holding some small round thing—a fruit perhaps, or possibly the age-old symbol of life. Even in the midst of a malicious desire to confute the Professor, Herbert Whitall would not deny his goddess her mead of praise.

"Perfect, isn't she?" he said. "Cretan, of course."

The Professor blew out his cheeks till they looked like twin balloons. Then he let all the breath go at once in a sound like "Pooh!" or "Pah!"

"Egypto-Greek!"

Herbert Whitall maintained a superior smile.

"Plenty of Egyptian influence in Crete. The ivory figures at Hagia Triada—"

Professor Richardson said, "Nonsense!" but the battle was suavely declined.

"Perfect anyway, my dear fellow. And Lila might

have stood for her. She doesn't like me to say so, but you can't help seeing the likeness. And we needn't dispute about perfection.''

The Professor grunted.

''Where's this dagger you're so cocksure about?''

Herbert Whitall held it out—a long, thin blade with an ivory handle delicately carved in a vine pattern—twisting stem, graceful leaf and swelling grape, the whole exquisitely balanced, easy to hold, and small enough to be a woman's ornament worn in the girdle or the hair.

''The story is that Marco Polo brought it back from China.''

The Professor snorted.

''That blade never came out of China!''

''I agree. It's of later date than the hilt of course. If Marco Polo really brought it home, the blade may have been broken, or he or someone who came after him may have thought they could better it. After all, Italy and Spain could claim to lead the world in the tempering of steel. This blade is undoubtedly of Italian workmanship. The dagger in its present form turns up in the dowry of Bianca Corner who married into the Falieri family in 1541. It is listed amongst her personal effects.''

''*An* ivory dagger is listed among her effects. After which nobody knows anything about it until the middle of the eighteenth century, when Lord Abington picked it up in Venice with this ridiculous Marco Polo story pinned to it. From that point, of course, the pedigree is quite straightforward!''

Herbert Whitall raised his eyebrows.

"Ridiculous?"

"Absurd!" said the Professor. "A fatuous fabrication! The sort of thing that could only impose on the ignorant and credulous!"

Mabel Considine put her hand on his arm and pressed it gently.

"Very pretty, isn't it? Those grapes! And do you see, there is a fly on one of them? But I'm afraid I don't like daggers and things like that. I can't help wondering whether they've ever killed anyone. And of course I suppose they must have done when they are as old as this one seems to be."

The Professor would have liked to go on being rude to Herbert Whitall. He didn't see why he should be interrupted. He blew out his cheeks again and said,

"Ask Whitall, and he'll tell you Marco Polo used it to stab Jenghiz Khan—ha, ha!"

The pressure on his arm increased. Mabel Considine was smiling at her host.

"What I was going to ask Sir Herbert was whether we couldn't hear some of his beautiful records. Such a very great treat. Of course there is plenty of music on the wireless, but if you want to hear the great soloists you have to go to gramophone records. It's really quite like a miracle to be able to say, 'Now I'll hear Kreisler, or Caruso, or Galli-Curci, or John McCormack.' And you have such a wonderful collection of those old records—quite out of the catalogue now."

"Shocking bad," said George Considine. "All scratch. Can't listen to them myself."

"George, *dear!*"

"Oh, have it your own way! You always do!"

She did at least on this occasion, Eric Haile coming up in support, and the whole party moved back into the room. The steel shutter was locked upon the precious ivories and the brocade curtain drawn across it again.

Eric Haile stepped naturally into the position of musical director.

"Now what shall we have? You mentioned Kreisler—or are we only to call upon the glorious shades? Mrs. Considine? Lady Dryden?"

Sybil Dryden had not a note of music in her. She could not have cared less. The whole thing was a bore. But so were the ivories, and they had at least been preserved from the quarrel which Professor Richardson had seemed determined to provoke. She smiled, said something vague about their all being so charming, and thought how embarrassing Mabel's girlish enthusiasms had become. To look sixty and behave as if you were sixteen was a social tragedy.

The Professor was joining in the choice of records now. He had, it appeared, a passion for tenor and soprano arias in the old-fashion Italian style. George Considine liked something he knew, something of the kind you can pick up and whistle. The four of them trooped off to the study in search of records.

Lila was sitting on one of the sofas with Adrian Grey. He was showing her sketches of a house he had been asked to alter. A little comfort and peace flowed in on her as she looked at the pictures and listened to his quiet voice explaining them. Miss Whitaker had gone out of the room.

Herbert Whitall came to sit by Sybil Dryden. After a brief glance at Lila and Adrian he said under his breath,

"Soothing syrup?"

"Yes—you had better let them alone. By the way, young Waring is here."

"Here?"

"He arrived at a quarter to seven and demanded to see Lila. I got rid of him. Herbert, he will ring up tomorrow. I think she will have to see him. He says he won't take his dismissal from anyone else, and he is a very stubborn young man. It is a pity, because of course it will upset her. But perhaps not such a bad thing in the end. If he makes a scene—and he probably will—he will frighten Lila. She can't bear anything like that. The more I think of it, the more I am inclined to believe that it may be quite a good thing. I shall be present of course."

He said, "Oh, well—" and left it at that.

Sybil Dryden passed smoothly to the arrangements for the wedding.

The party from the study came back, laden with records and all talking at once. Mabel Considine was really enjoying herself. She had a cult for John McCormack, and she had just found two records from one of the very few operas she had actually seen. She was talking about it as they all came back into the room.

"It was before I was married—and that's a very

67

long time ago, isn't it, George? Mother and I were travelling. We did Venice, and Naples, and Rome, and Florence, and Milan. Such a wonderful stained glass window in the cathedral there, on the left as you face the altar—all blue and green. I do hope it wasn't hurt by the bombing. And at Venice we went to the opera twice, and saw *La Favorita* and *Lucia di Lammermoor*. Or does one say heard—I never quite know. But I always think of it as seeing, because you hear it on the wireless of course, but it isn't the same thing, is it? I mean, when you've *seen* it you've got a sort of picture of it in your mind, and it does make a difference. The plots of operas are so very difficult and confused. And not knowing Italian—I'm sure I don't know to this day what *La Favorita* was about, even though we did see it. But *Lucia di Lammermoor* was easier, because of Sir Walter Scott, and I do remember these two tenor solos, because the young man who sang them was very handsome, and he had a really good voice. It's going to be such a treat for me, Sir Herbert."

She sat down on the sofa beside Lila and Adrian, her cheeks flushed, her girlish manner accentuated.

"You young people don't read Sir Walter Scott nowadays, do you? The opera is taken from *The Bride of Lammermoor*, and I haven't read it since I was fourteen, so I've got their names rather mixed up, but the girl was Lucy Ashton, and her brother was Henry—at least I think he was. He made her break off her engagement to the young man she was in love with. I'm not sure about his name.

68

There was someone called Edgar, and someone called Ravenswood, but I'm not sure whether they were the same person or not."

She gazed enquiringly at Adrian Grey. He laughed a little.

"I'm afraid I'm no use. *Ivanhoe* and *The Tailsman* are as far as I ever got with Scott."

She said, "I know. I read them all when I was fourteen, because I was in quarantine for three weeks in a house where there wasn't anything else to read. That is why I have got them mixed. But I remember about poor Lucy because it was such a dreadful story. Her mother and her brother made her marry the other young man, and she stabbed him on their wedding night and went mad, poor thing, and died. And this record which Mr. Haile is just putting on is what her real lover sings over her grave."

The two preliminary bars of the accompaniment put a stop to this stream of reminiscence. She leaned back with her eyes half closed, making little rhythmic movements with her hands as the air came floating out in John McCormack's beautiful voice: *"Bell' alma innamorata—bell' alma innamorata—ne congiunga il Nume in cielo."*

Lila sat looking down at the page which Adrian had turned, but she did not see it. She had never read the books she ought to have read. She had never read a novel of Sir Walter Scott's right through, though Uncle John had had them all. But she had once taken *The Bride of Lammermoor* from its shelf, and it had opened upon the scream of

69

terror and the Ashton family rushing in to find Lucy in her blood-dabbled night-dress staring with crazy eyes at the bridegroom she had stabbed. She had put the book back and dreamed a terrible dream about it in the night and then shut it away and never let herself think of it again. The picture came out of its shut-up place. It lay between her and Adrian's sketch—Lucy crouched upon the bed—the scream still sounding in the room—the blood—the dagger—the dreadful staring eyes. The dagger had an ivory handle with vine-leaves on it and a bunch of grapes. Where the blood had touched them the grapes were red—blood-red. John McCormack's voice mourned over Lucy's grave: *"Bell' alma innamorata—ne congiunga il Nume in cielo—bell' alma innamorata——bell' alma innamorata—"*

The picture began to swim before her in a mist. Adrian's hand came down on hers, steady and warm.

"Lila—what is it, my dear?"

She looked up at him, her eyes dilated.

"It's—a horrible—story—"

His voice was as kind as his hand.

"Well, it all happened a long time ago—if it ever happened at all. And by the time you get anything into Italian opera it doesn't seem to matter how many people are stabbed. Most of the cast have to be got rid of one way or another, with the hero and heroine in the limelight singing higher and higher till their very last breath. I'm afraid it always makes me want to laugh."

The picture dimmed and went away. The crazed eyes were the last to go—Lucy's eyes and the ivory dagger.

Adrian was smiling.

"The mourning lover is a gentleman of one idea. Have you counted how many times he says *'Bell' alma innamorata'*? I always mean to, but then McCormack's voice gets me and I really don't care."

Her colour was coming faintly back, the dilated pupils were normal again. She said,

"It's Italian, isn't it? What does it mean?"

He went on smiling.

"Something like, 'Fair beloved soul—we shall be united in heaven.' I don't know Italian—I'm just picking out the words everybody knows."

The record came to an end. Mabel Considine sprang up, went over to the radiogram, and demanded the Sextette, which proved to be quite unbelievably scratchy, with four of the performers providing loud background music, Caruso manfully shouting his way to the front, and Galli-Curci, crystal clear, hovering above the din.

When it was over Herbert Whitall directed a faint frown and a definitely sarcastic voice at Eric Haile.

"I really don't think we need bring in exhibits out of the Chamber of Horrors. May I suggest that we now hear something that we can listen to without wrecking the nervous system? Amazing to think that one used to pay a guinea for that sort of thing!"

Mabel Considine was shocked.

71

"Oh, but Sir Herbert, they were wonderful! On the old gramophones, I mean."

"I'm afraid I can't agree. We just didn't know any better—that was all."

Eric Haile smiled and shook his head. The Professor rushed into noisy disagreement.

"I never heard such nonsense in my life, and I'm sure one hears enough one way and another! The pre-electrical record was made for the pre-electrical gramophone. The effect was remarkably pleasing. Of course if you go and put the poor thing on to an electrical machine, the result is just a massacre. But I maintain, and I shall continue to maintain, that the old records were good enough on the old machines."

Herbert Whitall quite definitely sneered.

"Of course if you really want the violin to sound like a flute!"

"I do nothing of the sort!"

"My dear fellow! Why not just put the clock back altogether and prove how superior the stage-coach was to the Daimler or the Rolls Royce?"

The blood was mounting to the Professor's crown.

"It didn't kill so many people!"

"Well, there weren't so many people to be killed, were there? Anyhow I notice that you condescend to an autocycle. To be entirely logical, you should still be wearing woad and living in a cave."

He got a red malevolent glare.

"And if I were, do you know what I should do? I should come round some dark night to your cave

72

and hit you over the head with my neolithic axe—and then where would you be?"

"Still in the twentieth century, I hope."

Professor Richardson burst out laughing.

"Think you've got the last word, Whitall? I wouldn't be too sure if I were you!"

Eric Haile's dark eyes went dancing from face to face. They saw George Considine on the edge of embarrassment, a record in his hand. His wife, her attention caught by the rasp in the Professor's voice, her hand at a fluttering end of hair, the desire to be helpful plainly written upon her face. It gave her rather the look of an anxious hen. Lila and Adrian bending over those eternal sketches. Amiable fellow, Adrian, but a bit of a bore. Come to think of it, so was the lovely Lila. Probably just as well. Beauty and brains would be a formidable combination—too formidable for Herbert Whitall. Sybil Dryden had had both. Wasn't there something about "the monstrous regiment of women"? He thought the cap would fit her pretty well. But she could meet her match in Herbert. A cold devil—a cold, calculating, sneering devil. If he went on baiting Richardson, there would probably be a brawl. Better black them out.

He put on a magnificent orchestral record of a Bach toccata and fugue and turned up the volume control. An ocean of sound surged out and filled the room.

CHAPTER 12

It was at half past ten, when the Considines were saying good-night in the hall, that Miss Whitaker came down the stairs in her outdoor things—dark navy coat, small navy hat, umbrella and handbag. She went up to Herbert Whitall and spoke to him in a low voice. No one could hear what she said, but everyone could see that he was not pleased. He frowned, set his thin lips in a disagreeable line, and said,

"Very sudden, isn't it? Suppose I say no?"

George Considine, who was the nearest, did hear that. He also heard the reply, in which Miss Whitaker's voice was a little raised.

"I should go all the same."

She turned abruptly and went over to where Mabel Considine was winding her head in a wisp of scarlet chiffon and pinning an elderly Shetland shawl across her chest.

"Mrs. Considine, I wonder whether you would kindly give me a lift as far as the village? I can catch the last bus into Emsworth. I have just had a telephone message from my sister. She is ill, and I think I ought to go to her."

"Oh, my dear—of course! But so late! And if you miss the bus—Are you sure you must go?"

"Quite sure. My sister is all alone there with her little boy. And I shan't miss the bus—there is plenty of time."

Mabel Considine thrust her arms hurriedly into the sleeves of what looked like a gardening-coat, added a massive scarf in the colours of the golf club of which George was a member, and said good-night all over again.

The door was opened, admitting a gusty draught. Someone said it was blowing up for rain. Lady Dryden moved back towards the drawing-room. The door banged, and Professor Richardson was understood to say he must be getting along.

Adrian and Lila had remained in the drawing-room, where Eric Haile was stacking the records preparatory to putting them away in the study. As Lady Dryden came in, Lila got up. The moment which she always dreaded had arrived. It was bed-time, and Herbert would kiss her good-night. She said in a fluttering voice,

"I'm tired—I think I'll go up now—"

Aunt Sybil wasn't pleased. She looked down her nose and said,

"I think you had better wait and say good-night to Herbert," and all at once it came over Lila that she would have to. Because if she tried to go up now she might meet Herbert in the hall and have to say good-night to him there, and that would be much, much worse, because they would be alone, and when they were alone he kissed her in a way that was indescribably different and dreadful. A little shudder passed over her. She went to the hearth and stood there, holding out her hands to the fire.

She turned with a start as someone came into the room, but it was only Marsham to help with the records. It came to her to wonder what a man like Marsham would be like when he wasn't being a butler. She had no idea why this thought should have come to her. He was a very good butler. Everything in the house went smoothly as clockwork. But underneath, when he wasn't making up the fire, waiting at table, drawing the curtains, and putting the cushions straight, what would he be like then?

It was only just lately that Lila had begun to have thoughts like this. They came to her sometimes when she looked in the glass and saw herself in one of her new frocks. No one who looked at her as she was looking at herself would know how she was feeling deep down underneath. So every now and then when she looked at somebody else—at Miss Whitaker, at Eric Haile, at Sybil Dryden, and, just now, at Marsham, she had a queer frightened feeling that perhaps they were really quite different underneath. Just as she herself was different and they didn't know it.

Marsham came over to the fire, trimming it, pulling the logs together. He looked exactly as he always did.

And then Herbert Whitall came in, and she forgot everything else. Lady Dryden moved to meet him.

"We were just waiting to say good-night. I'm

taking Lila off to bed. Your country air makes us all sleepy."

He smiled.

"You mean my country air—or my country guests?"

"My dear Herbert! The Professor is anything but soporific. Do you really enjoy quarrelling with him?"

"Oh, immensely. You see, I have a number of things which he would give his eyes to get, so he crabs them. If he could persuade me that they were fakes, I should get rid of them, and then, even if he didn't manage to get them himself, he wouldn't be aggravated by seeing them in my possession. Even if he can't persuade me he can perhaps plant a thorn here and there, or at the very least he can blow off steam."

She looked at him curiously.

"And what do you get out of it?"

He laughed.

"My dear Sybil—can you ask? What used you to get out of it when you came into a room and knew that none of the other women could touch you? Wasn't it meat and drink to you to be envied and—hated?"

Under the impact of the past tense her features had sharpened. He smiled.

"Pleasant—wasn't it? Well, that's what I feel like when I see Richardson, Mangay, and the others full of envy, hatred and malice over my ivories. Petty of course, but that's how we are. Any toy is good enough to fight over. And a thing that isn't worth fighting for isn't worth having."

He looked past her at Lila. It was a long look without passion in it—the look of the connoisseur in the auction room, cold, appraising. As he came towards her, she felt sick and shaken. Now he was going to touch her, kiss her. She couldn't scream or run away. If she did—would Aunt Sybil still make her marry him?

His hand fell upon her shoulder. He bent and kissed her cheek.

"Good-night, my lovely Lila. Sleep well and dream of me."

It was over. Her heart always seemed to stop for the moment of the kiss. She felt as if she couldn't breathe—everything in her was tight and cold. But now it was over.

She went upstairs with Sybil Dryden and said good-night. When five minutes had gone by it would be safe to lock the door. Aunt Sybil wouldn't come back.

When the key had turned she took a long breath, tipped hot water into the basin, and washed away Herbert Whitall's kiss.

CHAPTER 13

For a time all the normal sounds of an occupied house went on—water running; a door opening and closing again; footsteps on the stair, on landing and passage; the sound of voices muted to the edge of what could just be heard; small hushed movements in this or that of the bedrooms; the shutting of a drawer; the click of an electric light switch. And then, with a gradual fading out of all these things, that curious transition state during which the silence of a house which is still awake passes imperceptibly into the silence of a house which is very deeply asleep.

It was just before this transition period that Marsham made his final round of the house. The windows had all been fastened hours before, and the front door locked when Professor Richardson had followed the Considines. He shot the two bolts, top and bottom, and turned into the passage which divided the rooms which looked out upon the gravel sweep from those which faced the terrace and the view.

At the study door he paused, and stood for a moment listening. There was a sound of voices from within. As he said afterwards, he supposed that Sir Herbert was having a smoke and a drink with Mr. Haile, who was staying the night. Since Sir Herbert was often very late and he was not required to wait up for him, he did not find anything unusual in the fact that the gentlemen should be sitting over the fire with their drinks. He could hear two voices, but could distinguish no words. This is what he said afterwards. At the time, he lingered a little longer than was exactly necessary, but not so long as to lay himself open to a charge of eavesdropping. When he moved to go, it was with a slight shrug of the shoulders, and he had not taken more than a couple of steps before he turned back again. One of the voices had been raised. He stood for a moment, and then took his way to the end of the passage and through the green baize door which screened the back stairs.

Lila Dryden did not undress. She had no settled plan in her head, she was just waiting. Presently, when everyone was in bed and asleep, she would have to think what she was going to do. Of course the easiest thing would be not to do anything at all. That was what she had been doing all this time—the easiest thing, the easiest way. It was like being in a car when someone else was driving—you didn't have to think, you just let yourself be carried along. Sybil Dryden was an extremely capable driver. She knew just where she was going, and how to get there. But tonight Lila had had a sudden horrifying glimpse of her destination. It was like seeing something in the flare of a lightning flash, and it had frightened her so much that she was almost ready to jump out of the car.

Lucy Ashton's crazed eyes, and the ivory dagger red with blood.

The picture rose, and there was no Adrian to send it back to its own horrible place. Her heart failed and her breath fluttered.

She got up, shaking from head to foot, went over to the hearth, and kneeled there. The fire had died down. But wood ash holds the heat for a long time. A comfortable warmth came from it, it helped her to stop shivering.

But she had not come there to warm herself. When Sybil Dryden tried the handle of her door before dinner, she had slipped Bill's letter under the wooden kerb which guarded the hearth. She had read it, she had hidden it, and she had lied about it. Now she lifted the kerb and pulled it out, a little dusty and crumpled. Bill never wrote long letters. He got on with what he had to say, and when he had said it he stopped. This was almost too short to be called a letter at all. She knelt there in front of the pile of wood ash with the glow at its heart and read what he had written.

"Lila—I've got to see you. If you want to marry Whitall you can marry him. If you don't want to, I'll take you to Ray tonight. I'll be outside the window of the room on the left of the hall as you come in from half past eleven onwards. Show a light, and I'll knock three times so you'll know it's me.

Bill"

It was a way out. She could pack a suit-case. She could put on a dark coat and skirt and her fur coat, and when the big clock on the landing struck the half hour after eleven she could slip downstairs and get out of the window in the Blue Room, and Bill would take her away. She always wondered why it was called the Blue Room. Perhaps it was blue once, long ago. It wasn't now. There was some very dull tapestry work on the chairs, and an ugly modern picture of a girl with a green face which Herbert said was very clever.

These things were in the confusion of her mind, all mixed up with listening for the clock to strike, showing a light in the Blue Room, and waiting for Bill to knock on the window. Bill would take her away, and she need never see Herbert again. . . .

Aunt Sybil would *make* her. Herbert would make her. She couldn't really get away from them.

Bill would take her away. He would take her to Ray. Then she would have to marry him. He would make her. Ray would make her. She didn't want to marry him.

She knelt there for a long time. She didn't know what to do. She went on kneeling until she began to feel giddy. Then she got up and huddled on the couch at the foot of the bed with the eiderdown pulled round her, because she was dreadfully cold, and you can't really think when you are cold. She tried very hard to think, but it wasn't any use. Bill said, "Come down and show a light, and I'll take you away." Just for a moment she thought she could do it, but she couldn't really. Sybil Dryden would never let her do it. However softly she opened her door, however softly she crept, Sybil would hear her. Sybil would come out of her room. Or Herbert. She had a most awful picture of being trapped in the dark, with no one to hear if she cried out. The room rocked and filled with mist. She couldn't do it.

And then quite suddenly it came to her that she needn't do it. Bill would wait, and then he would go away. And he would come back in the morning, because if Bill said he had got to see her, he would go on till he did. And it wouldn't be nearly so frightening in the daytime. And she could tell Adrian and ask him—and ask him—

She drifted into an exhausted sleep. At first it was very deep. Then it began to be shot with dreams, like vague terrifying shadows—passing, fading, coming again. She did not know what they were, she only knew that they were dreadful. She moved among them like someone groping in a fog. She didn't know where she was going or why. Something drove her. The dreams went too. They all drove together without any power to stop, like leaves driving in the wind—weak, fluttering leaves in a bleak and dreadful wind.

Suddenly the wind stopped. There was a stillness. Lucy Ashton's eyes looked into hers.

She woke under a blaze of light. She was in the study. The overhead light was on, the room was as bright as day. Herbert Whitall was lying sprawled across the carpet. He was dead. She had never seen a dead person before, but she was very sure that he was dead. There was blood on his shirt-front. She drew a long sighing breath. Then she saw the blood on her white dress—a bright splash of it all down the front. Blood on her dress, and blood on her hand. It was her right hand, and it was dreadfully stained. On the floor at her feet lay the ivory dagger.

CHAPTER 14

Bill Waring heard the half hour strike from the village clock, two notes so faint that if his ears had not been on the stretch he would not have heard them. The wind was setting that way, or he would not have heard them at all—a soft wind, rather high up. It drove the low cloud which darkened the face of the sky, and it moved and rustled the tree-tops, but down on the level of the drive, under the shadow of the pillared portico which screened the front door, the air scarcely stirred.

Bill stood in the shadow of the portico. He could see the front door, the windows of the rooms on either side of it, and the windows of the flanking wings to the east and to the west. None of these windows showed any light at all. If he crossed the wide sweep of the drive and stood back from the portico he could see the whole front of the house. There was not a light in any of the rooms, nor had

there been since he came. He had left his car outside the gate because turning it on the gravel was
going to make too much noise, and if he left it in
the drive it wouldn't be facing the right way.

He had been waiting a bare ten minutes, when
the clock struck. It was a bit early for everyone to
be asleep in a house like this, so he didn't really
expect Lila to be punctual.

His will was set to see her. It was a tough and
obstinate will. It was set. But against it, and not
for the first time, there moved a small, cold breath
of doubt. It would not affect what he did, but quite
insensibly it changed his thought about what he
was doing. Adrian Grey's sister Marian had said
to him a year ago, speaking of Lila, "She's very
lovely, and she's very sweet, but the man who
marries her will have to be her father, and her
brother, and her nursemaid, as well as her husband." He hadn't cared then, but he wasn't so sure
that he didn't care now. A vague daunted feeling
of what life with Lila would be like had begun to
tinge his thoughts. He had not been two months
out of the country before she had let herself be
pushed into saying she would marry Herbert Whitall. Well, he was here to see that she had fair play.
If she wanted to marry the man she could marry
him. If she didn't want to marry him, he would
take her to Ray. After that he supposed they would
be married. The thought did not raise his spirits at
all. They remained dark and clouded. He began to
think about Ray, and found it a relief. She would
know what to do, and she would look after Lila.

He found himself wishing strongly that she was here.

It was about this time that he thought he heard something, or someone, moving. The sound came from the direction of the drive. Afterwards he was to be pressed as to just what kind of a sound it was, and for the life of him he couldn't say. It wasn't anything as definite as a footstep, and it was overlaid by the continual soft stirring of the wind in the tops of the trees. It might have been someone coming up the drive on the grass verge and going off by the path which led round to the other side of the house, but neither he nor anyone else would have thought of that if every moment of the time when he stood waiting under the portico had not been sifted out again and again. And in the end all that you could say was that someone could have come up the drive in that way. What he heard was no evidence that anyone had done so. Any creature of the night could have been about its own secret business—cat, dog, fox, badger, owl.

He listened, but the sound didn't come again. Four notes sounded faintly from the village clock, and then the twelve strokes of midnight. He waited a little longer and then began to walk along the front of the house, taking the left-hand turn. The gravel gave place to a wide paved walk. It was old and mossy, and his feet made no sound.

As he came round the corner and up on the terrace he was quite out of the wind. It was not very dark. He could distinguish the stone balustrade and see how the ground dropped ledge by ledge. The woods on either side moved in the wind he could no longer feel. He turned from the prospect, and saw that there was a light in the corner room.

He did not know that the room was Herbert Whitall's study. He had never been in the house in his life except that evening, when he had waited in the room to the left of the front door. That was where he had asked Lila to meet him. She was to come down, and she was to show a light, and he was to knock three times so that she would know that it was he. There had been no light in the room outside which he had waited, but there was a light in this corner room. He wouldn't put it past Lila to have muddled the whole thing up. He would have to investigate. There were two windows which showed a light. One of them was a long glass door. The real window showed only a dim glow, but the curtains of the door had been carelessly drawn. They left a two inch gap, and a long, narrow streak of light came through it, to lie in a crooked shaft on two descending steps and the damp stone beyond. The reason he had not seen it at once when he came round the corner was that there was a great dark bush of something on either side of the steps. As he passed between them, his sleeve brushed the right-hand bush and the smell of rosemary came out on the soft night air.

He looked through the gap in the curtains, and he saw Lila's gold hair underneath the light. She was turned a little away, so that he did not see her face—only the hair, the line from cheek to chin,

and her white neck a little bent as if she were looking down. She was wearing a long white dress.

He must have pressed on the door, because it
moved under his hand. It had been ajar, opening
towards him, and he had pushed it to. Well, that
made everything quite simple. He groped for the
handle, moved to avoid the swing of the door, and
stepped into the lighted study.

Lila stood looking down at her right hand, which
was red with blood. There was blood on her
dress—a long smear. On the floor at her feet was
a dagger with an ivory handle. It lay there as if it
had just dropped from her hand. There was blood
upon the hilt and upon the blade. And a couple of
paces away Herbert Whitall lay dead in his evening
clothes with blood on his shirt.

The eye may receive an impression too quickly
for the brain to deal with it. The impact is too shocking. Reason and common sense rebel—the sense
which is the common heritage from centuries of
law and order. It is difficult immediately to believe
in a violent breach of the common law.

Bill Waring stood where he was, his shoulder
brushing the curtain which he had pushed aside.
It came to him that Lila hadn't moved or turned
her head. He had pushed the curtain, the runners
had gone swooshing back along the rail, but she
hadn't turned her head. He looked past her to the
far side of the room and saw that the door stood
open into a passage. There was a light in the passage, but not a bright one. The study light was
very bright. It showed everything. It showed Adri-

an Grey in dressing-gown and pyjamas coming into the room and putting a hand behind him to shut the door. When he had shut it he said, "Lila—" in just his quiet usual way.

She moved for the first time, for the first time looked away from her bloodstained hand and the fallen dagger. A long, cold shudder ran over her. When Bill came forward, when he too said her name, she looked at him quite blankly, and looked away.

Adrian did not move. He put out his hand as he might have done to a child, and all at once she ran, crying and sobbing, to throw herself into his arms.

CHAPTER 15

They closed about her. The sobbing stilled. He looked at Bill Waring across the golden head that was pressed against his shoulder and said in his quiet voice,

"He's dead, isn't he? Did you kill him?"

Bill stood where he was. He had that stunned feeling. It showed in his voice as he said,

"No—did you?"

Adrian shook his head.

Bill said, "Did she?" And then, with mind and voice waking from their shocked stupor, "No—no—it's not possible!"

Adrian didn't speak. He felt Lila draw a long trembling breath. He felt her suddenly a dead weight in his arms. If he had not been holding her so closely, she would have fallen. He picked her up and carried her over to the deep couch which stood at an angle to the fire. When he straightened himself after setting her down, it was to find that Bill had come across and was looking down over the back of the couch.

"What is it?"

"She's fainted. It's just as well. Why are you here?"

"I came to take her away. I told her to meet me. I said I'd be outside the room to the left of the hall."

"Then why are you here?" He emphasized the last word.

"She didn't come. I thought I would walk round the house. I saw a light—I saw Lila. The door was ajar. I came in."

"You're sure you didn't kill him?"

"My God, no! He was dead. She was standing there, like you saw her, with the blood on her hand."

They faced each other across the sofa with Lila between them, much too intent upon her and upon one another to be aware of anything else. If the handle of the door had turned, if the door had swung gently in, the movement would not have reached them.

It did not reach them.

Bill said, "What are we going to do—get her back

to her room? There's her dress—there's nothing to be done with a stain like that." His mind baulked. All that blood wouldn't wash out without leaving a mark. If they burned the dress it would be missed. But Lila must be got out of it.

Adrian shook his head. He said quietly,

"No. It can't be hushed up. Whatever we did, the dress would give us away. Too many people saw her in it tonight. You've got to clear out, and at once. If you don't, you're for it—and it drags Lila in. Where are you staying?"

"The Board. But I checked out at half past ten. I wasn't going back. If Lila was coming with me, I was taking her to Ray Fortescue. If she wouldn't come, there wasn't anything for me to stay for. I've got my car."

"You were going back to town?"

"Yes."

"Then go—and get a move on! It's the only thing you can do. This is my story. I couldn't sleep, and I heard someone moving. My room is across the landing from Lila's, and when I opened my door I saw her going down the stairs. I knew she sometimes walked in her sleep, so I followed her."

Bill's eyes were hard on his face.

"Does she walk in her sleep?"

"Oh, yes. She used to do it when she was at school—that's a solid bedrock fact. I followed her and saw her go into the study. Herbert Whitall was lying there on the floor with that ivory dagger a little way off. Lila was bending over him. I wasn't a moment behind her, so she couldn't possibly

91

have stabbed him. She got the blood on her hands and dress touching him. He had been dead some time—his hand was cold when I felt it."

"Is it cold?"

Adrian said, "It will be before the police get here."

"Will it?"

"Of course. Let me finish. Lila woke up and fainted with the shock. Push off, Bill! It's the only thing you can do. My story will stick all right—it's quite a good one. In fact, except for a minor detail or two, it happens to be the truth."

Eric Haile came into the room and shut the door behind him.

"Hullo, Waring!" he said. "I don't know whether you'll agree with me, but I don't think Grey's story is quite good enough."

Nobody spoke for a moment. The feeling of being in some incalculable kind of nightmare deepened. The ordinary link between cause and effect was gone. Anything might happen at any moment.

Adrian had turned. Bill came round the end of the sofa. Then he said,

"What exactly do you mean by that, Haile?"

Eric Haile smiled.

"Just what I said—the story isn't quite good enough." He moved to stoop over the body and touch the lifeless wrist. "Not quite accurate either. He's still warm. Whenever it was done, it wasn't so long ago. And I really don't think that anyone who was in the drawing-room this evening can have any difficulty in guessing who did it. You weren't there, Waring, but Adrian was. Also some people called Considine, and a Professor Richardson. Mrs. Considine has a passion for John McCormack, and we put on a record of his from *Lucia di Lammermoor*. Mrs. Considine was at some pains to give us the story of the opera—Lucy Ashton going mad on her wedding night and stabbing the bridegroom who had been forced upon her. The lovely Lila was considerably affected. She undoubtedly perceived that there was a certain parallel. Adrian had to hold her hand. Very agreeable for both of them. Just previous to this interesting scene the ivory dagger with which poor Herbert seems to have been stabbed had been a good deal in evidence. Well, I ask you! It does all rather hang together, doesn't it?"

Adrian left the couch and came forward.

"Look here, Eric—"

"My dear Adrian, I'm not looking anywhere— I'm ringing up the police."

"I don't know how much you heard, but what I said was true. I did see Lila come out of her room, and I did follow her down the stairs. Everything else apart, there simply wasn't time for her to have stabbed him."

Eric Haile walked round the body to the writing-table and took up the telephone receiver.

"You can tell that to the police," he said.

CHAPTER 16

Ray Fortescue woke in the night with the sound
of the telephone bell in her ears. It had stopped
ringing before she was really awake, and for a moment she wasn't sure whether she had heard it or
not. She had time to blink at the darkness and
to wonder who could possibly be calling her up
in the middle of the night before it rang again.
She said, "Blast!" jumped out of bed, turned
back to snatch the eiderdown, and groped her
way to the little hall, where she put on the light.
It was so exactly like Cousin Rhoda to have a wall-
instrument immediately opposite the door of the
flat, thus achieving the minimum of privacy and
the maximum of discomfort. She clutched the eiderdown round her with one hand, lifted the receiver with the other, and heard Bill's voice say,
"Ray—" She knew it was his voice, because it did
things to her, but if it hadn't been for that, she
wouldn't have known it. She stopped bothering
about the draught under the front door or whether
the eiderdown was slipping. She only thought
about Bill.

"What is it?"

"Ray? It *is* Ray?"

"Yes, Bill. What is it?"

"Something has happened."

"What?"

"Whitall is dead—murdered."

A most awful icy cold that had nothing to do with draughts drove in on Ray. She said, "How?" and Bill said,

"He was stabbed."

She had begun to shake so much that she could hardly hold the receiver. There was a rushing sound in her ears. Through it Bill's voice came urgently.

"Ray—Ray—are you there? Don't go away!"

"I'm here."

Whatever happened, she would always be there if Bill wanted her.

"Then listen! You've got to help! Nobody knows who did it—but Lila was there. I don't mean at the time, but it must have been soon afterwards. Adrian says she was walking in her sleep. We're afraid she touched the dagger—there was blood on her hand and on her dress."

"Bill, how do you *know*?"

"Oh, I was there too. I was going to take Lila away."

She said on a sharp frightened note,

"Bill, for God's sake don't say things like that! Not on the telephone—not to anyone!"

"My dear, we're past all that. Haile walked in on us. He isn't quite sure whether Lila did it alone, or whether I helped her, but I rather gather he thinks we were in it together."

"Bill!"

"Never mind about that. Listen, because the police will be here any moment, and then I probably shan't be able to telephone. I want you to come down here. There's a train at eight-thirty. I'll meet you if I can, but you may have to take a taxi at Emsworth. Lila's had the most dreadful shock, and you are the only person who can help her. You and Lila have always been like sisters. No one has the right to keep you out."

"I'll come, Bill."

He said, "Thanks," and hung up.

When she had put back the receiver she picked up the eiderdown and went into the bedroom. It was dark, it was cold. Her feet were like ice, and so was her heart. She got into bed, pulled the clothes about her. Herbert Whitall had been murdered, and everyone was going to think that Bill had done it. He had come back from America to find that Lila was going to marry Herbert. He had gone down to Vineyards to take her away, and whilst he was there in the middle of the night Herbert Whitall had been stabbed. What else could anyone possibly think?

Herbert Whitall had been stabbed.

Bill wouldn't stab a man. It just wasn't a possible thing. He could have hit Herbert Whitall—he could have hit him hard enough to kill him. But he couldn't possibly have stabbed him.

The thought was like a little glow of warmth at her heart. Through all the dreadful days to come it never went away. She began to think, to plan.

She switched on her bedside light and looked at

the time. It was just after half past twelve. Eight hours before she could catch that train. She would get up and begin to pack at six. There were one or two telephone calls she would have to make. Fortunately, nothing ever waked Rhoda. She would have to allow a quarter of an hour or twenty minutes for telling Rhoda and letting her fuss. Not more, because her temper wouldn't stand it, and Rhoda was really frightfully kind. She could manage with one suit-case. She kept her mind on what she would have to take, and she had got as far as house-shoes, when the telephone bell rang again. This time she ran to it eagerly, because it might be Bill.

It was Sybil Dryden. The hard, clear voice was unmistakable. When you were with her there was a sort of sweetness that lay on the surface like polish, but on the telephone the sweetness was gone. You felt that you were being told what to do, and that it was up to you to get on and do it, even if you were only being invited to tea.

It wasn't an invitation to tea. The voice said,

"Ray, is that you?"

"Yes, Lady Dryden."

"Mr. Waring has told you what has happened. We are all in the study waiting for the police, so I heard what he said. Mr. Haile thought it best that we should stay together." A touch of the grand manner here. Even at a moment like this Sybil Dryden could convey how much she appreciated the dictatorship of Eric Haile. She went on now without a pause. "Mr. Waring rang off before I could

97

stop him. I heard him telling you to come down by the eight-thirty. That won't do."

"Lady Dryden—I've got to be with Lila—you mustn't try and stop me."

"I am not trying to stop you. The house is not mine, and I have no say in what goes on here, but I imagine that Mr. Haile will hardly object to your coming. I want you to take a later train, because I want you to get Miss Silver to come here with you."

Ray didn't think she had ever heard the name before. She echoed it.

"Miss Silver?"

"You won't know her name—it never gets into the papers. She is a private detective. I have known about her off and on for years. She has helped friends of mine, and she is absolutely reliable. Here is the address—write it down! Miss Maud Silver, 15 Montague Mansions, West Leaham Street. Ring through at half past seven and make as early an appointment as you can. You have got to see her, and you have got to persuade her to come down here with you. She is fond of young people. Tell her about Lila and enlist her sympathies."

"Lady Dryden, I don't really know what has happened."

The voice came back insistently.

"I heard what Mr. Waring told you. Lila was walking in her sleep. She found the body—a most dreadful shock. You understand—Miss Silver must be persuaded to come down. You must ring me up when you have seen her and let me know the result, and your train. I will see that you are met."

In the study at Vineyards Lady Dryden hung up the receiver and turned from the table. No more than a yard away one of Herbert Whitall's lifeless hands lay palm upwards on the dark carpet. Nothing could be moved until the police came, and none of them must leave the room. Someone had spread a handkerchief over the dead man's face, but he must not be moved. The ivory dagger must not be moved. The blood must not be washed away. The dark carpet had swallowed it up, but it was there, and there it must stay.

Sybil Dryden skirted the body and came back to the upright chair from which she had risen to go to the telephone. She was wearing a flowered dressing-gown—pale colours on an ivory ground. Her hair was hidden under a lace cap. Her face was pale and set.

Lila was still on the sofa where Adrian had laid her down. He sat beside her with a hand on her shoulder. Every now and then she gave a stifled sob. When this happened he bent and said something which no one else could hear. But she never answered him or lifted her face from the cushion into which it was pressed.

Bill Waring stood with his arm along the stone mantelshelf looking down into the fire. There was an old-fashioned clock on the shelf with a slow, heavy tick. It marked the interminable minutes one by one.

Eric Haile sat on the arm of one of the big leather chairs. Whether by accident or design, he was between the rest of the party and the door. His bright malicious glance went to and fro.

Marsham was in the hall, waiting to admit the police. Mrs. Marsham had been told to dress and make coffee. Frederick had not been roused. The whole house waited. Nobody spoke.

Then all at once everyone stirred. Bill Waring straightened himself. Lady Dryden turned her head. Eric Haile got to his feet. There was a tramp of feet in the passage. Marsham opened the door and announced,

"Inspector Newbury—"

CHAPTER 17

"I don't know what folk are coming to, ringing up before eight in the morning!"

Emma Meadows spoke her mind with the freedom to which her long years of service entitled her. She had brought in the early cup of tea which Miss Silver considered an indulgence, and instead of waiting for it in her comfortable bed, there she was, three parts dressed and in the act of pinning on the net which controlled a neat curled fringe. The hair was mousy in colour, abundant, and with no more grey in it now than it had had for the last twenty years. Removing her new bright blue dressing-gown with the practically indestructible hand-made crochet trimming skilfully transferred from its crimson flannel predecessor, Miss Silver stood revealed in a slip petticoat of grey artificial silk and a neat white spencer whose high neck and long sleeves had also been adorned with a narrow crochet edging. She smiled benignly upon her faithful Emma, took a sip of the tea, and remarked that people could not always choose the moment when they required assistance.

Emma's large, pleasant country face remained overcast.

"They did ought to learn to contain themselves," she said. "At everybody's beck and call—that's what they think you are. And what you ought to say to them is that you need your food and rest the same as others and you don't start work till ten o'clock."

Miss Silver's small neat features remained placid. This kind, solicitous service and the affection which prompted it were amongst the blessings for which she daily returned thanks to Providence. She had left school to enter what she herself called the scholastic profession with no expectation of anything but a lifetime of toil in other people's houses, and an old age in which her exiguous savings might or might not suffice to keep her out of the workhouse. When, by a curious change of circumstances, she found herself transferred to her present profession, she did not anticipate that it would provide her with the modest comfort which she now enjoyed. Her flat, her faithful Emma, her ability to help those who were in trouble, were the subject of her daily gratitude.

She sipped her tea, smiled kindly upon Emma Meadows, and stepping to the wardrobe, selected her second-best dress, a garment of sage-green wool which had been her best during the previous winter. When she had put it on she fastened the neck with her favourite brooch, a rose carved in black bog-oak with an Irish pearl at its heart.

"I have someone coming to see me at half past eight, Emma," she said. "She will join me at breakfast. If there is not enough fish for two more fishcakes, we shall have to open a tin of dried egg."

Emma said gloomily that there would be enough fish—"though why people can't have their breakfasts in their own houses passes me."

Miss Silver smiled.

"You are very good to me, Emma," she said.

Half an hour later Ray Fortescue was shown into a room which in other circumstances would have amazed her very much. The walls were covered with a bright flowery paper and a number of pictures in old-fashioned frames of yellow maple. The pictures were all reproductions of the more famous works of the great Victorian artists—"The Huguenots"; "Hope," drooping over her darkened world; "The Black Brunswicker"; "The Stag at Bay." Oddly shaped but very comfortable chairs with carved walnut frames, bow legs, and spreading laps. Curtains of the bright shade formerly known as peacock-blue. Upholstery of the same material. And a blindingly new carpet in a mixture of blue and brown which had cost so much that Miss Silver's conscience was not always quite at ease about it. Yet what was she to do? The old blue carpet, nursed through the war, patched and darned in the post-war years, had actually become unsafe. Signs of complete disintegration had appeared—Emma had caught her foot in a hole and only just escaped a heavy fall. Carpets were a wicked price, but the affair of the Urtingham pearls had proved very remunerative. So she told her conscience to be sensible and put her hand in her pocket. Even now, before breakfast and coming into the room with a client, she could not help thinking how well it looked. So cosy, and the colours blended in such a pleasing manner.

A small fire had been lighted on the hearth. As Ray took the curly chair on one side of it and watched Miss Silver settle herself on the other, she was wondering what Sybil Dryden imagined this mousy little person was going to be able to do to help Lila and Bill and all of them. She might have stepped out of any of those photographic groups which cluttered up the family album of the Victorian and Edwardian periods. And in every case you would have picked her out as the governess. Ray's eyes strayed from the bog-oak brooch to the black woollen stockings and the rather shabby slippers with the beaded toes. But Lady Dryden usually knew what she was doing. You didn't always like it, but you could see why she did it.

She had sent her to Miss Silver. She had said that she was fond of young people. This certainly seemed to be true. Lifting her eyes from the beaded slippers, Ray realized that the room was full of photographs of young men and women, young mothers and babies. Some of the photographs were getting old, but nearly all the people in them were young. And they were all over the place—on the mantelpiece, on the bookshelves, on a couple of small tables. Everywhere in fact except on the big plain writing-table.

Her eyes came back again to Miss Silver's face. The small capable hands were engaged with some soft knitting. She was being looked at in the firm encouraging way which had induced so many clients to open their hearts.

"What can I do for you, Miss Fortescue?"

"Lady Dryden sent me."

"Yes, you told me that."

"Something dreadful has happened."

In spite of herself her voice shook. She had meant to be quite terribly controlled and business-like, and her wretched voice had gone back on her right at the start.

Miss Silver said, "Yes, my dear?" very kindly indeed, and Ray bit her lip and burst into tears.

She hadn't been so ashamed of herself for years. Angry too. The anger helped. She dabbed fiercely at her eyes with her glove—because you never can find a handkerchief when you want one. And then Miss Silver was offering her a neat folded square and saying,

"Pray do not mind about crying. It is sometimes a great relief."

Ray stopped wanting to cry. She said,

"No—no—there isn't time—I've got to tell you."

It wasn't crying that was going to be a relief, it was telling Miss Silver. She couldn't get it out fast enough.

"We're in dreadful trouble. Lila Dryden is my cousin—our mothers were sisters. Sir John Dryden adopted her. He was only a very distant relation, and Lady Dryden isn't a relation at all."

Miss Silver coughed.

"She is a cousin of Lady Urtingham's. I have met her there."

Ray went on.

"Sir John was a dear. He died four years ago. Lila is lovely. Miss Silver, I've got to make you understand about Lila. She's lovely and she's sweet, but she just can't stand up for herself. She can no more say no when Lady Dryden says yes than she can fly up to the moon. She is afraid of people when they are angry and she can't stand up to them—she just does what they want her to do."

Miss Silver's needles clicked. She remarked that Lady Dryden had a commanding manner.

Ray nodded emphatically.

"She takes a lot of standing up to. Lila can't do it. You've got to understand that—she *can't*."

Miss Silver coughed.

"There has been some special instance in which she has failed to do so?"

Ray nodded again.

"Lila and I went down to stay with a great-aunt. She is an old pet. I've been there a lot, but it was Lila's first visit. Bill Waring is a nephew of her husband's—on the other side of the family, you know. I've known him always, but he hadn't seen Lila before. He just fell down flat, and they got engaged. That was about four months ago." She paused, and added, "Lady Dryden wasn't at all pleased."

Miss Silver looked across the pale pink vest she was knitting for her niece Ethel Burkett's little Josephine.

"Was Mr. Waring not in a position to marry?"

Ray's colour came up brightly.

"They wouldn't have had a great deal. But he is in a very good firm, and they think a lot of him. He has had one or two things patented. That is what he went out to America about."

Miss Silver coughed.

"A most interesting country. Is Mr. Waring out there now?"

"No, he has just come back. I wanted Lila to go and meet him, but she wouldn't. I had to do it. I had to tell him that Lila was going to marry Sir Herbert Whitall in a week's time."

Miss Silver said, "Dear me!"

She gazed mildly at Ray, and drew her own conclusions from the colour in her cheeks and the brightness of her eyes. A very definite and touching interest in Mr. Waring. Warm feelings and a generous heart. A candid nature, ill adapted to concealment of any kind. She said,

"Pray continue."

"He had had an accident—he had been in hospital—Lila didn't get his letters. Lady Dryden always said it wasn't an engagement. She never meant to let Lila marry him. Sir Herbert was a very good match—lots of money, and a beautiful old place which he has bought and done up. I was away—I'm just between jobs at the moment. There wasn't anyone to stiffen Lila up, and before she knew where she was Lady Dryden had her trying on her wedding dress and about three hundred people asked to the wedding."

The needles clicked rather sharply.

"And Sir Herbert Whitall was satisfied?"

Ray looked at her with a kind of stern anger in her face.

"He liked it. He was that kind of man—if he could get something away from somebody else he would think a lot more of it. He collected things— ivories—frightfully old and rare. He wasn't in love with Lila. He just wanted to collect her, and if he could snatch her away from Bill, that made it more exciting."

"He knew of her engagement?"

"It wasn't given out, but he knew all right."

Miss Silver coughed.

"Miss Fortescue, you are speaking of Sir Herbert Whitall in the past tense. Has anything happened to him?"

Ray's hands took hold of one another. She had taken off her gloves. The knuckles stood up white.

"Yes—yes—that's why I've come to you. They were all down at Vineyards, Sir Herbert, and Lady Dryden and Lila. And Bill went down to get Lila away. He went down yesterday. I tried to stop him, but he *would* go. I did try to stop him. And he rang me up in the middle of the night to say that Herbert Whitall had been murdered. He was stabbed with an ivory dagger. And they think Lila did it—or Bill." Her voice caught in an anguished gasp and went on again—"Or *Bill.*"

CHAPTER 18

Well, she had burned her boats, and she didn't care. Miss Silver must be blind, deaf and idiotic if she didn't tumble to the fact that Bill Waring was the centre of things as far as Ray Fortescue was concerned, and she wasn't reckoning on Miss Silver being anything of the kind. By just what imperceptible degree she was passing, or had passed, from wondering why Lady Dryden had sent her on such an apparently futile errand to an almost desperate anxiety that Miss Silver should be induced to come down to Vineyards, she could not have said. The originals of all those photographs smiling from their old-fashioned frames could have told her that they too had travelled the same way.

Ray sat there and wondered at herself. She had cried in front of a woman whom she had never seen before. She had as good as told her she was in love with Bill. And she didn't care. She had no idea why, but she *didn't* care. It might have been the gentle ordinariness of Miss Silver's manner, with its domestic background and its effect of taking the most surprising things for granted. It might have been the touch of fireside authority carrying her right away back to nursery days. It might have been the pink knitting. She didn't know and she didn't care. She went on telling Miss Silver everything she knew. It gave her the most extraordinary sense of relief. When she had finished she felt weak, and empty, and quiet.

Miss Silver coughed in a very kind manner and said briskly,

"And now, my dear, we will have some breakfast. Emma will have it ready for us. Fishcakes—and do you prefer tea or coffee?"

"Oh, Miss Silver, I couldn't!"

Miss Silver was putting the knitting away in a flowered chintz bag. She said with great firmness,

"Indeed you can, my dear. And you will feel a great deal better when you have had something to eat. Emotion is extremely exhausting, and Emma makes very nice fishcakes. And perhaps you would like to wash your face."

Ray washed her face, and it made her feel a good deal better. She also ate a fishcake and some toast and drank an excellent cup of coffee. The horrible things which she had been on the point of accepting lost some of their substance and became incredible again. Someone in *Alice Through the Looking-Glass* had said she could believe two impossible things before breakfast. Or was it three—she couldn't remember. What she did feel perfectly

109

sure about was that it was much easier to believe any number of impossible things before breakfast than afterwards. There didn't seem to be nearly so much room for them when you had had a fishcake, and toast, and coffee.

Miss Silver was coming to Vineyards. She said a beautiful piece straight out of a book about not coming down to prove that anyone was innocent or that anyone was guilty, but just to discover the truth and serve the ends of justice. And then she looked up trains, and went away to pack a bag, and told Ray to ring up Lady Dryden.

It was rather horrid to get a policeman at the other end of the line. Ray had to go on saying, "Please, may I speak to Lady Dryden?" for quite a long time before anything happened. The policeman went away, and the telephone bill totted up, but in the end Lady Dryden was produced. She sounded so exactly like herself that Ray felt it had been worth waiting for.

"Twelve-thirty at Emsworth? My dear, do speak up! It is twelve-thirty? . . . And she is coming? None of you young people speak into the mouthpiece. . . . She is? . . . I will arrange for you to be met. Now, Ray, don't go away! I want you to listen. There will be the inquest, and the funeral, and Lila must have some black. I am all right, because I came down in a black coat and skirt and my fur coat, but she has nothing. I am ringing up the flat, and Robbins will have a suit-case all ready for you to bring down. There is the black coat and skirt from Mirabelle, only do make sure that Robbins has put in the white crepe-de-chine blouse and not the shell-pink. And the black wool dress with high neck and long sleeves. It will do for afternoon or evening. I don't suppose we shall dress, but one can't sit about in a coat and skirt all day. Oh, and the black suède shoes. Robbins is so dreadfully apt to lose her head. . . . I think that is all. I can get her some black gloves in Emsworth. Now are you sure you have got all that? Coat and skirt—white crepe-de-chine blouse—black woollen dress—shoes. Oh, and of course a hat. There is a small black tricorne of mine which would do. Don't let Robbins give you the velvet one. It's not suitable."

Ray hung up, and admired. She didn't like Sybil Dryden, but she admired efficiency. Lady Dryden was certainly efficient. She was organizing Lila's appearance at the inquest and funeral of her bridegroom in exactly the same way as she had organized the arrangements for her wedding. Ray had sometimes wondered whether Lila really would go through with the marriage. She wondered still more whether it would be possible to get her through an inquest and a funeral. But if it was humanly possible, Lady Dryden would do it, and make sure that Lila presented a properly bereaved appearance.

Miss Silver was efficient too. Her bag was packed, and a taxi procured, Lady Dryden's suit-case collected from a tearful and rather incoherent Robbins, and the train to Emsworth caught with five minutes to spare. As it left the station, Ray felt as if she was leaving the comfortable everyday

111

things she knew behind her and being carried into a strange intolerable dream where all the values were different and all the rules were mad. In no other state could Lila and Bill be cast as suspects in a murder case.

The carriage was full of pleasant ordinary people. The train chugged on like any ordinary train. Miss Silver produced her pale pink knitting, carefully done up in a white silk handkerchief. She and Ray had corner seats. She sat there knitting rapidly in the Continental manner, her hands held low, her eyes quite free to watch the passing landscape or the faces of her fellow travellers. She wore a black cloth coat of many years' service and an aged tippet of yellow fur. The beaded slippers had been exchanged for strong laced shoes. Detective Inspector Frank Abbott of Scotland Yard, whom she not infrequently reproves for extravagance of speech, has been known to declare that Miss Silver has only one hat, and that it is fifteen years old if it is a day. This is not the case. She has always possessed at least two hats, a straw for the summer and a felt for winter wear. In fact, she usually has two of each, since at stated intervals a new one is acquired and its predecessor relegated to second-best. All of these hats are black and of an invariable shape, though there are seasonal variations in the shape of ribbon bows and little bunches of flowers. The current hat was in its second autumn. It had a meek black ribbon bow on one side and a tight bunch of pansies and mignonette on the other. The bow was clamped to the hat by a jet buckle. The pansies were transfixed by a dangerous-looking steel hat-pin. Nothing could have been more consolingly commonplace. Nobody could have looked less like a private detective.

The train chugged on.

CHAPTER 19

Lady Dryden met them at Emsworth, having successfully cut out one of the three Whitall cars from under the very noses of the police, Eric Haile, and an extremely disapproving chauffeur. She ordered Ray and the luggage into the back, and installed Miss Silver beside her in front. Being an excellent driver, she was able to negotiate the narrow Emsworth streets and give Miss Silver her opinion about Mr. Haile at one and the same time.

"He may think himself in a position to give orders, but it is more than possible that he will find he is mistaken. He is Sir Herbert's nearest relation—in fact the only one he has. But the whole position is still quite uncertain. There was to be a new will in anticipation of poor Herbert's marriage to my niece, and of course everything will depend on whether it was signed or not. If it was, there will of course be a substantial provision for Lila, and the executors will take charge of everything. Mr. Haile may be an executor or he may not, under either of the wills or under both of them, but until his position is clear, I must say I think it would be in better taste if he did not give himself quite so many airs of authority. One cannot help wondering whether he does not know more about this question of the will than he chooses to admit."

Miss Silver gazed mildly at the traffic and allowed her to talk. The rural towns of England abound in streets which might well have been conceived in a spirit of prophecy to confound the motorist and restrain his insensate desire for speed. All the approaches to the Market Square in Emsworth are blind and narrow. The corner of a very picturesque old house renders it almost impossible to take the Station turning without mounting the pavement. A drinking-fountain of majestic proportions and calamitous ugliness efficiently obstructs the approach to the Town Hall. A by-pass has been talked of for the last thirty years, but may very likely take another thirty to materialize.

Miss Silver was not nervous in a car, but she experienced a slight feeling of relief when they emerged upon a more modern road. Not really very broad, it appeared by contrast to be spacious. She had no affection for old houses, which she rightly considered to be dark and deficient in drainage. She was therefore able to gaze with pleasure upon the rows of small villas which bordered it on either hand, each with a trim autumn garden which displayed salvia, lobelia, marigold, and michaelmas daisy. The roofs of coloured tiles were gay in a gleam of morning sunshine, and she approved

114

the bright curtains which replaced the Nottingham lace of her own generation.

As they drew near the last of the houses, Lady Dryden said,

"They have called in Scotland Yard."

Ray felt a stab of fear, she didn't quite know why. She gave a little gasp which no one heard. Sybil Dryden went on speaking.

"So many of Sir Herbert's activities and interests were in London. I must say it is a relief to feel that the whole thing will be dealt with at the highest level. The Inspector from Emsworth has been quite civil, and I am sure he is a very good officer, but naturally these country policemen cannot have the same experience. I have nothing to complain about in Inspector Newbury's manner. He and the Police Surgeon both realized at once that Lila was in a very severe state of shock. Dr. Everett gave her a sedative and told me on no account to leave her alone. She was, of course, quite unfit to be questioned. And no wonder! Eric Haile absolutely would not permit any of us to leave the study until the police arrived. Imagine keeping a delicate girl in the room with her murdered fiancé! She had fainted, you know—of course I don't know how much Ray has told you."

Miss Silver coughed.

"Let us assume that I do not know anything at all. Just tell me everything as you saw it and heard about it yourself."

The story of the evening came out, told in a very clear and succinct manner. A picture of Lila Dryden emerged. A young girl, not very robust, looking forward to her marriage, but nervous as the day approached, overdone with town engagements and fittings—"So we were snatching this week-end to give her a rest. She used to walk in her sleep when she was at school, you know, and when it started again last week I put my foot down and said no more parties. Unfortunately she seems to have wandered out of her room last night and come upon poor Herbert's body. She must have touched him, because there was blood on her hand and on her dress. Fortunately, Adrian Grey heard her leave her room and followed her. He has been in charge of the alterations at Vineyards, and he has known Lila since she was a child. He realized that she was walking in her sleep, and went down after her, but she must have touched the body before he got there. You can imagine the shock when she came to and saw poor Herbert lying dead."

Miss Silver said,

"Dear me! A truly dreadful situation. Mr. Waring was also present, was he not?"

Lady Dryden's voice hardened.

"Mr. Waring is an extremely obstinate and interfering young man. He had been given his dismissal and he had refused to take it from me. I had told him that if he insisted on it, Lila would see him in the morning, and he must needs come up in the middle of the night to try and persuade her into an elopement. If he finds himself suspected of poor Herbert's murder, he has only himself to thank. I hope it will not turn out that he had anything to do with it. But when you consider the circumstances—his assertion of a non-existent engagement, his obstinate determination to force himself upon Lila, his presence in the study immediately after the murder—well, one cannot be surprised that the police suspect him."

"He hasn't been arrested—"

Ray tried to get the words out, but they wouldn't come. Her throat closed on them, her lips were numb. She heard Miss Silver ask the question for her.

"He has not been arrested, Lady Dryden?"

"No—not yet. I expect they will wait for the Scotland Yard people. By the way, perhaps you had better not refer to that. Two of the staff at Vineyards come in from the village, and the head housemaid from Emsworth. She is a very nice superior woman, and she has a cousin who is married to Inspector Newbury. She lives next door to them, and she had heard all about the murder from her cousin and about Scotland Yard being called in before she came out here this morning. She should not, I suppose, have repeated it."

Miss Silver coughed.

"It will be better not to refer to the matter. Lady Dryden, what can you tell me about the weapon? Miss Fortescue tells me that Sir Herbert was stabbed."

"It was a dagger with an ivory handle. He collected old ivories. This was supposed to be very old. He was showing it to us in the drawing-room after dinner. That is the curious thing. He has a

117

collection of these ivories, and they are valuable. They are kept in an alcove off the drawing-room, and it is secured by a steel shutter. He opened it after dinner last night because Professor Richardson was there and he wanted to see this dagger. They had some kind of dispute about it. The Professor did not seem to think it was so old as Herbert said it was. He was really quite rude about it. And then Mrs. Considine suggested music, and Herbert locked the dagger away."

"He locked the dagger away again?" said Miss Silver in an enquiring voice.

"Yes. We all saw him put it back on the shelf and lock the sliding shutter. There is no doubt at all that he put it away. The question is, when did he get it out again, and why. The Considines and Professor Richardson went away at half past ten. Lila and I said good-night and went upstairs. Some time between then and midnight the ivory dagger was taken out again and Herbert was stabbed with it."

A pair of fine wrought-iron gates came into view. They stood open to the road, with a tree and shrub border beyond them. Lady Dryden turned in between the gates.

CHAPTER 20

Ray found that she was not to be allowed to see Lila until after lunch. Lady Dryden was emphatic.

"You can stay with her the whole afternoon if you like. She is not to be left alone. Mary Good is with her now—the nice woman who comes out from Emsworth. Lunch will be ready, and you must come in. If we do not have proper meals we shall all break down, and that won't help anyone."

They had lunch, and Ray made herself eat. Miss Silver produced a marvellous line of small trite observations about the countryside. Ray was always to remember her remarking that she considered it draughty, and that changes in the weather were more noticeable than they were in a town.

They were a party of five. Eric Haile took the head of the table. Watching his assured manner and air of being very completely at home, Ray was reminded of something her old nurse had said about a woman who was putting on airs—"She thinks everything becomes her." Ray considered that fitted Mr. Haile very well. He had a quiet way with Marsham. He played the host to the manner born. He thought everything became him.

The other two staying in the house were Mr. Grey and Miss Whitaker. She knew Adrian Grey, and could feel thankful that he was here. Miss Whitaker was Sir Herbert's secretary, and it seemed she had been away visiting a sick sister and had only got back a couple of hours ago. She was in black. She had dark circles under the eyes which she so rarely lifted that Ray couldn't have said what colour they were. She hardly spoke, and she only made believe to eat, but she drank a glass of wine and it brought a little colour to her cheek. Of course it must have been a frightful shock, coming back like that to find Sir Herbert dead. And of course she would be out of a job. Perhaps she had somebody depending on her—you never knew. Ray wondered how long she had been with Sir Herbert, and whether she had been fond of him.

Just for a moment Millicent Whitaker looked up. Ray saw that her eyes were dark, and hard, and bright. A little shiver ran down her back. She turned to Adrian Grey.

When they were coming out of the dining-room he said in a low voice,

"You have come to be with Lila. I am so very glad." Then, as they drew away from the others in the hall, "Lady Dryden isn't very good for her, I think. She *will* expect Lila to make an effort, and that isn't what she needs. She is like a child who has had a bad dream—she needs to be reassured and comforted."

They stood for a moment looking at one another, and Ray said,

"Yes."

She had known him on and off for years, but

not well, not like this. All at once she felt that now she knew him very well indeed. He was the sort of person you could be friends with. She felt that they were friends. She said in a quivering voice,

"Bill didn't do it."

"I'm sure he didn't."

"He might have hit him—he couldn't have stabbed him."

His quiet "No" was like a hand coming out to help you in the dark. She looked at him with a gratitude which told its own story and turned to the stairs.

"I must go to Lila."

"Yes. But just a minute. I don't know how she is, but it's possible she may want to see me. My room is just across the landing, and I'll be there all the afternoon. I'll come up with you and show you."

As they went up together he said,

"You see, she may think she did it, and I'm the only person who can tell her she didn't, because I was behind her all the way."

When Ray came into the room she couldn't see anything at all. The curtains were drawn close against the daylight, letting through a kind of shaded dusk just tinged with the blue and green and rose of a flowery pattern. After a moment her eyes cleared, and she saw the bed with someone lying on it. Then Mary Good got up and came forward in a print dress and white apron. Her voice when she spoke had a pleasant country sound.

"Is it Miss Fortescue? Her ladyship said you

would be coming to sit with Miss Dryden. I can't get her to take anything, but I'm keeping it hot by the fire. She did ought to have something.''

Ray said, "I'll see what I can do."

She had her eyes on the bed, but there was no stir, no movement. She went to the door with Mary Good. As she was stepping back into the room, the woman whispered,

"You're not afraid to stay with her?"

"Afraid?"

"Well, she seems quiet enough," said Mary Good.

Ray shut the door and went over to the bed. She felt sick with anger. Afraid? Of Lila? So that was the downstairs gossip—Lila had stabbed Herbert Whitall, and must be watched lest she did someone else a mischief! *Lila!*

She could see quite clearly now. Lila was lying stretched out rigidly with her face buried in the pillows. There was nothing to be seen of her except a cloud of hair, shadowy in the dusk of the room. Ray put a hand on the shoulder nearest to her and said,

"Lila—it's Ray. Aren't you going to speak to me?"

There was a faint tremor, instantly stilled.

"Lila—"

A hand came out and caught at hers. It was cold.

"Has she gone?"

"Yes."

"There isn't anyone else—only you?"

"Only me."

The hand pushed faintly.

"Lock the door—"

When she came back after turning the key Lila was sitting up. She had thrust the bedclothes back and sat stiffly upright with a hand on either side of her, pressing down upon the bed. She said in a strained, gasping way,

"Pull back the curtain—I can't see you—I want to see you."

Well, that was something to the good. If ever Ray had hated anything in her life she hated this horrid gloom. It was with considerable relief that she drew back the curtains of the nearer window and let in daylight and a pale gleam of sunshine. But she wasn't prepared for what the light would show her. She thought she knew Lila inside out, but she had never seen her like this. It wasn't just her pallor, or that she looked most dreadfully ill. The pale hair had lost its gold. It fell dank and tangled about her shoulders, and her eyes stared as if they saw something dreadful and couldn't stop seeing it.

She said, "Come here," and when Ray came she turned the stare on her and said,

"Did I do it?"

"Of course you didn't!"

"He's dead, you know. Herbert is dead. I don't know whether I did it. Adrian is the only person who knows, and they won't let him come. I *want* Adrian."

"He's just across the landing—he can come to you at once. He is waiting for me to let him know whether you would like him to come."

"You won't let Aunt Sybil in? I only want Adrian."

"I won't let anyone else in, I promise you. I'll go and get him."

It didn't take a minute, because he was waiting with his door ajar. She slipped across the landing, but before she was there he was out of his room and they were going back together. There wasn't a sound in the house until they were right at Lila's door. Then Lady Dryden's voice came floating up from the hall with its sweet polished tone. Ray could remember calling it a shiny voice when she was a child. She shut the door on it now and turned the key in the lock again.

Lila was just as she had left her. The same strained pose. The same staring look. It was fixed on Adrian now. She began to speak in that unnatural voice.

"Herbert is dead. He was stabbed. I saw him. But I don't know if I did it. They can't tell me, because they don't know. And I can't remember. Lucy Ashton killed the man they made her marry, and I can't remember if I killed Herbert. I didn't mean to, but I can't remember. You are the only person who can tell me. Did I do it, Adrian?"

"Of course you didn't!"

He was sitting on the bed beside her, but not touching her yet.

"Are you sure?" Her voice had a wavering note.

"I'm quite sure. Give me your hands. And let me cover you up—you'll get cold."

The pale night-dress was slipping from her shoulders. The tangle of hair fell over them. She went on staring at Adrian Grey.

"Are you sure?"

"Of course I'm sure. Now listen! You were walking in your sleep. I heard you come out of your room, and I followed you downstairs. You went into the study. Poor Herbert was lying there dead before you came. Hold on to that. He was lying there dead before you came out of your room and started to go downstairs. I was behind you all the way, and he was dead before either of us came into the study."

A shudder went over her.

"I woke up—and he was dead. And my hand was red."

"Yes, I know. You must have touched him."

She shook her head with a curious stiff motion.

"I wouldn't do that—I wouldn't touch him. I hated him to touch me." The shudder went over her again.

"You were walking in your sleep—you didn't know what you were doing."

"I wouldn't touch Herbert." She leaned towards him, lifting her hand from the bed and holding it out. "It was all red. How did it get like that? I wouldn't touch him—not however much I was walking in my sleep."

Under his air of quiet control Adrian Grey was aghast. What sort of crime had Sybil Dryden been prepared to abet, and what sort of crime had he been prepared to condone? If Herbert Whitall were not now lying dead, they would have been standing by whilst this child married him. He said in a warm, strong voice,

"There are a lot of things we don't know, but there is one you can be sure about—you had nothing to do with Herbert's death. You can be quite, quite sure about that."

"Can I?"

"Yes. He must have been dead before you came downstairs."

He had taken the hand she was holding out, clasping it firmly. All at once she gave him the other one. She was shivering a little. She said in a surprised voice,

"I'm cold," and he pulled the eiderdown round her and pulled up the pillows.

Ray came forward with the cup of soup which had been keeping hot by the fire.

"This will warm you, darling."

"Will it?"

Her voice had changed. The strain had gone out of it. It was comfortable to have Adrian's arm round her and to lean against his shoulder. She drank the soup and ate some of the chicken mould which Mrs. Marsham had sent up. She was warmed and fed, and the horrid feeling about not being able to remember was gone. She hadn't done anything dreadful after all. Adrian said so. A pleasant drowsiness began to come over her. When Adrian laid her back on her pillows and tucked her up she opened her eyes for a moment.

"I don't want Aunt Sybil to come."

"She won't if you go to sleep. But there's nothing to be afraid of, you know."

Half asleep and smiling, she spoke the thought that was in her mind—"Nothing to be afraid of. . . . She can't make me marry Herbert now. . . . "

CHAPTER 21

Miss Silver spent a not unprofitable afternoon. Unlike so many country houses, Vineyards was provided with an up-to-date system of heating which kept the whole house at a comfortable temperature. The drawing-room, so spacious, so well proportioned, would have been quite on the chilly side without it. As it was, she was able to enjoy a seat in the sofa corner and get on very well indeed with little Josephine's vest, whilst encouraging Lady Dryden to talk and receiving a great deal of information about everyone and everything—Lila's history from the time when her improvident young parents had been killed together in a motor accident—"And what would have happened to her, I can't imagine, if my husband hadn't come forward. They were quite distant cousins, and he was under no obligation to do so, but he was a childless widower at the time, and she was a pretty little thing. There was no legal adoption, but he treated her exactly as if she was his own child. Men are much more sentimental than women—don't you think so? I am fond of Lila of course, but I couldn't feel as if she were a child of my own. We were not married until some time later. He really did spoil and indulge her to an absurd extent. I have done my best to counteract it, but it is those early years that count. This marriage would have been the making of her—an older man upon whom she could lean, and complete security so far as money was concerned. I have never known anyone less fitted to struggle with the world than Lila is."

Miss Silver gave her slight preliminary cough.

"She was not provided for?"

Lady Dryden made an impatient gesture.

"Her parents had less than nothing. I believe my husband had to pay off a number of debts. He himself had losses, and he could not do very much. My own income is not what it was."

Miss Silver pulled thoughtfully at a pale pink ball of wool.

"Then you were quite satisfied about the marriage?"

"Indeed I was."

"And Miss Lila?"

Lady Dryden drew herself up a little.

"Ah—you've been talking to Ray. You really must not believe all the irresponsible things she says. Because I did not wish Lila to make an extremely foolish marriage with a young man who was not in a position to support her, she has no doubt presented me as a kind of cruel stepmother. Girls have these romantic ideas. But when you see

Lila I think you will agree with me that it would be the unkindest thing in the world to allow her to become a poor man's wife."

As her needles clicked and the pale pink vest revolved, Miss Silver agreed that romance was not always practicable.

"In everyday life it requires a great deal of courage and unselfishness if it is to be maintained."

Lady Dryden considered that this was the kind of thing to which there really isn't any answer. It did not appear to her to mean anything at all. She said, "Oh, yes," in a perfunctory way and went on to talk about Eric Haile.

"One of those charming people who spend a great deal more than their income. Though I don't think anyone knows what his income is. I should be surprised if he knew himself. I suspect that Herbert subsidized him a good deal."

"He has been staying in the house?"

"Only for the night. He has what he calls a cottage just on the other side of the village. He writes gossipy books about people's private lives. After they are dead of course, because there isn't any law of libel then."

Miss Silver coughed.

"You do not like him?"

Lady Dryden looked down her nose.

"I have nothing against him in a social capacity. He can be very entertaining. At the moment I think he is taking too much upon himself, and I resent it. This was to have been Lila's home, and Herbert is no sooner dead than Eric Haile behaves as if the whole place belonged to him."

"Is it possible that it does, Lady Dryden?"

"It can't be possible. Herbert told me himself a week ago that he was signing his new will."

"Did he say when?"

"Within a day or two—I certainly understood that it would be within a day or two."

"Did Mr. Haile know that?"

"I don't know. Herbert may have told him, or he may not. I will tell you one thing. They had an interview just before dinner last night. Herbert told me that he thought his cousin wanted to borrow money, and when I said I hoped the interview would be pleasanter than he appeared to expect, he laughed and said, 'Keep your good wishes for Eric. He's going to need them.' "

Miss Silver said, "Dear me!"

There was a tinge of complacency in Lady Dryden's voice as she went on.

"I said that sounded vindictive. He said that was what he was, and he repeated the word. So I don't think the interview can have been a pleasant one, or that Mr. Haile can have enjoyed it very much."

Miss Silver gave a thoughtful cough.

"And when they came in to dinner, did Mr. Haile appear to be upset?"

"Oh, no. But he wouldn't—he would never show anything. He has that social manner—no matter what he had in his mind, he would never allow it to show. No matter what it was!"

Miss Silver looked across her knitting with a very serious expression,

"Just what do you mean by that, Lady Dryden?"

Sybil Dryden rose from her chair and stooped down to put a log on the fire. Her back was towards Miss Silver. All her movements were graceful and controlled. She said,

"Mean? Oh, just what I said. I always do."

She came back to her chair, arranged a cushion behind her, and went on smoothly.

"I think I had better tell you about Miss Whitaker."

Just before tea Eric Haile came into the room. Lady Dryden at once said that she would go and see how Lila was getting on.

Having remained courteously upon his feet until she had left the room, Mr. Haile sat down in the chair which she had vacated and proceeded to make himself agreeable to Miss Silver. After a few generalities he said with a smile,

"Charming woman, Lady Dryden. Unfortunately she doesn't like me."

Miss Silver wondered what this was going to lead to. She maintained an attentive gaze and continued to knit. There was a brief pause as if he expected her to speak. Then he went on.

"You must not think me inhospitable if I say that I do not quite understand in what capacity you are here. Naturally, any friend who Lady Dryden feels would be a comfort or support to herself or to that poor girl is only too welcome. You are a friend of long standing?"

"No, Mr. Haile."

"Then it is a professional engagement? Lady

131

Dryden has mentioned that you were concerned in the recovery of Lady Urtingham's pearls."

"Yes, Mr. Haile."

He allowed himself to look a little surprised.

"But in this case there has not been any robbery. Nothing is missing—there are no pearls to be recovered."

Miss Silver again said, "No, Mr. Haile."

If she was aware of exasperation, it did not interfere with the progress of little Josephine's vest. She continued to knit smoothly and rapidly, and to regard him in a gently expectant manner. Eric Haile found himself unable to decide whether she was doing it on purpose. If she was, then she was deep, and he had better be careful. If not—well, she was easy, and he could go right ahead. He thought he would go on—but warily of course. He looked at her with great frankness and laughed.

"What I am trying to say is that whilst I am delighted to see you here, I would rather like to know whether your visit is a professional one."

Miss Silver coughed gently.

"I think you may call it so, Mr. Haile."

"Then—pray do not misunderstand me—just what do you hope to accomplish?"

She knitted in silence for a moment before she spoke.

"You referred just now to the Urtingham pearls, and you said that in this case nothing was missing. I cannot agree with you there."

"Indeed?" He stared at her. "And what do you suppose to be missing in this case?"

"The truth, Mr. Haile."

This was said with so much simplicity that he could have laughed. He did permit himself an indulgent smile.

"Well, well, there is that way of looking at it of course. But with regard to my cousin's death, I don't really think that we have very far to look for this truth you speak of. I'm afraid there can be no doubt that he was stabbed by Lila Dryden. Lady Dryden naturally does not choose to admit it, but the facts speak for themselves. Not very creditable facts, I am afraid. Sybil Dryden was pushing that unfortunate girl into what she considered a very advantageous marriage. Have you met Lila Dryden?"

"Not yet."

He threw up a hand.

"A lovely creature—quite unsophisticated—mentally still in the nursery. You had only to see her with my cousin to realize that she had an intense physical shrinking from him. To my way of thinking the whole thing was iniquitous. Then last night Herbert got out this ivory dagger, and there was a lot of talk about how old it was, and how many people it might have killed. They say he locked it up again afterwards—there is an alcove with a steel shutter behind that curtain over there—but I can't say I saw him do it myself. I was bringing in gramophone records from the study, and as luck would have it, Mrs. Considine asked for a John McCormack record from *Lucia di Lammermoor*. She not only asked for it, but she gave us a résumé of the plot, which is of course taken from Scott's *Bride of Lammermoor*. I expect you will remember that Lucy Ashton stabs the bridegroom who has been forced upon her on their wedding night."

Miss Silver inclined her head.

"A most painful story."

His tone took on a shade of condescension.

"I'm afraid the plots of operas are mostly that way. But it was an unfortunate moment to talk about Lucy Ashton. I thought Lila was going to faint. Anyone could see that she was abnormally affected by the story. To my mind there is no doubt that she later walked in her sleep and came across the dagger. Whether she was still asleep when she stabbed poor Herbert, there is no means of knowing. If she woke suddenly to find him touching her or holding her, I feel that anything may have happened. I have not the slightest doubt that that is how my cousin met his death. She was not, of course, responsible for her actions, and no jury would find that she was. But Lady Dryden is simply shutting her eyes to the facts when she looks for any other explanation."

Miss Silver looked down at her knitting. She might have been counting the stitches, or she might not. After a moment she said,

"How well you put it, Mr. Haile. And how extremely interesting."

Lady Dryden came back into the room as she spoke. Her manner was a little more commanding than usual. No one would have guessed that she had just been obliged to admit defeat. In a minor matter, it is true, but she was not accustomed to have her wishes set aside. And by Ray Fortescue! She would have a word with Ray presently, but at the moment it was, of course, impossible to risk throwing Lila back. Ray, like Eric Haile, was taking too much upon herself.

She had gone up to find all the curtains drawn back and Lila on the sofa in a pale blue dressing-gown looking really quite cheerful, with Adrian Grey more or less holding her hand. And all Ray had to say was, "We thought we would have tea up here with Lila. And I've been telling her about Miss Silver, so perhaps she would like to come up too." It had really left her with nothing to say. She simply couldn't risk upsetting Lila, and Ray knew it. There would be something to be said later. But Lady Dryden knew how to make a virtue of necessity. She was doing it now, and in the grand manner.

"Lila has had a refreshing sleep and seems to be quite herself again. I wonder if you would care to join her and Ray for tea, Miss Silver?"

CHAPTER 22

Detective Inspector Frank Abbott and Inspector
Newbury drove up to the house together at just
after five o'clock. It had turned cold and was beginning to be wet. The house felt agreeably warm
when they came into it.

As Marsham stood back from the front door,
which he had closed behind them, he received a
shock of surprise. The Inspector from Scotland
Yard looked a great deal more like a guest than
accorded with his sense of the fitness of things. He
had been in very good houses, and he knew. Even
if he had still been in service with the Earl of Drum-
ble he would without a qualm have admitted this
tall fair young man on any social occasion. Very
good clothes too. Savile Row if he was a judge,
and he thought he was. Not too new, and worn
the way a gentleman ought to wear his clothes—
as if they were the right and proper thing for him
to wear and he didn't have to give them a thought.

Lady Dryden, who was coming down the stairs,
received the same impression, though she would
not have put it in quite the same way. She had a
moment of wonder as to who this distinguished-
looking young man could be, and one of angry
surprise when he was presented as Detective In-

spector Abbott from Scotland Yard.

"The new Police College product, I suppose," was her comment to Adrian Grey, who had followed her.

Adrian supposed so too. He had had only a fleeting glimpse of the two Inspectors as they turned into the passage leading to the study.

"What did you say his name was?" He had an idea that he had seen the tall, slim figure and the fair slicked-back hair before.

"Abbott," said Lady Dryden rather as if the name were an offence to her. "Detective Inspector Abbott."

Adrian felt a tinge of amusement. Even at a time like this Sybil Dryden appealed to his sense of humour. He proceeded to gratify it.

"Then it's Frank Abbott. He's related to everybody all over England, and I've met him. I thought I knew that back. He looks as if he had been kept on ice ever since the family came out of the Ark, but I believe it's mostly manner. His grandmother was old Lady Evelyn Abbott, and a noted dragon in her day. She quarrelled with his father and cut Frank out of her will when he went into the police. The money all went to a granddaughter."

"Oh, there was money?"

"One of those shipping fortunes."

Miss Silver, coming downstairs about half an hour later, encountered a short, alert little man who was giving very perfunctory attention to Lady Dryden's remarks about her niece's health. She caught the words "extremely delicate from a child," and had no difficulty in arriving at the conclusion that the gentleman to whom they were addressed was Dr. Everett, the Police Surgeon. As she passed him, he set a determined foot upon the bottom step.

"Well then, I'll just go up and see for myself. There'll be someone with her, I take it, so I needn't trouble you."

"But, Dr. Everett—"

"Now, Lady Dryden, it's no manner of use, and you're not helping her or yourself. If she's fit to be seen, they must see her, and if she isn't, I'll say so. You mustn't expect me to take my opinion from you or from anyone else. And you may take it from me, if she's any way fit, it'll be best for her to get it over, so I'll just be going up." He suited the action to the word, and at a very brisk pace.

Lady Dryden stood where she was with an angry flush on her face. Miss Silver gave a slight admonitory cough.

"These enquiries are painful, but they must take their course. Believe me, it is not wise to oppose them. I gather from what he said that the Inspector is here."

"Two of them," said Lady Dryden. "There is a man from Scotland Yard with Inspector Newbury."

Miss Silver looked brightly interested.

"Indeed? May I ask his name?"

"I believe it is Abbott."

Miss Silver coughed in a pleased sort of way.

"Really? How very pleasant. Such an able officer. And an old friend of mine."

138

Dr. Everett made his appearance on the landing and began rapidly to descend the stairs.

"A remarkable improvement. That's a very sensible girl you've got with her. Nice girl—level-headed. Best thing possible for Miss Dryden. And she's perfectly fit to make a statement. Of course she needn't. I've told her that. Always play fair. She's got a perfect right to refuse, or to hold her tongue until she can see her solicitor. But she'll have to see the Inspectors and tell them so herself. I'll be there." He went briskly off in the direction of the study.

Miss Silver considered her course of action. She had no wish to be intrusive, or to put herself in Frank Abbott's way. It would not be very long before someone or other would mention her presence at Vineyards. Meanwhile she had spent quite an informative half hour with Lila Dryden and Adrian Grey, to say nothing of the afternoon's conversations with Lady Dryden and Mr. Haile. She felt that she had plenty of food for thought, and that it would be pleasant to finish little Josephine's vest. She proceeded in the direction of the drawing-room.

It was, however, no more than a few minutes later that Lady Dryden followed her in a formidable cold rage. She had been refused permission to be present while Lila was questioned, and she strongly suspected that it was Dr. Everett who had instigated the refusal. She relieved herself by some very caustic remarks, and subsided finally into a state of icy resentment. For the first time in her life

139

she was up against circumstances which she could not control and people whom she could not manipulate. The whole structure of the law, taken, as we all take it, for granted, emerged as a factor not to be diverted or compelled. Instead of a safeguard it had become a threat. She knew what it was to be afraid. She sat staring into the fire, and had no more words.

Upstairs Lila was supporting the ordeal of being questioned with perfect calm. Since Adrian was sure that she hadn't killed Herbert, everything was quite all right. The immense relief of knowing that nobody could make her marry him now really left no room for anything else. Inspector Newbury and Inspector Abbott sat side by side and asked her a great many questions. Some of them she could answer, and some she couldn't. When she didn't know the answer she said so. It really wasn't frightening at all.

"Why did you go downstairs, Miss Dryden?"

"I don't know. Adrian says I was walking in my sleep."

"Is that what he told you to say?"

Lila's blue eyes opened quite wide. They were very beautiful eyes.

"Oh, no—he saw me."

That was Inspector Newbury. Then the London Inspector.

"Did you go down to meet Mr. Waring?"

"Oh, no. I was going to wait and see him in the morning."

"He wrote and asked you to meet him?"

She gazed at him earnestly.

"Oh, yes. And I didn't know what to do. I thought, and thought, and I didn't feel as if I could go down. Everything was so empty, and everyone in bed—except perhaps, I thought, Herbert might still be there, and if I went down—" Her colour went. She said in a whisper, "I couldn't."

"You were afraid of him?"

"Oh, yes—" a shudder shook her—"*dreadfully.*"

"Then why did you go down?"

Ray stood behind the couch. The young man with the mirror-smooth hair and the cold blue eyes was trying to catch Lila out. She had to bite her lip to keep back angry words. But there was no need to be angry. Lila wouldn't be caught, because she was speaking the truth. She just looked at him and said,

"But I didn't—at least I didn't mean to. It was cold, so I sat down on this couch and pulled the eiderdown over me. I had to think whether I would have to go down or not, and I thought I wouldn't. I thought if I didn't go down, Bill would come back in the morning, and that would be a great deal better. And then I must have gone to sleep. I didn't mean to go down—I didn't really."

"You know you did go down?"

"I didn't know I was doing it."

"You know you went down to the study?"

Her eyes widened.

"I woke up there."

"Go on, Miss Dryden—"

"Herbert was dead."

"How did you know he was dead?"

"I thought he was—"

"What made you think so?"

She said, "Blood—" in a whispering voice. "On my hand—and on my dress—"

"And that made you think Sir Herbert was dead? Did you think you had killed him?"

She shook her head.

"I didn't think—it was all too dreadful. Adrian was there. He says I didn't. He says he was just behind me."

"Did you dream when you were walking in your sleep?"

"Oh, no—I don't. At least I don't remember it if I do."

"Do you often walk in your sleep?"

"I used to when I was at school."

"And lately?"

"Aunt Sybil said I came out on the landing one night last week. I didn't know I did."

"And you don't remember dreaming last night?"

She shook her head.

"No—I just woke up. And Adrian was there."

CHAPTER 23

It was about three-quarters of an hour later that Miss Silver, coming through the hall, was aware of Adrian Grey emerging from the passage which led to the study. He was not alone, and his companion was Detective Inspector Abbott. She had been about to go upstairs, but she paused and waited for them with a smiling face and an outstretched hand.

Frank Abbott took the hand and reciprocated the smile. Adrian Grey having mentioned that there was a Miss Silver staying in the house, he was by no means unprepared for the appearance of the lady whom he had been known in moments of expansion to address as "Revered Preceptress." They were, all jesting apart, on a footing of deep attachment, and, upon Frank's side, of a most unfeigned respect. As always in the presence of a stranger, she addressed him with formality.

"Inspector Abbott—this is indeed a pleasure!"

Frank, on his side, was equally punctilious.

"My dear Miss Silver! Mr. Grey told me that you were here. Perhaps we could have a talk—if you can spare me a little time?"

Adrian passed on, and they were alone. Miss Silver coughed.

"I should appreciate the opportunity."

Frank shed his formal manner.

"Then come along to the study and give me the low-down on everything and everyone."

She said, "My dear Frank!" but her tone was an indulgent one.

They went down the passage together and came into the study.

No trace of the tragedy remained. Herbert Whitall's body had been removed long ago. The photographer and the fingerprint man had done their work. The room had been ordered. The light which had shone down upon such a terrible scene now disclosed no trace of it. There was not even a stain on the deep-toned carpet to show where the ivory dagger had dropped from Lila's bloodstained hand—if indeed it had so dropped. The couch upon which Adrian Grey had laid her stood at its accustomed angle to the fire. A bed of glowing ash sent out a pleasant warmth.

Miss Silver sat down on the sofa, not too near the fire, because the room was really very comfortable, whilst Frank Abbott arranged himself in a casual attitude on the arm of one of the big chairs. When she had opened her knitting-bag and extracted from it little Josephine's vest and a crochet-hook she found him regarding her with a quizzical smile.

"Grey tells me that you have been here since one o'clock. You therefore already know all. How much are you going to tell me?"

She drew on a pale pink ball and began to finish

144

off the neck of the vest with a neat crochet edging.

"My dear Frank, you sometimes talk very great nonsense."

He laughed.

"Well, I would like to know who did it. Was it the lovely Lila?"

"I do not think so."

"No more do I. But if it were not for one extraordinarily lucky fact, I should say that nine juries out of ten would hardly leave the box—unless they were so overcome by her looks that they couldn't bring themselves to believe the evidence. I mean, just consider it. I suppose you have heard about the scene in the drawing-room last night—the *Lucia di Lammermoor* business, with a John McCormack record on the gramophone and Mrs. Considine imparting the story of the opera—the unfortunate Lucy going mad and stabbing her bridegroom. I've just had it all from Haile, and he says Lila Dryden was a good deal affected. I gather she didn't like her bridegroom much better than Lucy liked hers. Grey tried to soft-pedal the whole thing, but you can imagine that the prosecution could make a good deal of play with it. Well, the guests go away at half past ten. Everyone goes upstairs except Whitall, who is in the habit of sitting up late. Round about midnight Lila Dryden comes down, presumably to meet the devoted Bill Waring. A note from him urging her to elope was found in her room. For some reason she opens the glass door in the study instead of the window indicated by him in what, I believe, they call the Blue Room. I can't think of any reason why she should have done this, but apparently she did. She is interrupted by Herbert Whitall. She turns round from the window, sees him, picks up the dagger which is lying on the writing-table, and strikes blindly with it. As luck will have it, she hits a vital spot. He staggers back and falls. The dagger drops from her hand, staining her dress. Then Mr. Bill Waring, who has got tired of waiting in front of the house, comes up on to the terrace, sees the light, finds the door ajar, and walks in. And at practically the same moment Mr. Adrian Grey comes in by the open door from the passage. He and Bill Waring see each other, and they both see Lila Dryden. She faints. Adrian Grey puts her on the sofa—and by the way, it is rather illuminating that it was into his arms she threw herself and not Bill Waring's."

Miss Silver said primly, "He is a very old friend."

"So everyone tells me. Well, he puts Lila on the sofa, and he and Bill have a short dramatic conversation which interests them both so much that neither of them notices that the door has been opened. This time it is Mr. Haile who butts in, but not at all obtrusively. He stands and listens. Here's his statement of what he heard." He opened an attaché case which he had set down in the lap of the chair, took out a typewritten sheet, and began to read.

"Waring said, 'I came to take her away. I told her to meet me. I said I'd be outside that room to the left of the hall.' Grey said, 'Then why are you here?' and Waring said, 'She didn't come. I thought

146

I would walk round the house. I saw a light—I saw Lila. The door was ajar. I came in.' Grey said, 'You're sure you didn't kill him?' and Waring said, 'My God, no! He was dead. She was standing there like you saw her, with the blood on her hand.' After that they talked about what they were going to do. There was a stain on her dress. They didn't think it would come out, and if they destroyed the dress it would be missed. Grey told Waring to clear out and get back to town. If he stayed he would drag Lila in. He had got to get out. Grey said he would say he heard Lila come out of her room and followed her down the stairs, that he was behind her all the way, and that Herbert Whitall was dead when they reached the study. Lila must have touched him and got the blood on her that way. He had been dead some time. When he had said all this, he said it was a good story and it would stick. And I came into the room and said I didn't think it was quite good enough."

He folded up the statement and tossed it back into the case.

"There, gentlemen of the jury—that is the case for the prosecution, and a pretty damning case it is."

Miss Silver let the adjective pass without reproof.

"And what is the case for the defence? You mentioned an extraordinarily lucky circumstance."

"Oh, it's the medical evidence. Bill Waring says he heard twelve o'clock strike before he started to walk round the house. Whether you accept that or not, Haile says he looked at the clock as he came

147

into the study, and it was just after ten past twelve. He rang up the police at once, and they were there in half an hour. Dr. Everett was out on a case in this direction, and they picked him up on their way. Well, he swears that the man had been dead for an hour at the very least, and the postmortem bears that out. If Lila Dryden stabbed him she wouldn't have just stood there for a good half hour or so. The same applies to Bill Waring and Adrian Grey. Granted they were both in love with Lila Dryden—and that gives either of them a motive for getting rid of Whitall—why in heaven's name should they hang about on the scene of the crime for half an hour? It doesn't make sense, and I think it lets them out. Besides *stabbing*—it's really not the sort of thing you would expect either of them to go in for. I can see Grey reasoning with Whitall, and I can see Bill Waring knocking him out, but I can't see either of them stabbing him with a gimcrack fancy dagger. I don't know how that strikes you?"

Miss Silver coughed.

"Very much as it strikes you, my dear Frank. I have not as yet had an opportunity of meeting Mr. Waring, but from what I have heard of him it would not seem to be at all in character that he should stab Sir Herbert. There would, for one thing, be no need for him to do so. I understand that he is a powerful young man. If, for instance, Sir Herbert had interrupted Miss Dryden's projected elopement and proceeded to resist it by force, it would, I gather, have been an easy matter for Mr. Waring to knock him down. He has been described to me as an expert boxer."

Frank nodded.

"As you say. Two hearts that beat as one! Quotation from classical poem whose author I forget. To proceed. Setting Lila Dryden, Adrian Grey and Bill Waring aside for the moment, what ideas have you?"

The crochet-hook went in and out, making a delicate shell pattern about the neck of little Josephine's vest.

"None, I think, that I can formulate at the moment. There are, however, a few points." Her gaze dwelt upon him thoughtfully. "The ivory dagger. It was, I understand, exhibited to Sir Herbert's guests last night, and afterwards locked away by him."

"Yes, that is so. As to the locking away, Adrian Grey, Mrs. Considine and Professor Richardson are all prepared to swear to that. Lila Dryden says she didn't notice it, but he always locked his ivory things away. Lady Dryden says she wasn't interested. Miss Whitaker was not in the room, and Mr. Considine and Mr. Haile were talking about gramophone records and not taking any notice."

"Then how did it come about that the dagger was here in the study, conveniently to a murderer's hand?"

"Oh, I think that is easily explained. Whitall had an argument with the Professor about its authenticity. I expect old Richardson stung him up, and he went and fetched the dagger after the others

149

had gone up. It would be quite a natural thing for him to do. And there is this support for the theory that he did do it." He got up, went over to the writing-table, and came back with a small cylindrical object in the palm of his hand. "You see what it is—a jeweller's magnifying-glass. It had rolled under the table. They've been over it for finger-prints, so it doesn't matter about handling it. A bit of a muddle, I gather, but a good plain mark of Whitall's thumb right on top."

"You think he was examining the dagger?"

"Yes, I think we may assume that he was. In which case it would be lying there on the table, and very handy for anyone who wanted to do him in. Any other points?"

Miss Silver drew her wool through a loop and fastened it off. The neck of the little pink vest was finished. She turned her attention to a sleeve.

"Yes, Frank. There is my position in this house."

"Well, I'm never surprised to see you, because you do keep on cropping up. But I was just won-dering how you came to be here—so soon."

Miss Silver gave a gentle cough.

"Lady Dryden called up Miss Fortescue between the discovery of the murder and the arrival of the police. She told her to get in touch with me and bring me down here as soon as possible."

"You know Lady Dryden?"

"I have met her. She is Lady Urtingham's cousin."

"Well, well. And the point you wish to raise?"

"My position in the case. I am not entirely happy

150

about it. I have said to Lady Dryden what I say to every client—I do not come into a case to prove anyone innocent, or guilty, I come into it to discover the truth and to serve the ends of justice. Lady Dryden replied that her niece was innocent, and that the discovery of the truth would prove her innocence. I went on to say that in any criminal case, and particularly in a murder case, a very strong light is turned upon the thoughts, the actions, and the lives of everyone directly or indirectly connected with it. I pointed out that it was not always possible to say what will or will not come out. She drew herself up and said that she and her niece had nothing to hide. I told her that if she were not really willing to be taken at her word, I could retire from the case, but if I undertook it I must have a free hand and feel myself at liberty to consult with the police. She replied coldly that neither she nor Miss Dryden had anything whatever to conceal, and that her sole object in retaining my services was to arrive at the real facts of the case."

Frank's fair eyebrows lifted.

"I am reminded of 'Perhaps it was right to dissemble your love, but—why did you kick me downstairs?' Do you usually press a client as far as that?"

There was a silence long enough to be marked before she said,

"No, Frank."

"Meaning?"

"I think that, in spite of her disclaimers, Lady

Dryden has something to hide."

"Then why import you into the case?"

The crochet-hook went in and out, making little pink shells. Miss Silver coughed.

"She was very much alarmed about her niece's position. She was desperately anxious to avoid an arrest and the consequent blow to her own social position. She had heard exaggerated stories, and believed me to have some influence with the police. She hoped that I should be a channel through which her views might percolate. Those, I think, were her reasons for sending for me in the first place, and for retaining me after I had made my position clear. I do not wish you to think that I believe her to have been directly concerned in the murder."

"You said she had something to hide."

"Yes. I have asked myself why she should have been forcing her niece into this marriage."

"It was like that?"

"Very much so. And I have wondered about her motive."

Frank Abbott regarded her quizzically.

"One has heard of it being done, you know. The lovely Lila is a social asset. Lady Dryden would expect her to make a brilliant match. Bill Waring is merely a nice chap with decent prospects. The late Whitall had what it takes nowadays—enough capital to live on till the cows come home. Lady Dryden may have wanted to wipe the eye of her dearest friends, whose plainer daughters were making better matches. Or she may have wanted some of that capital." He paused, and added, "Or do you mean anything more sinister than that?"

Miss Silver had begun upon the edging of the second sleeve. She said gravely,

"I think so. I have understood both from Lady Urtingham and from Miss Fortescue that the late Sir John Dryden was a wealthy man, and that he was devoted to the child whom he had adopted. On the way down in the train Miss Fortescue said that the marriage with Bill Waring would have been quite possible with what he is getting now and what Sir John left Miss Dryden. Yet Lady Dryden had been at some pains to impress upon me that, owing to substantial losses, her husband had not been able to do what he wished, and that her own resources were very limited."

"And what do you think that adds up to?"

Miss Silver coughed.

"I should like to know the terms of Sir John Dryden's will—how much was left to Lila, and who were the trustees."

Frank whistled softly.

"Well, we can do that. In what way do you think it may be relevant?"

"There may have been a money motive for the murder. It could be a strong one. You see, there is the question of Sir Herbert Whitall's will. There was an old will which was to be superseded by one made in anticipation of his marriage to Lila Dryden. The marriage was to have taken place next Thursday, but no one seems to know whether Sir Herbert had in fact signed the new will."

Frank Abbott laughed.

"You have been here—what is it—a matter of six hours. Wasn't I right when I said I was sure you already knew everything there was to know?"

Her glance reproved him.

"My dear Frank! Lady Dryden and I were together in the drawing-room for the greater part of the afternoon. She believes, or is very anxious to persuade herself, that Sir Herbert had already signed this new will. She says he informed her a week ago that he was on the point of doing so. On the other hand, I can see that the attitude adopted by Mr. Haile fills her with apprehension. He has certainly assumed a good deal of authority."

"Next of kin, isn't he?"

"I believe there is no other relative. Lady Dryden informs me that he was in the habit of borrowing from his cousin—that Sir Herbert informed her last night before dinner that he was expecting an application of this nature from Mr. Haile and intimated that it would be refused. She says Mr. Haile arrived early and did have an interview with Sir Herbert."

Frank said, "I see." He got up and stood with his back to the fire. "There's something to think about there. If the new will was signed, presumably Lila Dryden would get a large share of the money, and Lady Dryden would profit. That might give her a motive for bumping Herbert off. But it's a poor one. There would have to be something more than that, and they seem to have been on perfectly good terms. On the other hand, if Haile knew, or believed, that the old will was still in force, and that he benefited under it to any considerable extent, he would have quite a strong motive for putting Whitall out of the way before a new will could be signed, especially if he was pretty badly broke and had just been refused a loan. Do you know, I rather begin to fancy Haile as a suspect. Let us consider him in that light. The butler says in his statement that he went round the downstairs rooms as usual at eleven o'clock, but when he got to the study he didn't go in because he heard voices. Says Sir Herbert was in the habit of sitting up late, and he thought he was there with Mr. Haile. Haile says he did look in for a moment or two after the others had gone upstairs, but by eleven o'clock he was undressed and ready for bed. Says Grey passed his room when he had the door open and must have seen him in his pyjamas. Grey duly corroborates. Of course a person who had gone upstairs could just as easily have come down again, and neither Marsham nor Grey would have any reason to be very exact about the time. But on the face of it, it doesn't seem so likely that it was Haile who was in the study with Sir Herbert. We won't rule him out, and we will continue to consider him. He was so very conveniently on the spot to walk in on Grey and Waring with the lovely Lila in what could hardly have been a more compromising situation. It seems to me just a little bit too opportune. He says he couldn't sleep, got up, and went to look out of the window. His room is at the side of the house, and there is a path between shrubs, and a flat paved walk right under the house. That's the way Bill Waring came. Haile says he looked out, and thought there was someone on the path between the shrubs. He says he can't say he exactly heard or saw anyone. He just thought there was someone there, or something—it might have been a dog or a cat. Now, curiously enough, Bill Waring says very much the same thing. He says he thought someone or something was on the shrubbery path when he was waiting in front of the house. He is just as vague about it as Haile. Neither of them will go farther than thinking there might have been someone there. Bill Waring says he didn't start to go round to the study until a good ten minutes later, and that doesn't fit in with Haile, because Haile says he thought he ought to investigate, so he put on a coat and came downstairs. He says he was going to go out on the terrace by way of the glass door in the study. When he got to the door from the passage he heard voices, opened the door an inch or two, was appalled at what he heard, and decided to listen in. Well it could be true, but I don't think it explains why he came downstairs. Either he saw, or perhaps heard, something a good deal more definite when he looked out of his bedroom window than he is prepared to admit, or he had some other reason for going down to the study. You don't hurtle out into the night because you think there may be a stray cat in the grounds—there's bound to be more to it than that. I daresay he looked out of his window and heard whatever it was Bill Waring heard, but it must have been at least twenty minutes later that he walked into the study and told Adrian Grey his story wouldn't wash."

Miss Silver had completed the second sleeve of little Josephine's vest. She broke the pink wool thread, pulled it through the last loop, and said,

"There is certainly a discrepancy."

He nodded.

"I think Mr. Haile's affairs will bear looking into. If he inherited under the old will, and knew that he was going to be cut out under the new one, you get a pretty strong motive."

Miss Silver coughed.

"'The lust of gain, in the spirit of Cain,' as Lord Tennyson says."

"The *mot juste*, as always!"

She coughed again.

"Mr. Haile would have a strong motive, as you say. He has been at some pains to impress upon me that Lila Dryden must have committed the crime, either walking in her sleep, or in a fit of temporary derangement."

Frank came back to his seat on the arm of the chair.

"A curious business sleep-walking. How much does anyone really know about it? The person is asleep, the mind somewhere else. But some of the senses seem to operate. Or do they? The sleep-walker moves about a house, goes out—on a roof, into a garden—they've been known, I believe, to walk for miles. He goes where he wants to go, he doesn't bump into things, and as a rule he doesn't come to any harm. What guides him? Does he walk by sight, or by some sense that we don't know anything about?"

Miss Silver had taken out her knitting-needles and was casting on. She said in a thoughtful voice,

"I do not know. I knew a woman once who told me a very curious story. She was a Devonshire woman, and she was friendly with a farmer's wife in the neighbourhood. This woman woke up in the night and found her husband gone. She supposed that he had got up to attend to one of the beasts, and she turned over and went to sleep. When she woke again it was beginning to get light. She heard her husband coming up the stairs. When he came into the room she spoke to him, but he did not answer, and she saw that he was asleep. He had on trousers and boots. He came in with a big bunch of heather in his hand. He laid it down on the counterpane, pulled off his boots and trousers, and got into bed, all without waking. He slept for about half an hour, and then woke up without the least idea that he had left his bed. He did not know that he had ever walked in his sleep before, and he had no recollection of any dream. And the nearest place where he could have picked the heather was up on the moors seven miles away. He had risen, dressed, walked fourteen miles in the night, and come back with his bunch of heather. That is a true story. I do not feel at all able to explain it."

"Nor I. But I suppose he must have had his dream about the heather, and come and gone in it. And then forgotten the whole thing. And that

I suppose is what Lila Dryden might have done—
if it were not for the medical evidence. She could
have dreamed she was Lucy Ashton, stabbed Whitall in her dream, and forgotten all about it when
she woke again. But the medical evidence being
what it is, I think it rules that out. Even if Grey is
lying when he says he followed her down from her
room, I can't believe she just stood there for that
extra half hour which has got to be accounted for.
If Whitall was dead half an hour before Grey and
Waring reached the study, then I don't believe that
Lila Dryden was there when he was killed. She
wandered in afterwards. You agree?''

"Yes, I think so."

"Then I must get back to Haile and the question
of whether he is suspect number one. He is doing
his best to throw suspicion on Lila Dryden. The
question is, did he have a motive for killing Herbert
Whitall? If he knew that he was coming into the
money under the old will, and that the new will
had not been signed, then he did have a motive.
Look here, what about having the secretary in? She
would probably know whether the will had been
signed or not. Anyhow it's worth trying."

As he got up and went over to press the bell,
Miss Silver stopped knitting for a moment. If he
had been looking in her direction he might have
received the impression that she was about to
speak. She did not, however, do so, and by the
time he returned to his seat she was counting
stitches in an abstracted manner.

CHAPTER 24

It was Marsham who answered the bell. Asked to
find Miss Whitaker and tell her that Inspector Abbott would be glad to see her, he came over to the
fire, put on a couple of logs, and departed on his
errand. Miss Silver, having confirmed that she had
the right number of stitches on her needles, was
knitting in her usual smooth and rapid manner
when Millicent Whitaker came into the room.
Frank had moved to the writing-table. He noted
her pallor, her black dress, a certain rigidity in her
movements, and thought she showed more signs
of shock than Lila Dryden did. She had been a long
time with Sir Herbert. It was not impossible that
she had been attached to him.

When she had taken the chair which he had
placed for her, he said,

"I won't keep you, Miss Whitaker, but it occurred to me that you might be able to help us."

"*Us?*"

As she spoke the one word, her eyes went to
Miss Silver in the sofa corner. Frank gave her his
cool official stare.

"Yes. Miss Silver is here as Lady Dryden's rep-
resentative. If you object to her presence, I will ask
her to leave us. Have you any reason to object?"

"Oh, no reason at all. I just wondered." There was a clipped sound about her speech. She seemed in a hurry to close her lips upon the words and have done with them.

Frank Abbott said,

"Sir Herbert's solicitors will be coming down tomorrow, but meanwhile I thought you might be able to help us in the matter of the will. Sir Herbert was making a new will in anticipation of his marriage, but there seems to be some uncertainty as to whether this will was signed or not. Lady Dryden believes that it was."

"She would," said Millicent Whitaker.

"May I ask whether you mean anything by that?"

"Oh, no, nothing. Why should I? I suppose the wish may be father to the thought—that is all."

"Well, you have really answered my question— haven't you? Now, do you know whether Sir Herbert had signed that new will?"

"I haven't the slightest idea."

"You were his secretary. Did nothing of the correspondence go through your hands?"

"There was not much correspondence. Sir Herbert dealt with the matter personally. He has been up at his flat in town a good deal. He would call on his solicitors and give his instructions verbally."

"And were you in London, or down here?"

"Sometimes one and sometimes the other, according to what suited Sir Herbert's convenience."

"But he told you a good deal about this will?"

"I wouldn't say that."

"And about the old one?"

"I really know very little about either."

"Did you know that Mr. Haile was a beneficiary under the old will?"

For the first time, she hesitated. It struck him that if she knew and didn't want to say, she would have to consider whether he could catch her out. If she did know, someone else might know that she knew. The thought had just time to present itself before she said,

"I really couldn't say. Sir Herbert would say things—I didn't know whether he meant them, and I didn't take a lot of notice."

"He did speak of Mr. Haile being a beneficiary?"

There was a spark in the fine dark eyes—a bright malicious spark.

"He spoke of cutting him out of his will."

"Meaning out of this new will?"

"I suppose so."

"When did he say this, Miss Whitaker?"

She looked down into her lap. Her voice went flat again.

"It was yesterday."

"He was talking about Mr. Haile?"

"Yes."

"What did he say?"

The spark glowed again.

"He said Mr. Haile would be dining here and spending the night. On his usual errand. He called it a fool's errand and said Mr. Haile should have no more money out of him. 'Not even after I'm dead,' he said. 'I'm tired of him, and when I'm

162

tired of anyone their name comes out of my will.' "
The last few words came with an extraordinary
edge to them. She half rose from her chair, and
said, "Is that all? Because that's all I can tell you."

"Just a moment, Miss Whitaker. You were away
last night, were you not?"

She resumed her seat and said sharply,

"I made a statement to Inspector Newbury. It
was read over to me, and I signed it. My sister is
not strong, and I had a telephone message that
made me anxious. Mr. and Mrs. Considine gave
me a lift to the village when they went away at half
past ten, and I caught the last bus to Emsworth. I
spent the night with my sister at 32 Station Road.
I did not get back here until ten o'clock this
morning."

She might have been reciting a lesson, but with
that underlying sharpness. Frank had an impression of every door being locked and every window
barred. Against what? He would have very much
liked to know. He let her go, and she went out,
walking a little as if there was armour under the
thin black woollen dress.

When she was gone he pushed back his chair
and came over to the fire.

"Well, what do you make of that?"

Miss Silver's needles clicked.

"What do you?"

An eyebrow rose.

"Animus against Haile. Possibly against others.
Possibly against the late Herbert. Considerable insistence on the perfect alibi for the perfect secre-

tary. Newbury is going into the question of the alibi. He's a very thorough fellow. As to the animus, there seems to be quite a lot of it knocking about. Haile has it in for Lila Dryden. Lady Dryden and the perfect secretary have it in for Haile. A curious and rather unnatural partnership."

Miss Silver coughed.

"What makes you say that, Frank?"

"I really don't know—it just struck me that way. Lady Dryden rather busy with her own importance. Perfect secretary probably not caring about being treated like a blackbeetle. Just something on those lines. Did I hit a bullseye by accident?"

"I think you may have done. I thought I would let you see Miss Whitaker before I told you of a conversation I had with Lady Dryden."

"Another?"

"We were together for most of the afternoon."

"And she had something to say about Miss Whitaker?"

"A good deal."

"As what?"

"It was very well done. Miss Whitaker had been such an invaluable secretary. Sir Herbert had depended on her in every way. Really too much, if she might say so. These associations tend to become a little too intimate. There had, of course, been some talk. There always is. Miss Whitaker is quite a good-looking woman. Naturally, she herself did not believe the stories. If there had been any foundation for them, Sir Herbert would hardly have been refusing to allow her to resign her position."

Frank whistled softly.

"Oh, she wished to go, did she?"

"So Lady Dryden said."

"Well, if she really wanted to go, he couldn't make her stop."

Miss Silver coughed.

"I put that point. Lady Dryden intimated that there might be ways in which pressure could be brought to bear, adding, 'I believe she had some expectation of being remembered in his will.' "

"The question then arises as to which will. It looks as if the perfect secretary might have been down for a legacy in the old will, and was being told that it wouldn't get into the new one unless she stayed put. By the way, I wonder why he wanted her to stay."

"He seems to have relied upon her a good deal. She had been with him for ten years, and he was used to her. If there had been an affaire between them it was probably over, and he was too cold and selfish a man to consider her feelings in the matter."

"Do you think she cared for him?"

"I do not know. She is certainly suffering from shock. It is impossible to say whether it has gone deeper than might be expected in the circumstances. To arrive back after a few hours' absence and find that her employer had been murdered would naturally be a severe shock to any young woman. She would hardly have stayed ten years in Sir Herbert's employment if it had not suited her to do so. So abrupt an end to ten years' service would be, to say the least of it, discomposing."

Her use of this word caused Frank Abbott to slide a hand across his lips. Miss Silver would certainly not expect him to smile at this juncture, and he was not at all confident of being able to disguise a keen if momentary amusement. Beneath a cool and rather highbrow exterior he concealed a sense of humour which had sometimes landed him in trouble. He expressed agreement, and rose to his feet.

"Well, I must be off, or Lady Dryden will be offering me a meal in the housekeeper's room. It might, of course, be informative, but the Marshams wouldn't like it. Association with the police is very lowering to the social standards. I will go and see how bad the food at the Boar can be. Bill Waring is also staying there. Perhaps we shall mingle our tears over cabbage-water and bad dried egg. Go on having conversations with all and sundry. Another instalment of this great murder mystery tomorrow. Expect me when you see me."

An affectionately reproving glance followed him to the door.

When he had gone Miss Silver began to put away her knitting. Their talk had lasted for quite a time, and she had made a good start with the second pink vest. As she lifted the knitting-bag, something rolled from her lap to the floor. Bending to pick it up, she discovered it to be the magnifying-glass which Frank Abbott had taken from the writing-table to show her. During their subsequent conversation it had lain unregarded in her lap, screened by the flowery chintz of her niece Ethel Burkett's birthday gift. The old knitting-bag had been really quite worn out. This one was delightfully gay, with bunches of flowers in the most tasteful colours and a lining of a deep coral pink. Miss Silver admired it almost as much as she rejoiced in the affection which had prompted the gift. Even at this moment half her mind was upon dear Ethel and her children—so warm, so loving. She had a mere modicum of attention left for the magnifying-glass, and that of a surface nature. It must be very uncomfortable to use such an instrument for any length of time. The thought just came and passed. She got up and went over to the writing-table with the intention to replacing it there.

And then, as she turned it in her hand, by one of those unforeseen chances something caught the light and her attention. The overhead light was bright above the table. She had excellent sight. What she saw was no more than a scratch just inside the metal rim. She turned the glass, and perceived that it was not one scratch but a series of scratches, and that these scratches formed initials. They were by no means new, and only by holding the magnifying-glass in one position could they be seen at all. If there had not been so strong a light overhead they might not have been noticed.

Miss Silver made out the initials to be Z.R. After gazing at them for some moments she dropped the magnifying-glass into her knitting-bag instead of replacing it upon the table.

CHAPTER 25

When the two Inspectors had left Lila Dryden's room Ray Fortescue waited long enough to let them get well away and then ran down into the hall. She wanted to telephone to Bill, and she wanted to find out how she could do it. There was a telephone in the study, but that wasn't any good, because the policemen were there interviewing people. A house organized and improved by Herbert Whitall would probably be stiff with extensions, but she didn't know where she should look for them. There would be one in Sir Herbert's bedroom, but the idea of using it made her feel as if someone had dropped an icicle down her back.

She rang a bell, and Frederick came to answer it. She had seen him vaguely when she arrived, but she hadn't really noticed what a tall, pale slip of a boy he was. He really was very pale indeed. Not so nice being in a house where there has been a murder and the police keep coming in and out as if the place belonged to them. She produced a friendly smile, and said that she wanted to telephone.

Frederick looked sideways like a startled colt. His lip twitched as he opined that the police would be in the study. Ray liked boys. She thought this one wouldn't be more than seventeen. Her heart warmed to him. A year or two earlier he could have had a good cry, but you don't cry if you can help it when you are six foot one. She thought he was having pretty hard work to help it.

"I know," she said. "But I expect there's an extension, isn't there?"

"Oh, yes—in the Blue Room. I don't think there's anyone there."

He showed her the way, and displayed a tendency to linger.

Ray said, "Thank you very much. I'm afraid I don't know your name."

"Frederick, miss."

"Well, Frederick, do you think you could wait in the hall while I put through my call? Because I may have to go out for a little, and if I do, perhaps you would find Mary Good for me and ask her to come up and stay with Miss Lila."

"Oh, yes, miss." He got as far as the open door, took hold of the handle, twisted it nervously, and said all in a rush, "She didn't have anything to do with it, miss—not Miss Lila, did she? I mean, there's things you can believe and things you can't and that's what I couldn't believe, not if it was ever so."

Ray gave him one of her best smiles.

"Thank you, Frederick—that's very nice of you." Frederick clung to the handle.

"They won't go to make out she did it, will they? Nor yet Mr. Waring. Ever such a nice gentleman, I thought he was. And a cruel shame not letting

169

him see Miss Lila when he come all that way."

What Marsham would have thought of this conversation, Ray did not care to speculate. She had a feeling herself that perhaps it had better stop. She said,

"Thank you, Frederick. Now if you'll just shut the door, I'll get on with my call."

She had never fully realized the beneficence of the telephone until just in a moment with a brief click it gave her Bill's voice, speaking from the Boar.

"Hullo!"

She said, "It's Ray," and heard his tone warm as he answered her.

"Ray! I wondered how I was going to get on to you. I thought it wouldn't be considered exactly tactful if I rang up, but I was getting to the point where I was going to crash in and chance it."

She thought, "He wants to know about Lila. I'm only a kind of extension of the telephone." Out loud she said,

"Lila is quite all right. She had a good sleep this afternoon, and then she got up on the sofa and we had a tea-party in her room—Adrian Grey, and Miss Silver, and me."

He didn't seem tremendously interested in the tea-party.

"Ray, I want to see you. Could you come out to the gate? We could sit and talk in the car. I don't suppose I'd better come up to the house."

"No."

"Do you mean no, you can't come, or no, I'd better not come up to the house?"

"I mean no, you'd better not come up to the house. I'll come and meet you."

"All right—I'll stop just this side of the gate."

She left Mary Good with Lila and went down the drive in the dusk. When she turned out of the gate Bill was there, walking up and down on the grass verge of the country road. He put an arm round her shoulders.

"Good girl! Punctual to the minute."

"Do we get into the car, or do we walk up and down?"

After being shut up in a warm house all the afternoon she thought it would feel good to walk with Bill in this cool, soft air.

"Well, I don't know. They may have put someone on to shadow me. I think we'd better sit in the car. I want to talk."

When they were shut in together he came back to Lila, as of course she knew he would. But it wasn't quite what she expected. He had turned round to face her, his back in the angle between the door and the driving-seat. From his voice she knew just the kind of frowning look he had.

"What has Lila got to say about it now she has come round?"

She told him.

"Do you mean to say she doesn't remember anything at all?"

"Nothing between going to sleep on the sofa in her room and waking up with Sir Herbert lying dead on the study floor."

"Do you think she is telling the truth?"

"I'm quite sure of it."

"Then she really was walking in her sleep?"

"Oh, yes. She does, you know, when she is worried or upset. She used to do it at school. Miriam St. Clair woke up with a cold hand on her face one night and screamed the place down."

He said in a dogged voice,

"Then she did it in her sleep."

"Bill! She didn't do it at all!"

"I don't see how you can get away from it. She wasn't responsible of course. But she had been holding that dagger—her hand was all red."

"Bill, you're mad! Lila couldn't kill anyone if she tried. And she wouldn't try."

"You didn't see her standing there like I did."

"I don't care what you saw. If the police thought she had done it they would have arrested her. They came up and saw her after tea—the Scotland Yard man and the local one. I could see they didn't think she had done it—not by the time they went away anyhow."

Bill said gloomily, "I can't think why."

She let some real anger into her voice.

"Because they've got eyes in their heads and some sense in their brains! And because Adrian Grey swears that he was just behind her all the way from her room, and there simply wasn't time for her to kill Herbert Whitall. I mean, there would have been a scuffle and a pretty heavy fall. Adrian would have been bound to have heard it."

"My dear child, Adrian Grey would swear the moon was made of green cheese if he thought it

172

would get Lila out of a mess."

"Oh!"

Bill went on in tones which reached a new depth of gloom.

"I suppose you know what happened when she woke up?"

"No, I don't."

"I came in from the terrace, and he came in from the passage. And Lila woke up. Just like that. She saw Whitall lying there, and the dagger—and her hand. And then she saw me. Get a good hold on that, will you—she saw me first, before she saw Adrian, and I wasn't any good to her. She kind of shuddered away, if you know what I mean. But as soon as she saw Adrian she fairly chucked herself into his arms. Well, there's only one thing you can make of that, isn't there?"

"She had just had the most awful shock. She didn't know what she was doing."

"She knew which of us she wanted all right," said Bill. "When you have had a shock like that you don't reason, you act on instinct. Lila's instinct didn't take her to me, it took her to Adrian."

"Oh, Bill!"

"Don't sit there saying, 'Oh, Bill!' Do you suppose I want to marry a girl who shudders when she looks at me and flings herself into somebody else's arms? Because if you do, you had better start thinking again."

Ray was silent, because she didn't know what to say. She had too many insurgent feelings, and they wouldn't go into words. What she really

173

wanted to do was to put her arms round Bill and kiss the hurt away. She clamped her hands together and sat as far back in her corner as she could get. Anyhow it was a good thing that he could talk about it.

He went on talking.

"If they don't think Lila did it they are absolutely bound to think it was me. I can't imagine why they haven't arrested me already. They found my note to Lila, so they know I had asked her to come down and meet me. Only I didn't say the study—I said that room just inside the hall door. I told her if she wanted to marry Whitall she could, but if she didn't want to, I would take her away to you. I can't imagine why she went down to the study instead."

Ray found words.

"Darling, you don't *listen*. She—did—not—know—what—she—was—doing."

"That's what you say. I want to know how she got that blood on her hand."

Ray felt cold through and through.

"She must have touched him—or—or the dagger."

"Ray, can you believe that Lila would touch a dead body? Or that dagger, in cold blood?"

Ray was up against the one thing she really could not believe. She had to fall back on,

"She didn't know what she was doing."

"Then why did she do it?"

They sat facing one another. Feature and expression were hidden by the darkness, yet each knew the other so well that this darkness was only a black

174

screen upon which memory could throw its pictures. Bill holding doggedly to what he had said and saying it all over again, as if battering repetition was an argument in itself. Ray on the defensive—quick thrust and parry to meet his bludgeon blows, eyes wide and the colour in her cheeks like a flame. How many times had they fought each other to a standstill over something that wasn't worth a tenth part of all that force and fire? Things that didn't matter. And this thing that mattered more than all the world because it was a matter of truth and honesty between them. It wasn't Lila's guilt or innocence which was in question, it was their own integrity.

Bill said roughly,

"You won't face facts. Women never will."

"I'm not *women*—I'm myself. I'm facing the fact that Lila didn't do it. I don't care how much evidence there is—*she didn't do it*. If you cared for her you'd know that."

There was a long and rather horrid silence. Ray had the same feeling which had overwhelmed her when in a fit of rage she had thrown a stone through the drawing-room window. She was seven years old again, with that dreadful sense of irrevocability. When you break something, it's broken, and you can't put it together again.

In the end Bill said in rather a surprised voice,

"I suppose I don't. I suppose I never did."

Ray couldn't get her words steady.

"What—do—you—mean?"

"You know perfectly well what I mean. If we're talking, let's talk. Lila was the loveliest thing I'd ever seen, and I went in off the deep end. I didn't know a thing about her—I didn't care if there was anything to know. If I'd married her, we'd have been damned unhappy. I've been realizing that bit by bit ever since I got home."

Ray said with shaking lips,

"Then why did you come down here and start all this?"

"How do you mean, start all this? I wasn't going to have her pushed into marrying Whitall if she didn't want to, and I wasn't going to be dropped in Lady Dryden's tactful accidental sort of way as if I was something that hadn't really happened, or if it had it wasn't the kind of thing you would talk about in a drawing-room."

A gust of silent laughter swept Ray's anger away. She went on shaking, but it was the laughter that was shaking her now.

"Bill—*darling!*"

"Well, that's how I felt. I was going to bring her to you if she wanted to get away. And if she didn't want to get away she had got to break off our engagement properly."

"And is that what you want her to do now?"

A movement in the darkness told her that he was shaking his head.

"No—there's no need. It's broken off all right. She doesn't want me any more than I want her now. She made that quite plain when she turned her back on me and flung herself into Adrian's

176

arms. He's a good chap, and he'll look after her. I should say it was going to be a whole-time job!" He gave an odd half-angry laugh. "Marian Hardy told me it would be, months ago. I don't think I'm cut out for being a nursemaid."

Ray was struggling with the feeling that everything was going to be all right now. It was completely irrational. It was like having balloons under your feet and being floated up into the clouds. Presently the balloons would go off with a bang and let you down. Just at the moment she couldn't make herself care. She did manage to say that she thought she ought to go in.

Bill acquiesced.

"My police spy will be getting bored. He might even come along and arrest me just to relieve the monotony."

"Bill—you don't really think—"

"Well, to tell you the truth, I can't imagine why they haven't arrested me already. If Adrian is such a good liar that they really believe it wasn't Lila who did it because she wasn't long enough out of his sight, then I don't see how they could help believing it was me. In any case I don't see why they haven't arrested one of us. It looks as if they had got their eye on someone else. Let's hope they have."

Ray got out of the car, and they walked up the drive together. Just short of the gravel sweep he put on arm round her and said out of the blue,

"It makes a lot of difference having you here."

"Does it?"

177

"Yes. Why are you shaking?"

"I'm not."

He said, "Liar!" kissed her somewhere between her cheekbone and her ear, and went off down the drive at a run.

Ray went into the house with stars in her eyes.

CHAPTER 26

A deep concern about the case in which she found herself involved and the moral reprobation with which it was natural to her to regard the crime of murder did not prevent Miss Silver from bestowing grateful appreciation upon the comfort with which she was surrounded at Vineyards. She would not have cared to live in so much luxury for any length of time, but she could appreciate and enjoy it for the moment. The newest kind of spring mattress on her bed, the pretty eiderdown, so light, so soft. The warm, even temperature, so different from that of so many country houses where old heating systems and new taxation made even the most modest degree of warmth impossible. Only too well aware of this, she never came down into the country without due provision. It was her habit to change for the evening into the silk dress worn for best during the previous summer, and silk being no protection against draughts, to reinforce it by the addition of a black velvet coatee with a fur collar. This garment, most warm, most comfortable, was declared by Frank Abbott in his more irreverent moods to be of an origin so obscured by the mists of antiquity as to give it a kind of legendary character. Tonight, having arrayed herself in navy blue with a pattern of little yellow and green objects which resembled tadpoles, she fastened it at the neck with her bog-oak rose and added a string of small gold filagree beads. The coatee hung in a spacious mahogany wardrobe upon a plump hanger covered with pink satin, but she would not require it. Not only was there this delightfully even temperature everywhere, but there would also be a log fire in the drawing-room, and the brocaded curtains, lined and interlined, could be trusted to exclude the least suspicion of a draught.

To some the thought of such an evening as lay before her might have been daunting, but Miss Silver was able to look forward to it with interest. Here was none of that deep personal grief which would at once have roused her sympathy. Her mind would be free to deal with the many interesting aspects which the case presented. Whilst regretting that she had as yet had no opportunity of meeting Mr. and Mrs. Considine, Professor Richardson, and Mr. Waring, she was sure of ample food for thought in the opportunities which this evening would provide for a closer study of the household at Vineyards.

Lady Dryden, cold, proud, dominant, yet so unexpectedly communicative. A contradiction of type is always of interest. Mr. Haile, with his air of being so very much at home. Lila Dryden, lovely and helpless. The dark girl, Ray Fortescue, quick with feeling and impulse, yet under steady control. Miss Whitaker—she thought a good deal about Miss Whitaker. People do not shutter every window and bolt every door if they have nothing to hide. Mr. Grey—it required no great degree of perception to discover his devotion to Lila Dryden. She thought it was no new thing. Since he had known her from a child, it would be natural for him to have loved her with an increasing steadiness and warmth. She had not spent an hour in their company without discerning that the link between them was a strong one.

The domestic staff—two girls from the village and Mary Good from Emsworth. None of the three in the house at the time of the murder, since they all went off duty at nine. Of course people were not always where they were supposed to be, nor did they always remain there, but the police would at least have made certain that the two girls had reached their homes, and that Mary had caught the Emsworth bus.

She passed from them to the Marshams—butler and cook. Mrs. Marsham she had not seen. She knew nothing about her. She might be fair or dark, large or small, temperamental or calm. Beyond the fact that she was Marsham's wife and an extremely good cook, her personality was a blank. Of Marsham, observed during lunch and occasionally encountered since, she did not feel that she knew much more. He had the face and port which have gone very well with episcopal robes. A mitre would have suited him. The pastoral crook would have been held with dignity by that large and carefully tended hand. His step, like that of so many heavy men, was light. His voice was soft, his manner irreproachable. But when you had observed these things there appeared to be no more to observe. The attributes of his office wrapped him about like the fabled cloak of darkness. Behind it the man, as distinct from the butler, walked invisible.

There remained Frederick, the seventeen-year-old footman. Enquiry had elicited that he had not been roused by the happenings of the previous night. After the discovery of the murder Mr. Haile had rung for Marsham. There was, apparently, a bell on the landing in the servants' wing. The Marshams had come down, but Frederick had slept on, and no one had thought to wake him. Yet, watching him at lunch, Miss Silver considered that it was he rather than Marsham who looked as if he had not slept. He was a fair-skinned boy of the type to which pallor is not natural. He was extremely pale. His hand shook when he offered her Brussels sprouts, and somewhere in the background he dropped a plate. At seventeen the nerves are not armoured against murder, but inextricably coupled with its shock there is in the young a flavour of excitement, an underlying sense of being in the midst of things. One's photograph in the papers— Frederick Baines! This flavour Miss Silver found to be entirely absent. No two natures are the same, and she did not allow herself to give its absence any particular importance. She merely kept it in her mind along with many other details observed and put away for due consideration. She went down to dinner in a meditative mood.

Dinner had not proceeded very far before she had decided the question of Mrs. Marsham's temperament. Imperturbable was the only possible word for it. No person suffering from shock or from a shaken nerve could have produced such a flawless meal. Whatever might be happening in the rest of the house, it was obvious that the kitchen remained unshaken. For the rest, everything proceeded very much as it had done at lunch. Mr. Haile played the pleasant host, Lady Dryden the formal guest. Adrian Grey appeared rather dreamy and abstracted, busy with thoughts of his own and emerging from them with reluctance when directly addressed. Ray Fortescue had her own thoughts too. The dark eyes shone, the wide mobile lips were not very far from a smile. A much less acute observer than Miss Silver could have guessed that she was happy. In this house and at this time it was an arresting circumstance and a pleasant one. Beside her, Miss Whitaker had the shadowed look of someone who is not really there. When anyone spoke to her she had to come back from a long way off. She took a spoonful from each dish and left it on her plate.

When they rose from the table Miss Silver enquired whether she might telephone, and was directed, as Ray had been, to the Blue Room,

Frederick preceding her to turn on the light. She thanked him, and when the door was shut, looked up the number of the Boar and asked for Detective Inspector Abbott. His rather blasé "Hullo?" became a friendly greeting as soon as he heard her voice.

"What can I do for you? I suppose it isn't a case of 'Fly, all is discovered!' is it? The parts of detective and murderer doubled by Inspector Blank. Edgar Wallace used to be rather fond of that trick."

"My dear Frank!"

"One must relax occasionally. Waring and I have just dined at separate tables, trying unsuccessfully not to catch each other's eye. The food, however, is good. Marvellous for a village pub, but I believe they do a roaring trade with sight-seers in summer. There's Vineyards, and a Roman villa, and several very hot-stuff gardens in the neighbourhood, I'm told. Anyhow they have their own hens, and whoever does the cooking knows how to make an omelette. I can't imagine why it should be so difficult. The French are not nearly so good as we are at things like governments and elections and paying their income tax, but they do have us beat to a frazzle over omelettes. I must ask the landlord if his wife is French. There was also some real cheese—not the awful oily stuff which comes done up in impenetrable shiny paper, and which I suspect of being one of the more subtle products of whale oil. But there—as you were about to remark, idle badinage should be kept within limits. Did you have something you wanted to say?"

A discreet cough came to him along the line. It proved to be a preliminary to Miss Silver going over to the French language, which she spoke after the honourable tradition of the Prioress in the *Canterbury Tales*. If not actually the French of Stratfordatte-Bowe, it was in the true line of descent.

"You will remember the magnifying-glass which you showed me."

"Certainly."

"Did you know that there were initials on it?"

"I did not."

"I discovered them by accident. I was replacing the glass upon the writing-table, when the light caught what I at first believed to be a scratch just inside the rim. On further examination I discovered that there were two initials."

"Are you going to tell me what they were?"

For his side of the conversation Frank considered that he might reasonably adhere to his native tongue. Miss Silver's French delighted him, his own did not. If he could not do a thing to perfection he would rather not do it at all. Except for an occasional quotation, he therefore preferred to leave French alone. "Wind in the head—that's what you've got, Frank my boy," as his respected superior, Chief Detective Inspector Lamb, was wont to say.

In the Blue Room Miss Silver gave a gentle cough. She said in English, "I think I had better do so," and then reverted to French. "The first is the last letter of the alphabet. The second is R. I felt that you should know without delay."

Frank Abbott gave a long soft whistle.

"Oh, it is, is it? Well, we shall just have to find out whose godparents searched the Scriptures for a name. It sounds as if one of the minor prophets might be involved."

"My dear Frank!"

She heard him laugh.

"I had to learn the whole list of them at school. It finished up with a most suggestive jingle."

She said, "That is all. I will now join the others. Shall I see you in the morning?"

"Undoubtedly."

Returning to the drawing-room, Miss Silver seated herself at a little distance from the fire. The chair which she had chosen stood at a companion-able angle to that from which Adrian Grey had risen at her approach. He put down the paper which he had been reading and said,

"Let me get you a cup of coffee."

Thanking him graciously, she awaited his return. From where she sat she could observe the little group about the hearth. Lady Dryden had finished her coffee. She had a book in her hand, and occasionally she turned a page, but Miss Silver received the impression that she was not really reading. She had, perhaps, produced as much social small talk as she felt necessary.

Eric Haile stood with his back to the fire with a cigarette between his fingers. Every now and then he put it to his lips and let out a faint cloud of smoke. Every now and then he addressed a smiling remark to Ray Fortescue in the sofa corner. When he did this she would look up from the magazine whose leaves she was turning and make some brief reply. Then she went back again, not to the magazine, but to her own private dream.

Miss Whitaker was not in the room.

Adrian Grey came back with the coffee-cup in his hand.

"I noticed you took half milk after lunch, and one lump of sugar. I hope that is right."

So he did notice things, in spite of that air of being somewhere vaguely in another world. She gave him the smile which had won the hearts of so many of her clients and said,

"How kind. Pray sit down, Mr. Grey. I should be so glad to have a little talk with you."

As he took the chair beside her he had the feeling that it was a comfortable and familiar place. If he had been in some private world, it suffered no intrusion, neither was he being asked to leave it. He had encountered a friendly presence. There was a sense of security.

She sipped her coffee in a thoughtful manner and said,

"I think you can help me if you will. You must have known Sir Herbert very well. Will you tell me about him?"

It was simply phrased and simply spoken. Adrian felt no disposition to resist. He spoke with perfect frankness and simplicity.

"I don't know what to tell you."

She smiled again.

"Whatever you choose. I am wondering a little how you came to be associated with him."

"Oh, that is easy. I was rather at a loose end. I had known him casually for some years, and when he asked me whether I would care to undertake the alterations he wanted made at Vineyards I jumped at it."

"He gave you a free hand?"

"Well, I wouldn't say that. I would put up my suggestions, and as a rule he took them. But not always. For instance, he would hang on to that horrible staircase."

Miss Silver set down her coffee-cup on a small occasional table.

"Thank you—no more." She opened her flowered knitting-bag, disposed the pink ball in such a manner that it would not roll, and resumed little Josephine's second vest.

"You say you knew him casually. But in such a close association as you imply you must have learned to know him better."

Their distance from the group at the fire and the low tone in which they were speaking gave the conversation as much privacy as if they had been alone. He hesitated for a moment, and then said,

"Oh, yes—a great deal better. We came together on some surface similarity in our tastes. We both fell for Vineyards, for instance. He could appreciate a beautiful thing when he saw it—he did appreciate beautiful things in his own way. What I discovered when I got to know him better was that there was

187

something rather abnormal about this appreciation."

Miss Silver gave her gentle cough.

"In what way?"

He looked at her with candid hazel eyes.

"If he admired a thing he wanted to possess it."

"That seems abnormal to you?"

"It does a little. But I have put it badly. He could hardly admire what belonged to someone else. Or if he admired it he must strain every nerve to get it for himself."

The thought of Lila Dryden rose between them as clearly as if she had come into the room and was standing there—lovely, fragile—something to be desired and possessed by Herbert Whitall.

Adrian said quickly,

"He was quite ruthless about it. He would rather have seen anything he wanted smashed than let it go to somebody else."

Miss Silver's needles clicked.

"You did not find it altogether easy to work with him?"

"Not altogether. But as far as Vineyards was concerned it wasn't too bad—I didn't see so much of him. He came and went of course, generally at the week-end, but for the most part I was here on my own."

Miss Silver put down her knitting for a moment and looked at him across the pale pink wool.

"I am going to ask you a very frank question. You may not care to answer it, but I hope that you will do so. Did you like Sir Herbert Whitall?"

He showed no hesitation in answering.

"I don't think he wanted to be liked."

"Had you any feeling of affection or friendship for him?"

He shook his head.

"That's the wrong way to put it. He didn't want those things—he had no use for them."

"What did he want?"

"Beautiful things that would belong to him—things other people wanted and couldn't get. He valued a thing much more if other people wanted it. And he liked power. His money gave him a lot of that, but it wasn't enough. He liked to have people on a string, so that they couldn't get away if they wanted to. He liked to know something about them which wasn't usually known—something they wouldn't like anyone to know. He mightn't ever use that knowledge, but he liked to feel that he had got it there to use."

Miss Silver had been listening with an air of absorbed attention. She coughed and said,

"Such a person as you describe would be liable to arouse feelings of acute resentment and even hatred. Quite a number of people might have been tempted to wish for his death."

The hazel eyes looked straight into her own. Adrian Grey said,

"Oh, yes, quite a number."

CHAPTER 27

At ten o'clock next morning Miss Silver was informed by Frederick that Inspector Abbott was in the study and would like to see her there. Not being as yet quite perfect in his part although a willing learner, this was Frederick's version of a much more politely phrased request. Miss Silver, however, took no exception to it. She had been about to embark upon a truly thankless task. Her niece, Gladys Robinson, a selfish and flighty young woman, so different, so very different, from her sister dear Ethel Burkett, had written to ask for a loan and to pour out a string of complaints about her husband, a most worthy man, though perhaps a little dull and a good deal older than Gladys. He had been considerably better off at time of their marriage, but he had been just as many years older, just as dull, and just as worthy. Miss Silver had long ago decided with regret that Gladys had married him for his income, and not for his moral worth. She wrote with increasing fretfulness of having to do her own housework. She complained that Andrew was mean. She so far forgot herself as to say, in terms whose vulgarity shocked Miss Silver profoundly, that there were other and far better fish in the sea. On the last page of this latest letter she had actually mentioned the word divorce.

In her reply Miss Silver had got no farther than, "My dear Gladys, I really cannot say how much your letter shocks me—" When, interrupted by Frederick with his version of Inspector Abbott's message, she laid down her pen with a sigh of relief, closed the blotter, and proceeded at once to the study.

Frank Abbott was alone. Coming forward to meet her, he enquired immediately,

"Where is the magnifying-glass? I suppose you have it."

Her glance reproved him. Her sedate "Good-morning, Frank" was a reminder that the formalities had not been observed.

When he had responded and replied to a solicitous hope that he had slept well, she answered his question by diving into her knitting-bag and handing him the magnifying-glass.

"I thought it best to take charge of it. In the circumstances it seemed inadvisable to leave it lying about."

"Oh, quite."

He took it to the window, turning it this way and that until the initials came into view. Then he came back and set it down upon the writing-table.

"Z.R. it is. And scratched on by his own amateur hand, I should say. Throws a sinister light upon Collectors' morality. You wouldn't think this sort of thing would be in any danger of being pinched, would you? But the Professor thinks it's safer to put his initials on it. By the way, I was right about the minor prophets—Zephaniah, Haggai, Zechariah, Malachi. Professor Richardson is Zechariah. And so what?"

She seated herself and took out her knitting. Little Josephine's second vest was well on its way. It was in a very thoughtful manner that she said,

"It would be easy to attribute too much importance to the fact that the Professor's magnifying-glass has been found in this room. I think you said that it had rolled under the table. I suppose you mean the writing-table?"

"Yes."

"It may have been mislaid on some occasion previous to the murder."

He shook his head.

"I'm afraid not. The room was thoroughly turned out the day before Whitall and his party came down here. And Richardson wasn't anywhere near the place until he came to dinner on the night of the murder."

"Did he not come into the study before dinner?"

"I don't know—it hasn't been mentioned. But we can easily find out." He went over to the bell and pressed it. "There are one or two other points I'd like to take up with the butler."

It was Marsham's habit to answer the study bell. He answered it now.

"Come in and shut the door. There are just one or two points where I think you can help me. This dinner-party on the night of Sir Herbert's death—can you tell me in what order the guests arrived?"

"Certainly, sir. Mr. Haile came early, just before

half past seven. He had an appointment with Sir Herbert and he was shown in here. Mr. and Mrs. Considine came next, and then Professor Richardson. They were all asked for a quarter to eight."

"And did the Professor come out here?"

"Oh, no, sir. Sir Herbert and Mr. Haile were having their talk. The Professor went into the drawing-room."

"Then Sir Herbert was not in the drawing-room when his guests arrived?"

"No, sir—he was in the study. It was gone eight o'clock before Sir Herbert and Mr. Haile came through."

"I see. And when the guests were going away, Mr. and Mrs. Considine went first, didn't they?"

"Yes, sir—at half past ten. They gave Miss Whitaker a lift as far as the bus."

"Ah, yes—Miss Whitaker. That was arranged beforehand?"

"No, sir. Miss Whitaker came up to Sir Herbert in the hall. She said she had had a message to say her sister was ill, and she asked Mrs. Considine if she would give her a lift to catch the bus."

Abbott's eyebrows rose.

"You mean that was the first Sir Herbert heard about it?"

"It would seem so. He didn't seem very pleased about it. He said suppose he was to say no, and Miss Whitaker said that she would go all the same."

Inspector Abbott made a mental note to the effect

that Miss Whitaker did not appear to be popular with the staff. He said,

"Oh, he said that. Just how did he say it—angrily?"

Marsham hesitated.

"It is not very easy to say. Sir Herbert wasn't one to get heated, sir."

"And Miss Whitaker, when she said she would go all the same—how did she sound? Was it said lightly?"

"Oh, no, sir."

"She was angry?"

"I certainly thought so."

"There was no more said?"

"No, sir."

"And she went with Mr. and Mrs. Considine?"

"Yes, sir."

"Was Professor Richardson in the hall all this time?"

"Yes, sir."

"He didn't go into the study—you're sure about that?"

"Quite sure."

"How long afterwards did he leave?"

"As soon as Mr. and Mrs. Considine had driven off."

"Then you are quite sure that he wasn't out here in this room at any time during the evening?"

Question and answer had followed one another rapidly. Marsham had hesitated only once, and then very briefly. Now there was a pause. He did not hesitate. He remained silent. Miss Silver's steady attention became a little more marked. Her fingers were busy, her eyes on Marsham's face. It remained expressionless.

Frank said sharply,

"That is what you said, you know."

"I beg pardon, sir—you asked whether Professor Richardson came out here before dinner or when the party was breaking up, and I said that he did not. Now you ask whether he was out here at any time during the evening."

"Well—was he?"

"I don't know, sir."

"And just what do you mean by that?"

"It's not very easy to say, sir—not in just a few words."

Frank Abbott, sitting sideways to the writing-table in a negligent attitude, allowed his cool blue eyes to scan the impassive face.

"Take as many words as you like," he said.

Marsham took them.

"You'll be aware, sir, that I made a statement to Inspector Newbury. I was asked a good many of the questions that you have asked me, and I answered them to the best of my ability. I was asked when I last saw Sir Herbert alive. I replied that it was just after Lady Dryden, Miss Lila, and Mr. Grey had gone upstairs."

Abbott nodded.

"I have the statement here."

He picked up a paper from the table, turned a page, and read: "'Sir Herbert came out of the drawing-room and went towards the study. I set

195

the drawing-room to rights and went out to my pantry. At eleven o'clock I made the round of the downstair rooms to make sure that all the fastenings were secure. When I came to the study I did not go in, because I heard voices. It was Sir Herbert's habit to sit up late. I thought Mr. Haile might be with him—'"

"Why did you think it might be Mr. Haile?"

"He was spending the night. I had seen Mr. Grey go upstairs, but not Mr. Haile. I thought he might be continuing his talk with Sir Herbert."

"You did not identify his voice?"

"No, sir."

"You know that Mr. Haile says he did go to the study for a drink, but that he only stayed a few minutes and was up in his room before eleven o'clock?"

"No, sir, I didn't know that."

"It is in Mr. Haile's statement, and it is corroborated by Mr. Grey, who says he saw Mr. Haile in his room with the door half open as he came back from having a bath. Mr. Haile was in his pyjamas, and it was then eleven o'clock. So it would not have been Mr. Haile whom you heard talking to Sir Herbert in the study after you had locked up."

"It would seem not, sir."

"In your statement you go on to say that having heard the voices and decided not to go in, you finished your round and went up to bed."

"Yes, sir."

"Then where does Professor Richardson come in?"

"Sir?"

"Look here, Marsham, you may be getting yourself into an awkward position. You have made a statement—you have answered questions put to you by the police. You could have refused to do so until subpoenaed by the Coroner's court. What you cannot do and get away with it is to make a false statement."

"Sir!"

"There is such a thing as a lie by implication. I daresay your statement is true so far as it goes. I daresay you passed the door of this room, heard voices, and thought that Mr. Haile was with your master. That is as far as the statement goes. And I'm telling you it doesn't go far enough, or why didn't you answer me when I asked you whether you were sure that Professor Richardson had not been out to this room at any time during the evening of the murder? There must have been something that made you hesitate. I am now going to ask you point-blank whether, after standing outside the study door and thinking it was Mr. Haile with Sir Herbert, you heard something that made you change your mind."

Marsham's face showed nothing. He said without any noticeable pause,

"It wasn't anything I could swear to."

"Well, I think you'd better tell me what it was."

"I had gone just past the door—"

"Yes?"

"Well, sir, I think I should tell you that I did hear something."

197

"What did you hear?"

Marsham said slowly,

"It wasn't words, sir. It was—well it was a sound. And it wasn't the kind of sound I would have expected Mr. Haile to make."

"I think you'll have to tell me what kind of a sound it was."

Without any other change in his expression Marsham blew out his large pale cheeks and emitted a sound that might have been "Pah!" or "Pooh!"

The effect was laughable in the extreme, yet neither of the two who were observing him felt any inclination to laugh. The absurd imitation might very well bring its subject to his death by hanging. Miss Silver had no means of identifying this subject. Frank Abbott had. He had, in fact, not so many hours before been an entertained spectator whilst two ruddy cheeks were distended like balloons in order to expel that contemptuous "Pooh!" or "Pah!" He said quickly,

"You recognized the sound?"

The contours of Marsham's face were restored to their usual heavy dignity.

"I wouldn't take it on me to swear to it."

"I'm not asking you to swear to it. I'm asking you what you thought at the time."

After a pause he said,

"I thought it was the Professor."

Frank gave a brief nod.

"You stopped for another moment or so by the door?"

"For no more than a moment, sir."

"Hear anything else?"

"I heard Sir Herbert say something. I don't know what it was."

"Did he sound angry?"

"I couldn't say, sir. Sir Herbert had a kind of cold way with him when he was angry. He wouldn't raise his voice—not to notice."

"And that was all you heard?"

"Yes, sir. I went along the passage, and when I had finished I went up to my room."

CHAPTER 28

The door closed upon Marsham. Frank Abbott let a full minute go by. Then, rising from his chair, he strolled across and opened it again. The long passage was empty. He returned to the fire, noted that it required attention, and made an expert disposition of two small logs and a large one. When he had finished and was dusting his hands with a beautiful handkerchief in harmony with his tie and socks, he observed in a casual tone,

"Just as well to be sure that he doesn't make a habit of leaning against doors."

Miss Silver looked at him across her pink knitting.

"You think he heard more than he is willing to admit?"

"Could be. No one ever tells everything they know—not in a murder case. I learned that from you when I was in rompers. I thought he was holding something back. Didn't you?"

"I do not know. I think he recognized Professor Richardson's voice a good deal more definitely than he admits."

"Oh, yes—quite definitely. Likes the old boy, I wouldn't wonder. Was not, shall we say, extravagantly attached to the late Whitall. None of the old retainer touch about our Marsham."

Miss Silver coughed.

"I have yet to encounter a single person who can be said to have entertained the slightest affection for Sir Herbert Whitall."

Frank's fair eyebrows rose.

"What an epitaph! 'Here lies the man whom no one liked.' What would you think about adding, 'and a good many people hated'?"

"I think it may prove to be in accordance with the facts."

"Nobody liked him—a good few hated him. That's the verdict, is it? Into which of those two classes would you put Miss Whitaker?"

"I would not care to say. There has been some strong feeling. She is undoubtedly suffering severely from shock."

"Well, she has been with him ten years. She may have been his mistress. I don't suppose she murdered him. Newbury looked into her alibi, and it seems all right. She left at half past ten with the Considines, caught the Emsworth bus, and got off at the station at eleven o'clock. The sister is a Mrs. West living at 32 Station Road. She says Miss Whitaker got there just after eleven and went straight to bed—they both did. She said she had had a bad turn, and her little boy hadn't been well. She rang her sister up because she was going to be alone in the house with him, and she wasn't any too sure of herself."

"She is on the telephone?"

"Yes, I asked about that. She has a masseuse boarding with her. She has the telephone, and allows Mrs. West to use it."

"And where was this masseuse?"

"Away for the week-end. The story hangs together all right. Miss Whitaker took the ten o'clock bus back in the morning."

Miss Silver went on knitting. From her expression Frank deduced that she still had something to say. He waited for it, leaning against the mantelshelf, the picture of an idle, elegant young man, fair hair mirror-smooth, beautifully cut dark suit. It was not very long before she coughed and said in a tentative manner,

"For how long has Mrs. West resided in Emsworth?"

He looked a little surprised. Whatever he was expecting, it was not this.

"Mrs. West? I don't know. Wait a bit, I believe Newbury did mention it. There was something about her being new to the place. It came up in connection with her being alone in the house with the child. He said she probably wouldn't know anyone she could ask to come in."

Miss Silver pulled on a pale pink ball.

"That is what I imagined. I think it probable that Mrs. West's move to Emsworth followed upon Sir Herbert's purchase of Vineyards."

"And the meaning of that is?"

"I am wondering whether Miss Whitaker's concern was so much for her sister as for a child who might have suffered if deprived of proper attention. May I ask whether Inspector Newbury mentioned the child's age?"

"Yes, I think he did—a little boy of eight. You mean?"

Her needles clicked. She said,

"It is possible. It would, I think, explain some things, and suggest some others."

As she spoke the last word, the door was opened. Frederick appeared, towering over the Professor. His "Professor Richardson—" was a superfluity, since that gentleman immediately bounded into the room, his bald crown gleaming, the ruff of red hair standing up about it like a hedge. His deep voice boomed.

"Well, Inspector, here I am! And what do you want with me? Newbury asked me all the questions in the world yesterday morning. You asked them all over again in the evening, and here we are again. I suppose you sit up all night thinking up new ones. It beats me how you do it."

As soon as he drew breath he was introduced to Miss Silver.

"Friend of Lady Dryden's? Much upset, I suppose. Can't imagine her upset, but suppose she is. I said so to Mrs. Considine—met her on my way here. And do you know what she said? She was at school with Lady Dryden, you know. Said she'd never seen her upset in her life. Didn't allow things to upset her—that's the way she put it. Said if there was a row or anything, Sybil always came out of it with everything going her way. I've known people like that myself. It's quite a gift. But they're not much liked—I've noticed that."

He had come up to the fire, and stood there, leaning over it and rubbing his hands. He turned about now and addressed himself to Miss Silver.

"The fact is, people who don't have any misfortunes are very irritating to their neighbours. No opportunities for popping in with condolences and new-laid eggs. No visits to the afflicted. No opportunities for the milk of human kindness to flow. Naturally it doesn't."

He was so ruddy, so glowing, so pleased with himself, that it became every moment more difficult to picture him in the role of first murderer. And the motive—a dispute over the authenticity of an antique dagger? Memory stirred and provided Frank Abbott with a vista of belligerent letters to the *Times*—about this, about that, anything. Disputes—the man's past had been fairly littered with them. But no corpses. Then why now? The whole thing appeared in a ridiculous light. Yet the fact remained that the Professor had certainly been in this room on the night of the murder, and that fact he would have to explain.

As the booming voice stopped, Frank said in his quiet drawl,

"Do you mind telling me which way you came in the other night?"

The Professor turned a pair of gleaming spectacles upon him.

"What do you mean, the other night?"

"The night Sir Herbert was murdered."

"Then how do you mean, which way did I come in? Which way does one usually come in? I came here to dine. I rang the bell, and I was let in by that six and a half foot of tallow candle, young Frederick What's-his-name. He'll tell you so if you ask him."

Frank Abbott nodded.

"Naturally. But that wasn't the time I was talking about. You dined here, and you went away at half past ten, just after Mr. and Mrs. Considine. What I want to know is, when did you come back, and why?"

"When did I come back? What do you mean, sir?"

"Just what I say. You came back—probably to this door on to the terrace. You attracted Sir Herbert's attention, and he let you in."

The Professor blew out his cheeks, and said, "Pah!"

Frank, listening to the sound, reflected that it really was more like "Pah!" than "Pooh!" It was followed immediately by the word "Nonsense!" delivered upon a growling note.

He continued equably.

"I don't think so. I think you did come to that door."

Professor Richardson glared.

"What you think isn't evidence, young man. What my housekeeper can swear to is. She will tell you I was in by a quarter to eleven, and that is that!"

"You were riding an autocycle?"

"I always do. It is not a criminal offence, I believe."

"It might be a convenient accessory. If you were back in your house in the village in a little over ten minutes you could have made the return journey in the same time. You had had some dispute with Sir Herbert earlier in the evening. He put forward a story which connected this ivory dagger with Marco Polo."

"Fantastic! Completely and ridiculously fantastic! And so I told him! The earlier authentic record goes back no farther than the eighteenth century."

"At which point Mrs. Considine intervened and asked to hear some of her favourite records. Well, you wanted to have the thing out. You went home, stewed over it a bit, thought of a lot more things to say, put your magnifying-glass in your pocket, and came along back. You knew Sir Herbert was given to sitting up late—you knew that he would be in this room. You came round on to the terrace, he let you in, went and fetched the dagger, and you took up the argument where Mrs. Considine had interrupted it. By the way, here is your magnifying-glass." His hand went into a pocket and came out again. He held it out with the glass upon its palm.

The Professor had a rush of blood to the head, to the face—one would almost have said to the hair. Sweat broke out upon him. He might have just emerged from a cauldron of boiling water. He said with a growl in his throat,

"What's that?"

"Your magnifying-glass."

"Who says it's mine?"

"It has your initials on it."

The red heat the man was in, his glaring eyes, the ferocity of the growling voice, threw back to the savage and the animal.

Miss Silver, continuing to occupy herself with little Josephine's vest, regarded the scene with an intelligent interest. Anger was both a disfiguring and a revealing passion. The old proverb ran, *In vino veritas*, but it was not the drunken man alone who spoke the truth. Anger could be as sovereign to loosen the tongue as wine. The Professor's tongue was loosened. He blew out his cheeks to their fullest extent. He made strange guttural noises. A cataract of words emerged.

"My initials are on a magnifying-glass—and the magnifying-glass turns up in this room! So very convenient! How do these things happen? Perhaps the experts from Scotland Yard can inform us! And because my magnifying-glass is here I have murdered Herbert Whitall! That is the next thing you will say, I suppose! Continue! Say it!"

Frank's manner became even cooler.

"Before either of us says anything more I had better caution you that anything you do say may be taken down and used in evidence."

The Professor broke into what was certainly laughter, though it had a very belligerent sound.

"All right—you have cautioned me. I needn't make a statement at all. I can consult my solicitor and all the rest of it. Bosh! I shall make any statement I like, and I don't require a solicitor to instruct me how to tell the truth! So I killed Herbert Whitall, did I? Perhaps you'll tell me why! Anyone except a homicidal maniac has got to have a motive. Where's mine? Tell me that, Mr. Clever from Scotland Yard!"

Frank went over to the writing-table and sat down at it. Drawing a writing-pad towards him and picking up one of Sir Herbert's beautifully sharpened pencils, he observed,

"Well, you did have quite a heated dispute with him."

The Professor ran his hands through his frill of red hair and hooted.

"Dispute! You call that a dispute! My good young man, my career has been punctuated with disputes! I didn't like Herbert Whitall—never met anyone who did. Entirely without veracity, human feeling, or scientific integrity—pah! But I never got as far as wanting to kill him. Why should I? If I didn't kill Tortinelli when he called me a liar on a public platform—if I didn't murder Mrs. Hodgkins-Blenkinsop when I had to listen to her talking pestiferous twaddle for two hours at a conversazione—

why should I assassinate Herbert Whitall? I tell you anyone who could endure that woman for two hours is a master of self-control. I tell you I wasn't even rude to her. My hostess implored me, and I restrained the impulse. I merely approached her and said, 'Madam, the statements which you have put forward as fact are inaccurate, your method in presenting them is dishonest, and I would recommend you to leave history alone and turn your attention to fiction. Good-evening!' " He broke into ordinary human laughter. "You should have seen her face! She weighs fifteen stone, and she gaped like a fish. For the first time in her life she couldn't think of anything to say. I left before she came round. Well now, you see I am a person of restraint and self-control. I preserve the scientific outlook— I am calm, I am detached. Why should I murder Herbert Whitall?"

The paper in front of Inspector Abbott remained blank. He said negligently,

"I didn't ask you whether you killed Whitall. I asked you whether you came back here on the night that somebody did kill him."

The Professor had approached the table. He now threw himself into a convenient chair, thumped the stuffed arm, and said,

"Oh, no, you didn't, young man—you didn't ask me anything at all. You *told* me I came back, which is a very different matter."

"Well, you did come back—didn't you?"

"Of course I came back! Why shouldn't I? Is there any law against it?"

"Would you care to tell me what happened?"

The Professor caught up the last word and hurled it back.

"*Happened?* Nothing happened! Except that I was able to give him a good setting-down about his ridiculous ivory dagger. Marco Polo indeed! Late seventeenth- or early eighteenth-century work, and so I told him!"

"But I believe you bid for it."

The Professor waved that away.

"Not for myself. Can't afford expensive fakes. A friend of mine, Rufus T. Ellinger, the beef king, cabled me to get someone to bid for it. Didn't go myself—didn't want to be associated with the thing. Ellinger had heard fancy accounts. He's a good judge of beef, but not of ivories. I told him it was pretty work, but the story was all moonshine. I told him the sum he could go to. Whitall outbid him, and that was that. Paid a pretty penny for it—much more than it was worth. Naturally he didn't like it when I told him he'd been had for a mug. Wouldn't admit it. Pah!"

"And you came back to have it out. Why did you go home? Why not just stay on after the Considines had left?"

The Professor now appeared to be perfectly amiable. His colour had relapsed into its normal redness. The crown of his head was no longer suffused. His voice had ceased to boom. He said,

"Ah! You think you've got me there, but you haven't. I went home for my magnifying-glass, and for a letter. Meant to bring them with me, but found

I hadn't got them. That's my housekeeper—she's always taking things out of my pockets. She says they'd burst if she didn't. The letter was from Robinet. He's the greatest living expert on ivories, and he knew all about this precious ivory dagger. Between us I thought we could bring Whitall down a peg or two, and so we did. I knew he sat up late, so I came round to this door."

Frank balanced the pencil in his hand.

"And he let you in?"

The Professor thumped the arm of his chair.

"No. The door was unlocked."

"What!"

Professor Richardson nodded.

"I just tried the handle—I was going to rattle it to attract his attention, you know—but it was open, so I walked in. Gave him a bit of a start." He grinned like a schoolboy.

Frank Abbott's eyes had become intent.

"Well, you came in. Was he surprised to see you?"

"I don't know whether he was or not. I said, 'Look here, Whitall, if that ivory dagger of yours is a day older than late seventeenth century, I'll eat it. Fetch it along, and I'll prove what I say, or Robinet shall prove it for you.' So he fetched it along, and I did prove it, though he was much too self-opinionated an ass to admit it in so many words."

"And then?"

The Professor stared.

"I went along home."

"Which way did you go out?"

"The same way I came in."

"Why?"

"Pah! Why does one do anything? It was the nearest way."

"It gave you a long dark walk round the house."

"And I have an excellent pocket torch. Look here, where is this getting us?"

Abbott said coolly,

"I just wondered whether it was because you didn't want to be seen. You wouldn't, would you, if Whitall was dead when you left him?"

The Professor thumped with both hands.

"Well then, he wasn't, and that's that! He was sitting where you are now with the dagger in front of him on the blotting-pad, looking about as sweet as verjuice. I went out, and before I got down the steps he was after me, locking the door in case I took it into my head to come back."

"He locked the door after you?"

The Professor gave one of his great roars of laughter.

"Jammed down the bolt! Couldn't do it fast enough! Afraid I'd come back and refute him some more!"

There was a pause. Then Abbott said,

"Do you know that Waring found that door ajar at a little after twelve?"

The Professor stared.

"Then someone must have opened it."

"Or left it open. If Herbert Whitall was dead when you left him, there would be no one to fasten the door after you—would there?"

211

The Professor grinned.

"Very subtle, young man! What do you expect me to say? He was alive when I left him, and he locked the door behind me. So you can put that in your statement, and I'll sign it!"

CHAPTER 29

When the Professor had made his statement and signed it, which he did with a fine zigzag of a Z and a "Richardson" of which the capital letter was the only one which could be identified with any certainty, he threw down the pen and enquired whether the police were going to make fools of themselves by arresting him.

"Don't mind me, if you want to be a laughing-stock! Get on with it!"

"And you will write to the *Times* about it? Well, I don't think we'll oblige you today, but you must understand that you will be called at the inquest, and that you should be available for further questioning."

The Professor gave his booming laugh.

"I shan't do a bolt, if that's what you mean!"

Miss Silver had been knitting thoughtfully. When Professor Richardson had banged the door behind him Frank Abbott strolled over to her and said,

"Well?"

She coughed mildly.

"An interesting character," she observed.

He sat down on the arm of the opposite chair.

"Oh, quite."

"In some ways so extremely uncontrolled, and yet capable of meeting a really alarming situation with considerable coolness. His argument, produced on the spur of the moment and after a really remarkable exhibition of anger, was, under the mannerisms with which it was presented, both adroit and cool."

Frank nodded.

"He has got a brain all right."

"A very good one, I should say."

He laughed.

"But you haven't really answered my question. What did you think of that cool, adroit argument of his? Did you find it convincing?"

"I am inclined to be convinced by it."

"Would you like to give me your reasons?"

Her busy hands rested for a moment. She looked at him in a very earnest manner and said,

"It is a question of motive. I cannot see why Professor Richardson should have desired Sir Herbert Whitall's death. There may, of course, be things that we do not know, but on the face of it the Professor had every reason to be pleased with the result of the interview which had just taken place. You can, of course, confirm his account of it by asking to see the letter from M. Robinet which, he declares, enabled him to confute Sir Herbert.

213

Having had the best of the argument, why should he proceed to violence? He would be much more likely to have arrived at a state of high good humour, no doubt very offensive to Sir Herbert Whitall but in no way calculated to produce a murderous impulse. There is also the fact that he apparently made no attempt to keep his voice down during the interview. The hour was not very late. It was only eleven o'clock. Anyone might have been passing along the passage. Marsham did in fact pass, and heard both his voice and Sir Herbert's."

"Oh, I did not suppose that he came here intending to murder Sir Herbert."

"What provocation could he have received sufficient to carry him to such an extreme?"

Frank raised an eyebrow.

"Does that temper of his require any extreme provocation?"

Miss Silver said in her most thoughtful voice,

"In small things, no. There is a great deal of surface disturbance, as we saw. He blustered and raged, but at a moment's notice control was resumed—if indeed it had ever really been lost. To use his own argument, if he has never assaulted anyone before, why should he now murder Sir Herbert Whitall?"

"In other words, you don't think he did it."

"I can see no reason why he should have done so."

As she spoke, the telephone bell rang. Frank went over to it, picked up the receiver, and said,

"Hullo?" Then his voice changed.

"That you, Jackson? Well, what have you got?"

There was a pause whilst a murmuring noise came from the instrument. After an interval Frank said,

"Forty thousand?" And after another, "Isn't that the old boy who had his picture in the papers with a hundred and one candles round a three-tiered cake? . . . I see. . . . All right. Thanks."

He hung up and came back to his chair.

"Well, there seem to be some signs of a rat down the hole you were interested in."

"My dear Frank!"

"The Dryden hole. I put a ferret down, and he's just come up to report."

Her glance held an indulgent reproof.

"I imagine you to mean that you have had some enquiries made with regard to Sir John Dryden's will."

"Right, as always! The excellent Jackson has been to Somerset House, and reports that Sir John left forty thousand pounds in Government stock in trust to his adopted daughter Lila."

"And the trustees?"

"Two of them—his wife Sybil Dryden, and Sir Gregory Digges."

This name, together with Frank Abbott's part in the telephone conversation, brought instant illumination to Miss Silver's mind. She took two newspapers, one world-famous for its moderate views and impeccable taste, the other of a livelier cast and given to pictorial illustration. Like Frank, she

215

immediately recalled the photograph of Sir Gregory Digges on his hundred-and-first birthday surrounded by descendants, all apparently in rapt contemplation of an enormous cake with candles on every tier.

Frank laughed.

"I see the name touches a chord. Well, there you are. The will was made getting on for twenty years ago, and I suppose Sir John wanted to pay the old boy a compliment. You know how it is with trustees—one of them does the work, and the others sign on the dotted line. Sir John obviously expected his wife to be the one who did the work. I begin to wonder how she did it."

Miss Silver was knitting again. She said in a reminiscent voice,

"Nineteen years ago. . . . Miss Lila was then about three, and Sir John was not married to Lady Dryden."

"Sure about that?"

"Oh, quite. I fear I cannot give you the date of the marriage, but it was some years subsequent to the adoption."

"Then her name must have been added later. Jackson didn't go into details. It would be quite a natural thing to do."

Miss Silver coughed.

"Lady Dryden certainly gave me to understand that Sir John had been able to do very little for his adopted daughter."

"Query—are her ideas so large that she regards forty thousand as chicken-feed? Or what? I wonder whether the late Herbert had had a look at Sir John Dryden's will same as Jackson. If he was marrying the lovely Lila he would take an intelligent interest in that forty thousand. But Lady Dryden says there was very little for Lila. How come? Herbert may have wanted to know that and a good deal more. He may have developed an inconvenient curiosity—even a menacing one. If the forty thousand was no longer there, it might be very awkward indeed for Lady Dryden. It would, in fact, explain why Lila mustn't marry Bill, and must marry Herbert though she quite obviously regarded him as poison." He glanced at his wrist-watch and got up. "Well, having given free rein to our imaginations and hung a great deal of fancy on a very small peg of fact, we had better come back to solid earth. From which mixed metaphors you may pick out any one you like and keep it with the assurances of my most profound esteem—an expression translated from the French. I'm going to try it on the Chief one day and watch him blow up. For the moment, if his train wasn't late, Mr. Garside, Whitall's solicitor, should be turning in at the drive. We are about to stage the great will scene and watch everyone's reactions. You are specially invited to attend."

Miss Silver gathered up her pink ball, her knitting-bag, and little Josephine's vest. She smiled, and said sedately,

"Thank you. It will be a most interesting experience."

CHAPTER 30

Mr. Garside was a thin, hatchet-faced man with a stoop and a deep lugubrious voice. He was very much shocked at his client's violent end, and at being, as it were, precipitated into the middle of a murder case. Such a thing had never happened to the firm before. Not in the three generations during which his family had been connected with it. Disapproval enveloped him like a mantle. He sat at the writing-table in the study, opened the small attaché case which he had brought with him, took out some papers, and looked down the room at the assembled company. To his right was Inspector Abbott of Scotland Yard with the local Inspector who had met him at the station. He considered that Inspector Abbott looked a good deal too young for the job, and that he would in all probability be inclined to give himself airs. He disliked him, he disliked his errand. The whole affair was, in fact, extremely distasteful. He directed his attention to the family.

Mr. Haile—he knew a good deal about Mr. Eric Haile. Sir Herbert had been quite outspoken about him on more than one occasion. Lady Dryden—handsome woman, looked very well in her black. The secretary, Miss Whitaker—there wasn't much he didn't know about her—looked shockingly ill. Miss Dryden now, who had lost her bridegroom only a few days before the wedding, she didn't look half so bad. Delicate of course and nervous, but that was only natural. A lovely creature. Ah, well, there was many a slip 'twixt the cup and the lip. She sat on the sofa in a plain black dress high to the neck and long to the wrist, Mr. Adrian Grey on one side of her and a little woman who looked like a governess on the other. He had heard her name, but for the moment it eluded him. Silver—yes, that was it—Miss Silver. Just what she was doing here, he could not imagine, and no one had taken the trouble to inform him. She had a flowered knitting-bag on her lap. He trusted she was not going to knit. Had he but known it, her sense of decorum, quite as great as his own, would have been equally affronted by the production of little Josephine's pink vest.

Inspector Abbott had also been contemplating the group about the hearth—Mr. Haile leaning against the mantelpiece, a suitable shade of gravity upon his handsome features—Lady Dryden in one of the big chairs—Miss Whitaker, as became her position, in a smaller one. Well, there they were—all the suspects, except Bill Waring and the Professor. He turned to the solicitor with a nod, and Mr. Garside picked up one of the papers he had taken from his case, cleared his throat, and addressed an expectant audience.

"I have been asked to make a communication to you on the subject of the late Sir Herbert Whitall's will. Since the two executors are present, Mr. Haile and myself, I will now proceed to do so. I do not know whether Mr. Haile is acquainted with the terms of the will—"

As he paused upon this, Eric Haile said,

"My cousin told me that he was putting me in as an executor, but that was some years ago. Beyond that I know nothing. He was not a very communicative person. I supposed that as he was going to be married, he would be making a new will. May I ask whether you are now talking of the old will or of a new one?"

There was a pause. No one could fail to be aware that the question and its answer were momentous. If the new will had been signed, Lila Dryden would be an heiress. If the old will were still valid, she would not get a penny. And who benefited then— the cousin, the secretary, or some person or persons unknown? Anything was possible, and when Mr. Garside opened his dry lips the secret would be out. He opened them now.

"Sir Herbert was in process of giving me instructions with regard to a new will, but he had deferred a final decision as to some of its terms. He intended to make that decision over the week-end, and to sign the will on Wednesday, the day before his marriage. I do not know whether he had indeed come to a final decision, or what that decision would have been. It is immaterial, since the will remained unsigned. It is therefore the old will which is operative, and under that will, as I have said, you and I, Mr. Haile, are named as executors."

Lady Dryden took the blow with courage. She lost some colour. It became apparent that what remained was the result of art, not nature. The hand which lay upon the arm of her chair tightened a little. Her eyes rested steadily upon the solicitor's face. Miss Whitaker in the small chair beside her drew a long, deep breath. Her hands relaxed the hold in which they had been clenched. There was no change at all in Lila Dryden's rather bewildered gaze. Eric Haile nodded and said,

"Well, let's get on with it. What are the terms of the will?"

Before Mr. Garside could speak Inspector Abbott said,

"Are you sure you don't know?"

He got a frank stare of surprise.

"I have said I don't."

"You have no idea whether you are a beneficiary?"

There was a slight shrug of the shoulders.

"One hopes of course. I'm about the only relation he had."

If it was acting, it was very good acting indeed. No protestations, no assumption of disinterest, no pretence of anything beyond a decent gravity and regret.

At a look from Abbott, Garside began.

"I do not propose to read the will *in extenso*— not at the moment. I shall, of course, hand Mr. Haile the copy to which as an executor he is entitled. If he would like to have it now—" He paused in an interrogative manner.

Eric Haile waved the suggestion away.

"No, no—later on will do. I don't suppose any of us are very much up in legal jargon. I don't know why you have to wrap things up so."

The lugubrious voice took on a hint of reproof.

"Where precision is indispensable words have often to be employed in a sense which is unfamiliar to the layman. I will therefore summarize the main bequests. They are as follows—"

There was another pause whilst he settled his pince-nez. It was not of any considerable duration, but it weighed heavily upon everybody present. Mr. Garside cleared his throat, held the paper from which he was about to read a little farther away from him, and announced,

"I will begin with the smaller legacies. Ten named charities will receive five hundred pounds apiece. These bequests will be free of legacy duty, as will also the bequest of ten pounds for each year of service to all members of his domestic staff."

It was at this moment that Miss Whitaker leaned forward, and that Lila Dryden turned her bewildered gaze upon Adrian Grey. If she had said, "What does it mean—what has it got to do with me?" the implication could not have been plainer. Herbert Whitall was dead—she didn't have to marry him after all. Then why did she have to listen whilst a lawyer read things out of his will?

Adrian put his hand over hers for a moment, and then took it away again. She wished that he had left it there. Something inside her had begun to shake. Her faint lovely colour came and went.

Mr. Garside pushed his pince-nez up on the right-hand side and continued.

"There is a bequest of five thousand pounds to Mr. Adrian Grey." Mr. Garside looked over the top of his glasses and explained. "This bequest is contained in a codicil added recently, but I include it, for convenience sake, amongst the legacies in the body of the will. There is also in this codicil a legacy of five thousand pounds and his collection of ivories to the South Kensington Museum." He paused here to clear his throat and cough.

Adrian Grey had flushed. He looked up as if he were about to speak, did in fact murmur something which nobody heard, and then stopped. The flush faded slowly from his face.

Mr. Garside said in his most funereal tones,

"The residue of the estate, together with any house property in his possession at the time of his death, to his cousin Mr. Henry Eric Haile."

Eric Haile stood where he was, and everyone looked at him. Or nearly everyone. Even Lila Dryden turned those large blue eyes of hers in his direction. The only person in the room who continued to look fixedly at Mr. Garside was Miss Whitaker. Her gaze was so intent, so expectant, that it actually affected him with a feeling of discomfort. He doubled over the sheet of paper from which he had been reading and dropped it upon the blotting-pad.

Eric Haile straightened himself. His colour had

risen a little, as well it might. The man who can hear unmoved that he has inherited a large fortune is either a saint or a person devoid of ordinary human feelings. The rise in colour and the brightening of the eyes showed that he was by no means unmoved, but nobody could say that he did not bear himself with dignity and good feeling. He said, the words hurrying a little,

"I didn't expect anything like that. It's very good of him. I thought there might be a legacy, but not anything like this."

Sincerity, or acting? Frank Abbott had been brought up on the immortal works of Lewis Carroll, *Alice in Wonderland*, *Alice Through the Looking-Glass*. A chance phrase from the Hatter's tea-party slipped into his mind and out again: "It was the *best* butter."

Mr. Garside, again adjusting his pince-nez, was engaged in speculating as to whether Mr. Haile had any idea of just how lucky he was. If Sir Herbert Whitall had lived four days longer, there might not have been even a ten pound legacy for his next of kin. He wondered if Mr. Haile suspected by what a very narrow margin he had become an exceedingly wealthy man.

It may be said that the two police officers were concerned with the same question. Their scrutiny of Mr. Haile failed to provide them with an answer.

Mr. Garside was putting his papers away in the attaché case.

"Perhaps, Mr. Haile, we could have a talk—" He

paused, glanced about him, and added the word, "elsewhere."

All this while Miss Whitaker had remained leaning forward and staring at him. The last vestige of colour had left her face. Except for the unnatural brilliance of the eyes it had a dead look. As he pushed back his chair preparatory to rising, she spoke with stiff lips.

"That isn't all."

"Well, yes, Miss Whitaker."

"It can't be! There must be something for me. He told me there was."

There might have been no one else in the room. Intensity of feeling isolates. It was present in her voice as she reiterated,

"He told me—he told me—"

Mr. Garside said,

"I am afraid—you may have misunderstood. You have, I believe, been Sir Herbert's secretary for some years."

"Ten." The word rang like a tolling bell.

The solicitor cleared his throat.

"You will, of course, receive ten pounds for each of those years—a hundred pounds. That would be, I suppose, the legacy to which Sir Herbert alluded."

She said in a low, shocked voice,

"A hundred pounds!"

And then suddenly she was on her feet and screaming.

"A hundred pounds! Is that what you call a legacy? I misunderstood, did I? A hundred pounds!

He told me he was providing for me, and for the child! He told me I was down in his will for ten thousand! Why else do you suppose I stayed on when I knew he was going to marry that girl? Do you suppose I wanted to? Do you suppose any woman would want to? I was doing it because I'd got to—that's why! Because he was making a new will—because I was down for ten thousand in the old one—and because he said he'd cut me out of the new will and never leave me a penny! So I would have had to stay and watch him putting her upon a pedestal and calling her his ivory goddess and getting a kick out of seeing how much I hated it—and him—and her!" Her voice broke and came down on a level menacing note. "And her! The fool—the little fool! What about her now? Aren't you going to arrest her? She was there with his blood on her hand, wasn't she? Wasn't she—wasn't she? Why don't you arrest her?"

On the last words she stopped. A shudder went over her. She put out her hands in a groping gesture and went down in a heap on the floor.

CHAPTER 31

At ten o'clock that evening Miss Silver said good-night to Lady Dryden and Ray Fortescue on the bedroom landing and went to her own room. Lila Dryden had come down to dinner, but had gone up again as soon as the meal was over. The gentlemen would probably sit up for a little while yet.

Miss Silver closed the door of her room, noted with pleasure that a small fire burned on the hearth, and drew a comfortable chintz-covered chair to a convenient angle in front of it. It was not her intention to undress or to go to bed for the present. She had engaged in a small harmless experiment, and she wished to see how it would turn out. Meanwhile the room was warm and cosy, and she had plenty of food for thought. Having no secure place in which to lock up notes which would necessarily be of an extremely confidential nature, she had made none. But this was, in fact, no handicap. As she ran through the names of those concerned in the case, whatever she might have noted down with regard to each of them was most exactly present to her mind. She went over them now.

First, the murdered man, Sir Herbert Whitall. Medical evidence gave the time of his death as probably not later than eleven-thirty. He was certainly alive and talking to Professor Richardson at eleven. He was certainly lying dead on the study floor at a little after twelve o'clock. Like so many British juries, Miss Silver had no absolute faith in medical evidence when it inclined to be dogmatic. She considered that there might well be a little more margin that Dr. Everett had allowed for. Without stressing this point she felt entitled to keep an open mind.

She considered the suspects.

Professor Richardson:—He was talking to the murdered man at eleven o'clock. In his statement he declared that he had left very shortly after that. He had not looked at his watch, but he had heard eleven strike from the village clock, and he had gone away soon after that. He thought he had been about twenty minutes with Sir Herbert. Not longer. Allowing twenty to twenty-five minutes for him to reach his house, to fetch M. Robinet's letter and the magnifying-glass, and return to Vineyards, twenty minutes with Sir Herbert would bring the time of the Professor's departure to a quarter past eleven. There could be no exact computation, but this would be near enough. The Professor swore that he left Sir Herbert alive. If the medical evidence was to be strictly interpreted, there remained a bare quarter of an hour during which someone else might have murdered him.

Miss Silver passed in review those persons who could have had access to Sir Herbert during that quarter of an hour. They included everyone who was known to have been in the house.

Lady Dryden:—It would have been quite possible for her to have come down to the study—perhaps to resume some earlier conversation which had not reached a satisfactory conclusion. The dagger was lying on the writing-table. She could have stabbed Sir Herbert. There was no doubt in Miss Silver's mind that Lady Dryden's conduct as a trustee was open to grave suspicion. If Lila Dryden's forty thousand pounds could not be accounted for, Sir Herbert Whitall would have to know the facts. It would not have been possible to hoodwink him. In view of what she had learned about him during the last two days, she did not find it difficult to believe that he would use this knowledge without scruple. If he got what he wanted, all would go smoothly. He wanted Lila Dryden. But suppose Lady Dryden to have become aware that she could not after all compel Lila to this marriage—she might in that case have found herself confronted with disgrace, even with imprisonment. There have been murders with less inducement than this.

Lila Dryden:—The girl who was being forced into a marriage from which she recoiled. No use to say that girls could no longer be forced into marriage. Wherever a strong will dominated a weak one such force could be, and was, employed. Miss Silver thought very seriously about Lila Dryden. That she would be capable of violence whilst in a waking and normal condition she found quite incredible. But there was the evidence of Adrian Grey and of Bill Waring to show that she had been in a state of

229

somnambulism. There was also the evidence of Lady Dryden and Ray Fortescue as to a previous history of sleep-walking. With her nerves strained and her mind recoiling from the marriage into which she was being pushed, she had been told the story of Lucy Ashton. Lucy had stabbed her bridegroom on their wedding night. Was it impossible that in some desperate dream Lila had gone down to the study and used the ivory dagger to stab Herbert Whitall? Might he not, either in her dream or in reality, have laid hands on her? Might she not have snatched up the dagger and struck blindly, not knowing what she did? Against this supposition, what was there? The evidence of Adrian Grey who said he had been close behind her from the time she left her room, and the medical evidence which said that Herbert Whitall had been dead for more than an hour when the police arrived. It was a little after twelve when Bill Waring and Adrian Grey had come into the study by opposite doors and seen Lila standing there with the dagger at her feet and Herbert Whitall's blood on her outstretched hand, Eric Haile coming in a few minutes later. The police were on the scene very soon after half past twelve. According to the medical evidence Sir Herbert should have been dead by half past eleven. Even if a considerable margin were allowed, was it possible to believe that Lila Dryden killed him and then remained standing over the body for anything between half and three-quarters of an hour? Miss Silver shook her head. She did not believe it to be possible. As to Adrian

Grey's evidence, it would, of course, have been gravely suspect were it not for the support it received from the time element and the fact that he certainly did enter the study from the passage just after Bill Waring had come in by the window. If he had not followed Lila Dryden as he stated, what brought him there at all?

She turned to Eric Haile. Most certainly he had what any jury would consider the strongest motive of all. His cousin's death at this juncture had made him an extremely wealthy man. Had Sir Herbert lived for even another four days, this would certainly not have been the case. There might have been a legacy, but in view of Sir Herbert's intended marriage it was unlikely to have been a large one. The pressing question arose as to whether Mr. Eric Haile knew of his prospects under the old will. He did know that he was an executor. He admitted that he had hoped for a legacy. *But what did he actually know?* Unless proof was forthcoming that he knew he would benefit substantially, the money motive lacked support. That he was habitually in financial difficulties seemed probable. Lady Dryden alleged that he had approached Sir Herbert for a loan on the evening of the murder and had been refused. This was corroborated by Miss Whitaker. He was seen in his room apparently ready for bed at eleven o'clock by Mr. Adrian Grey. He could very easily have come down to the study and stabbed his cousin at any time after eleven-fifteen, when the Professor went away. He certainly arrived in a very opportune manner when Mr. Grey and Mr. Waring were discussing what they should do. Like everyone else in the house, he could have killed Sir Herbert. But there was really no proof that he had done so.

She passed to another name.

Adrian Grey:—There was a money motive here too. There was some evidence, provided by himself, that his relations with Sir Herbert had included moments of strain. There was the motive of his deep affection and concern for Lila Dryden. Was it not possible that, instead of following Lila, he had preceded her? He could have been in the study at any time after Professor Richardson left. There might have been some reason for his lingering on the scene. He could have seen Lila come down the stairs. Or, what would be far more probable, having returned to his room and found himself unable to sleep, he could have heard her open her door across the landing, and then have followed her down just as he said. Oh, yes, a suppositional case could be made out against Mr. Adrian Grey. Miss Silver set it out clearly in her own mind.

Continuing with the persons in the house on the night of the murder, she arrived at the Marshams. Mrs. Marsham she had not even seen, but she was unable to consider her seriously. Only a cook with her mind on her work could have produced such food as had been set before her since her arrival at Vineyards. Marsham she had seen—had watched him under Frank Abbott's questioning. He had a majestic appearance and very good manners. He had comported himself with dignity. He had seemed unwilling to implicate the Professor, but had not withheld his evidence when questioned. Always keenly sensitive to any departure from the normal, Miss Silver could find only one slight instance of this in Marsham's behaviour. The study was his own particular charge, but after being questioned he had left the room without making up the fire. And the fire needed attention. The door was no sooner shut behind him than Frank Abbott was attending to it. She recalled that he had put on two logs. This trifling incident now came under her scrutiny. During her stay in the house she had noted Marsham's particularity with regard to the fires. The fact that he had not observed the study fire to require attention argued some considerable disturbance of mind. It might be the general disturbance occasioned by a violent death in the house, but in that case it would have been noticeable at other times and in other ways. This was not the case. She left it at that, and proceeded to the young footman.

Frederick:—She put him down as a nervous adolescent. Under eighteen and waiting to be called up for his military service. A nice intelligent lad. Not very experienced, but willing to learn. A good deal in awe of the butler. She thought for quite a long time about Frederick. He was too nervous. She knew fear when she saw it, and Frederick was certainly afraid. He had the scared sideways look, the sudden starts, the jerky movements, of a scared animal. He had a way of looking at Lila Dryden when she was in the room—a sudden quick glance, and then away again. That his nervous state had some connection with her was obvious to so acute an observer as Miss Silver. He might, of course, have fallen a victim to an attack of calf love, but she did not think the explanation lay there. There was none of the complacence, the variability of mood which accompany this state. She remained convinced that Frederick was frightened, and that the only possible reason for this must be that he knew something which was frightening him, and that this knowledge concerned Lila Dryden.

Those were all the people who were known to have been in the house after eleven o'clock on the night of the murder. She did not put Bill Waring into this category, since the only evidence relating to his movements, except that of Adrian Grey, came from himself. In his own statement he affirmed that, after waiting till past twelve o'clock for Lila Dryden to come to the rendezvous he had given her, he made his way round the house, noticed that there was a light in the study, found the door ajar, and went in. He had just parted the curtains and seen Lila Dryden standing near the body of Sir Herbert Whitall, when Adrian Grey came in through the open door on the opposite side of the room. Mr. Grey's evidence confirmed this. He came into the room and saw Lila Dryden and the body, with Bill Waring standing between the parted curtains. There was, therefore, nothing to show that Bill Waring had actually entered the house before the murder took place, and some support for his statement that he had that moment come upon the scene to find Sir Herbert dead. There seemed to be no reason why Adrian Grey should lie to protect him. There was nothing in their subsequent conversation as reported by Eric Haile to lend colour to any supposition of this kind. He had, it is true, what might appear superficially to be quite a strong motive for murdering Sir Herbert, but in Miss Silver's judgment it would not really bear scrutiny. The note in which Bill Waring had invited Lila Dryden to come away with him was both direct and practical. She could marry Sir Herbert if she wanted to, but if she did not want to, he would take her away to her cousin Ray Fortescue. Just that, and a simple arrangement for them to meet. No protestations, no vehemence, no threats. She found it impossible to believe that the young man who wrote that letter would have committed so foolish and melodramatic an act as murder by stabbing. It is true that she had not encountered Bill Waring personally, but she had received quite a strong impression of his character from Ray Fortescue and from Frank Abbott. Even Lady Dryden's slighting references had not been without their value. In point of fact, she could not bring herself to believe in Bill Waring as a murderer.

She came to the last of the suspects—Millicent Whitaker. There, beyond all shadow of doubt, was the oldest and strongest motive in the world—jealousy. Miss Silver here permitted herself a much hackneyed quotation—"Hell has no fury like a woman scorned." After ten years of close association Herbert Whitall was marrying another woman. And not only that. Whether from mere bluntness of feeling and regard for his own convenience, or from some more sinister and sadistic motive, he was insisting that she should remain in his employment. Insisting, and reinforcing his insistence with a threat. Under the will which he was about to supersede by a new one Miss Whitaker believed that she would inherit the sum of ten thousand pounds. If she left his employment she would not receive a penny, for herself or for her child. The first motive was most powerfully reinforced by another almost as strong. The two, taken together with Miss Whitaker's shocked and devastated looks, were truly impressive. But Millicent Whitaker had an alibi. At eleven o'clock she was alighting from the bus at Emsworth station. A minute or two later she arrived at 32 Station Road and according to her sister, Mrs. West, went straight to bed, only returning to Vineyards by the ten o'clock bus on the following morning. Miss Silver wondered whether Mrs. West possessed a bicycle. With a bicycle it does not take very long to cover seven miles on a clear road. Not being a cyclist herself, she could not be quite sure how long it would actually take. There might have been a dreadful urgency, a strong compulsion. There was no shadow of proof.

These were all the suspects now, both those within the house and those outside. She had, as it were, called them up and made them pass before her. She let them go again.

It was not a person now but an inanimate object upon which she focussed her thought—that long glass door which Professor Richardson had found unlocked at just before eleven o'clock.

Miss Silver leaned back in her chair and considered the door.

It was unlocked at eleven o'clock, but the Professor stated with emphasis that it had been bolted behind him when he went away. Yet Bill Waring had found it not only unlocked but ajar at a little after midnight. Since the fastening was of the old-fashioned kind by which the turning of the handle drives a bolt down into a socket in the threshold, there could be no question of its being opened from outside by someone in possession of a key. It could, therefore, only have been opened from within, and it had been so opened twice. Once before eleven o'clock—by whom and with what object?—and again after being locked by Sir Herbert at eleven-fifteen.

It was impossible to avoid the conclusion that the person who had opened it this second time was either Sir Herbert Whitall himself or his murderer. Professor Richardson was gone before a quarter past eleven. Had someone then come tapping on the glass and been admitted? Was this person expected? Or only so familiar that he—or she—would be admitted without question? Miss Whitaker would be such a person. Had she bicycled out from Emsworth and come tapping on the glass to make one last jealous scene, and in the end snatched up the dagger? Or had someone come along the dim passage from the sleeping house and through that other door to wreak some grudge or satisfy some greed, going back to the sleeping house again but first setting the door to the terrace ajar, so that it might be thought that the murderer came that way? Upon this point there was no evidence.

CHAPTER 32

Miss Silver looked at her watch. The hands stood at a quarter before midnight. She went to the mahogany wardrobe, unhung her black cloth coat, and put it on. She replaced her thin beaded slippers with a pair of Oxford shoes and assumed her second-best hat. At the open door of her room she paused and listened. A most profound silence had settled upon the house. On this floor at least nobody moved or stirred.

At the head of the stairs she paused again. A small light burned in the hall below. The carpet was thick and new, her feet made no sound upon it. Crossing the hall, she made her way to the Blue Room, where Bill Waring had had his interview with Lady Dryden, and which he had appointed as his meeting-place with Lila. The window, as she had noted when she had been in the room for the purpose of telephoning to Frank Abbott, was of the simple casement type—no locks, no bolts, no bars. She had merely to lift the latch, push open the right-hand half of the window, and step out. On the inside a low window-seat made the process extremely easy, whilst even on the outer side there was no more than a two-foot drop, and since the gravel of the carriage sweep came right up to the house there was no risk of leaving footprints.

Switching off the light in the room, she climbed out and drew the window to behind her. The latch would prevent it from shutting completely, but there was no wind, and she felt assured that it would remain as she had left it until her return. It might be that she would not require to use this mode of ingress, in which case she would of course make it her business to see that the latch was fastened from the inside.

With all this present in her mind as part of an orderly plan, she stood for a few moments so that her eyes might become accustomed to the darkness. At first she could distinguish nothing at all. Then what had seemed to be a black curtain resolved itself into the grey of a cloudy sky and the darker shadow of the trees about the drive. She was facing that way. Turning a little more towards the house, she was aware of the dense mass of shrubbery which flanked it. She had provided herself with a torch, but was unwilling to use it if the necessity could be avoided. By keeping close to the wall it would not be possible to miss the flagged path which Bill Waring had taken on the night of

239

the murder. There was, of course, another path beyond this one, winding through the shrubbery. It was in the direction of this second path that both Bill Waring and Eric Haile had located the slight sound which both deposed to having heard. Neither could say that it might not have been made by an animal—dog, or cat, or fox. As Miss Silver moved cautiously along the flagged path by the house she reflected that if it was a human being who had used that other and more deeply shadowed path, he—or she—must have been very familiar with it.

She reached the terrace steps and ascended them. Coming round the black bush of rosemary which screened the study door, she saw, as Bill Waring had done before her, that there was a light in the room. Where all the other windows showed black to the midnight sky, there came through the study curtains a just perceptible glow.

If she paused for a moment, it was not because this fact necessitated any disarrangement of her plan. When, earlier in the evening, she had entered the room and turned the handle of the glass door until the bolt which held it was released, she had had two objects in view—she wished to know whether the fact that the handle was no longer in the closed position would have escaped Marsham's notice, and also whether the fact that the bolt had been released would have caused sufficient draught to attract the attention of anyone who happened to be occupying the room. As regards the first point, it was Marsham's habit to draw the

240

curtains and latch the windows between six and seven o'clock. This from her own observation. She did not suppose that he would test the bolts again. He spoke of making his rounds upon the night of the murder, but it seemed unlikely that he would actually examine the fastenings, and he had specifically stated that he had not on that occasion entered the study, as Sir Herbert was there. It was her present purpose to ascertain whether any member of the household could have counted on his overlooking the fact that the bolt on the study door had been withdrawn. If Professor Richardson had found the door ajar at a little before eleven, that bolt must have been released by someone inside the house, and it must have been done between seven o'clock and, say, ten minutes to eleven. She herself had visited the study just after seven o'clock this evening—a very good time, because at that hour the servants were busy and the guests in their rooms.

She went up the two steps from the terrace and tried the door. It moved noiselessly under her hand, swinging outwards. There was not only a light in the room beyond, but there were two people there. From the other side of the curtains Eric Haile's voice said,

"What is it?"

If there was a moment when Miss Silver imagined that the words were addressed to herself, it passed as she heard Marsham say,

"Was there anything I could get you, sir?"

There was a hint of impatience about Eric Haile as he said,

"I didn't ring."

"No, sir. I was up late, and seeing the light under the door—"

"You wondered if I was lying murdered on the floor!"

As Marsham made some soft deprecatory sound, Miss Silver stepped into the space behind the curtains and pulled the door to behind her, taking care that it should not jar. As a gentlewoman, eavesdropping was naturally repugnant to her feelings. She would not, in her private capacity, have dreamed of listening to a conversation which was not intended for her ears. As a detective she had not infrequently conceived it her duty to do so. Mr. Haile's remark was in the worst possible taste—oh, very decidedly so.

By moving the middle fold of the curtain with great discretion she was able to see into the room. Both men were in her line of vision, Mr. Haile at the writing-table, and Marsham just inside the open door from the passage. As she watched, he shut it behind him and came forward.

"As a matter of fact, sir, there is something I would like to mention if you would pardon the lateness of the hour."

Eric Haile laughed.

"The later the hour, the clearer the brain! If I ever did any serious work—which I don't—I should start at midnight. Well—what is it?"

Marsham's face was without expression. His

voice betrayed some slight hesitation.

"I should not wish to be inopportune—and you will, of course, have had very little time to consider your domestic plans. I only wished to say that, when you have done so, Mrs. Marsham and myself would esteem it a favour if you would inform us at your earliest convenience—"

Eric Haile jerked an impatient shoulder.

"Good lord, man—come to the point! You want to know what I am doing about the place, and the staff—especially the staff. Is that it?"

"At your earliest convenience, sir."

Mr. Haile had a thoughtful look. If there had been a hint of bravado it was gone. He said,

"I don't know about this place—I haven't been into anything yet. But the flat in town—I shall keep that on of course. And I shall want a butler and a cook. Your wife is an extremely good cook."

"She has always been considered to be so, sir."

"And good cooking covers a multitude of sins, doesn't it!" He paused, and added with emphasis, "You think so—don't you?"

"Sir—"

"You know what I mean, don't you? Let's be plain about it. My cousin had discovered that you were fleecing him, and he was about to discharge you without a character. He told me so when I was in the study with him before dinner on the night he—died. If I were to give that information to the police, don't you think it would interest them?"

Marsham's face had gone grey, but he stood up to the blow.

"May I ask if you have said anything to the police, sir?"

"Not yet." He gave a short half laugh. "And just in case you should have any idea of removing an inconvenient witness, let me suggest that it would be very difficult to get away with another body on the spot marked X."

"Sir!"

"It would be quite incredibly stupid."

Marsham said with dignity,

"You are pleased to amuse yourself, sir. Perhaps you will permit me to make a personal explanation. You employed a very derogatory expression with regard to myself when you used the word 'fleecing.' I admit that I overstepped the bounds of legality in accepting a commission from the wine and cigar merchants patronized by Sir Herbert. When I was in service with the late Lord St. Osbert I had his authority to take my commission. He said they made enough out of him, and why shouldn't I make something out of them? I was with him for ten years, sir."

"And my cousin didn't see things in the same light as Lord St. Osbert?"

"No, sir."

Eric Haile gave his easy laugh.

"He didn't go into particulars, you know. I suppose you would like me to withdraw—or shall I say soften—the word fleecing."

"It is not an expression I should employ to describe the acceptance of a commission."

"Nor I!" He laughed again. "Are you going to

244

ask me to believe that Sir Herbert had no more grounds than that for dispensing with the really excellent services of yourself and of your wife?"

Marsham gave a slight deprecating cough.

"If you will excuse me, sir, you do not appear to have been quite correctly informed. I tendered my notice to Sir Herbert together with that of Mrs. Marsham a week ago. He was unwilling to accept it, and informed me that it would be to my advantage to stay on with him."

"You wanted to leave?" Mr. Haile sounded surprised.

"I was not happy in the position, sir. On the Saturday night Sir Herbert sent for me whilst I was superintending the laying of the dinner table. He informed me that he would not accept my notice, and offered me a rise of salary. When I refused it he so far forgot himself as to threaten me, saying that if I left, it would be without a character and with the police on my heels."

"All on account of a little matter of a commission? Come, come, Marsham! If I were to hand all this on to the police, how far do you think that story would take you?"

From where she stood Marsham's face was plainly visible to Miss Silver. Beneath its smooth and mannerly surface she was aware of something that did not flinch. He said in quite his usual manner,

"I should consider it inadvisable to import the police into the matter, sir. Everyone has some private affairs which he would not care to have intruded upon. Let us take the question of last Saturday night—or of any other night, sir. There are always a number of persons in a house any one of whom could be about his private business at an hour or in a place which might be considered compromising. By the police for instance. Their profession induces a very suspicious habit of mind. If I may say so, sir, it would be most unwise to import them into the matter under discussion."

There was quite a prolonged pause, during which Eric Haile looked fixedly at Marsham. There was no change in the butler's expression, which remained perfectly respectful. In the end Haile said gently,

"I take it you are suggesting something. What is it?"

"I was putting a hypothetical case, sir. There is, I believe, a somewhat vulgar proverb regarding the wisdom of letting sleeping dogs lie."

Haile rapped with his knuckles upon the edge of the table.

"And how long do they lie? Until they are hungry. And when they have been fed they will presently be hungry again—and again—and again."

Marsham's manner took on a faint shade of reproof. He did not care for the way in which his metaphor had been turned against him. He used the tone of one who has observed a social solecism but is too well bred to draw attention to it.

"I hardly think so, sir. The whole matter must naturally be a painful one—one would not willingly recur to it. That would be my point of view, and I imagine that it would be yours also. In my opinion the less said on the subject the better. If you will accept our notice and embody the kind appreciation which you have expressed regarding our services in a testimonial, it would, I think, be satisfactory to all concerned."

Eric Haile burst out laughing.

"What a thundering hypocrite you are, Marsham!" he said. "I don't know that I can bear to part with you, and I shall probably always regret it if I do. But, as you say, there are things which are better forgotten, and I might find myself wondering about this and that—from time to time, you know. So perhaps we are better apart. You shall have your testimonial. But I advise you to walk warily in the matter of—shall we say—commission. Or anything else that might be likely to interest the police. Good-night!"

Marsham said, "Good-night, sir."

As he turned to leave the room, Miss Silver opened the door behind her and stepped back. For a moment the darkness was bewildering. She closed the glass door without making any sound and waited until she could see her way. Then she went down the terrace steps, and along the paved walk by which she had come, to the window of the Blue Room, which she had left unlatched. A few minutes later she had reached her own room with a good deal to think about.

CHAPTER 33

"I could not have felt justified in keeping such a conversation to myself."

Miss Silver sat in one of the small armless chairs which the Blue Room provided. It had the low padded seat and back of the Victorian period and was tastefully covered with a cross-stitch pattern which represented wan lilies on a ground of deep ultramarine blue. Together with the other furnishings of this small room, it had passed with the house and had been sedulously preserved by the efforts of Adrian Grey. A Pre-Raphaelite influence was discernible. There was even an authentic Morris paper on the walls.

Whilst listening attentively to last night's experience Frank Abbott could not help being aware of how perfectly his Miss Silver fitted into these surroundings. The chair she had chosen had no doubt been specially designed for the use of ladies addicted to needlework. It afforded support to the back and for the swelling skirt of other days. In fact it resembled very strongly the furniture in Miss Silver's own flat, which she had inherited from a Victorian great-aunt. He really had to make an effort in order to give his entire attention to the business in hand.

"It was certainly quite a curious conversation," he said. "I wish I had been there."

Miss Silver coughed.

"I have repeated it as accurately as possible."

He nodded.

"You always do—you're a marvel at it. What I mean is, here were two people who obviously weren't coming into the open. In that sort of case it is not only what is said that counts. It is every tone, every inflection, every movement, the twitch of a finger, the flick of an eyelash, the atmosphere in the room, that counts. You have your impression from these things, and if I had been there I would have mine. Then if we pooled them and found they were the same—well, it would still not be evidence, but it would be something a little stronger than we've got at present."

Miss Silver inclined her head. She had cast on the stitches for little Josephine's third vest, which would complete the set. A pale pink frill about half an inch in depth now showed upon the needles.

Finding that she did not speak, Frank went on.

"Just let us see what we have got in plain words. Marsham comes into the study at an hour which suggests that he had been waiting about until everyone except Haile had gone to bed. That is the first point. He wanted to see Haile on a matter of urgency, and he wanted to be sure that they wouldn't be interrupted. I think that's a fair enough inference."

"I think so."

"Well then, he manoeuvres for position. He

doesn't want to stay on with Haile, but he doesn't say so. He lets Haile think that he would like to stay on. Obviously, he wants to find out whether Haile knows that he was under notice to leave, and why. Whitall may have told his cousin that he was dismissing Marsham for peculation. Haile evidently didn't believe that commission story, and nor do I. There was something more than that, and he had to find out whether Haile knew about it—either by word of mouth or because there was some evidence which might have come into his possession. So he asks what Haile is going to do about the house and the staff."

Miss Silver coughed.

"That is quite a fair summary."

Frank leaned forward from the arm of the chair on which he was sitting and pitched a log upon the fire. A shower of sparks flew high, and the smell of apple-wood came drifting back into the room.

"Well, Haile comes across with a good hard punch. Says his cousin told him Marsham had been fleecing him—an expression which Marsham characterizes as derogatory and not at all a suitable way of describing the comparatively harmless if irregular practice of taking commission. You will have noticed how skilfully Marsham's side of this conversation is conducted. Just the right amount of Lord St. Osbert, just a hint that he had condescended to a mere third baronet, and all the time the most perfect decorum of speech and manner. Is that how it struck you?"

"You have put it very well."

"To continue. Mr. Haile gives Marsham to understand that he doesn't believe the story about the commission. Says in effect that Whitall must have had some much more serious reason for sacking an excellent butler and a first-class cook."

Miss Silver stopped knitting for a moment and said with emphasis,

"She is more than that, Frank—she is quite outstanding. You will not, I know, overlook the importance of this factor. It explains Sir Herbert's determination to retain the Marshams in his service and makes it credible."

"You believe Marsham's yarn about Sir Herbert's threatening to put the police on him if he persisted in leaving?"

"Yes, I think so. You see, it would be all in character. Miss Whitaker was an invaluable secretary. We know that he was thwarting her desire to leave him by the employment of threats. I see no reason to suppose that he would scruple to do the same in the case of the Marshams. From what I have learned of his character since I have been in this house, I can believe that he would derive a perverted pleasure from using this kind of constraint. He could not have been unaware of Lila Dryden's feelings, yet he was determined to marry her. His conduct towards Miss Whitaker was not only cruel but in the worst possible taste. She had been his mistress, and she very properly desired to leave his employment before his marriage to Lila Dryden. He was using threats to induce her to remain.

251

I can readily believe that he would employ the same method of retaining the Marshams' services."

Frank regarded her quizzically.

"In other words you thought Marsham was telling the truth."

"With regard to that incident I should be inclined to think so."

"But Haile doesn't seem to have been impressed. Marsham says Whitall threatened that if he left, it would be without a character and with the police on his heels."

Miss Silver coughed.

"I feel convinced that Marsham would not have originated such an expression. It is foreign to his whole manner of talking. I received the very strongest impression that he was repeating what had been actually said to him by Sir Herbert."

Frank gave a little nod.

"That's a point," he said. "And here's another one. Haile comes back with, 'All on account of a little matter of commission? If I were to hand this story of yours to the police, how far do you suppose it would take you?' And now we come to what might, or might not, be a counter threat. I've got it all down as you told it me, and none of it's evidence. But Marsham says a piece to the effect that quite a number of people in the house might have been about their own private business on the night of the murder, and that he would consider it inadvisable to import the police into the matter— they've got nasty suspicious minds, and so forth and so on. Well, if that and what follows doesn't mean that Marsham has got something on Haile, I'll eat my hat. The bother is, it might be almost anything—an intrigue with Lady Dryden, a surreptitious raid on the whisky, or half a dozen other things. I don't suppose Haile has ever gone in for 'the white flower of a blameless life'—to dish up the revered Tennyson's most hackneyed quotation. But there really isn't anything you can put your finger on. All it boils down to is, Marsham knows something which Haile would prefer to keep dark, and they agree to part friends and mutually bury the past. If I have them up one at a time and put them through it, I don't suppose I shall get a thing. Marsham won't give Haile away, because he doesn't want to be given away himself, and the same goes for Haile. They've both got good headpieces and any amount of nerve. Marsham will probably admit to the commission, which is neither here nor there in a murder case, and Haile will say what we know, that his cousin was inclined to be too severe, and that he himself took a more lenient view and didn't want to be hard on the fellow, who really was a most excellent butler. You see, we shouldn't get anywhere. And if I tell the Chief all this, he'll tell me I've got highfalutin notions and can't see what's under my nose—there are two perfectly obvious suspects in Lila Dryden and Bill Waring, and why don't I get on with it and arrest them? I've had him on the telephone this morning—very British, full of the bulldog spirit, and totally lacking in bonhomie. Says I got my promotion too quick and it's given me wind in the head—setting up my fancy opinions against my lawful superiors, and so on. I hope he felt better when he had got it off his chest—I didn't. He can't get away today, but he'll be down bright and early tomorrow just to see I don't make a total mess of things. So if you can pull any rabbits out of the hat before then, I'm your slave for ever."

Miss Silver coughed reprovingly.

"My dear Frank!" she said.

CHAPTER 34

Emerging from the Blue Room a little later, Miss Silver encountered Ray Fortescue. The day was a blowy one, and she was very becomingly and suitably attired in a brown tweed skirt and a soft yellow cardigan and jumper. A scarf which repeated these two colours was tied over her dark curls. Miss Silver approached her with a smile.

"I see that you are going out. I wondered if I might speak to you for a moment. But I should not wish to detain you if you have an appointment."

Ray's colour came up brightly.

"Oh, no, it doesn't matter at all. I—I just thought it would be nice to get some air. There's something about this house—I suppose it's the central heating. It's very nice of course, but—I expect you know what I mean."

She had a horrid feeling that if the first part of this rather hurried speech declined a little from the ways of truth, the last few words were painfully accurate. Under a kind and candid scrutiny she became convinced that Miss Silver did indeed know exactly what she meant. She was going to meet Bill Waring, and there was no reason why she shouldn't have said so. She allowed herself to be shepherded into the Blue Room with the consoling reflection that it wouldn't do Bill any harm to have to wait.

Miss Silver seated herself and took out her knitting. She had observed a slight restlessness which suggested that Miss Fortescue might be in a hurry. On such occasions she found that the gentle, regular click of the needles had a soothing influence. Conversations conducted in a hurry were of very little value.

When after a few moments Ray had not taken a seat, Miss Silver invited her to do so.

"Pray, my dear, sit down. I will not keep you, but I am really anxious to ask your opinion on a matter to which I have given a good deal of thought."

The note of mingled frankness and authority carried Ray back to the schoolroom. She dropped into the nearest chair and said in rather a startled voice,

"What is it?"

Miss Silver pulled on her pale pink ball.

"It is the matter of the young footman, Frederick. I do not know if you have observed him at all particularly."

Ray showed frank surprise.

"Oh, yes. He is a nice boy. His people live in the village. Mary Good was telling Lila about them."

Miss Silver knitted placidly.

"Indeed? Now that is just what I was hoping for—a little information about Frederick. Pray proceed."

A hint of distress came into Ray's voice.

"But, Miss Silver, you don't think he had anything to do with it? I mean, he really is a nice boy—everyone says so. He's just waiting to be called up, you know. And then he wants to go to one of those vocational places they have now and train for something. He doesn't want to stay in service—he's just putting in time. He's frightfully keen to get on, because there's a girl, and he's planning to save all he can, so that they can get married by the time he's twenty-one."

Miss Silver coughed.

"And did Mary Good tell your cousin that also?"

"Oh, no, he told me that himself. I asked him what he was going to do when he'd finished with the Army, and it all came out. I like boys, you know, and they'll always talk to me. As a matter of fact it was his being so sure about Lila that broke the ice. He came in here to show me where the telephone was on that very first day and quite burst out with it. I thought he was rather a lamb, because about every other person in the house was going round glooming and believing the worst."

Miss Silver found these remarks of considerable

interest but rather lacking in clarity. In the tone of one who encourages a backward pupil she said,

"Perhaps you will tell me what Frederick actually said."

"I will if I can. I don't know that I remember exactly. . . . Oh, yes, he sort of burst out like I said—'Miss Lila never did it!' I'm sure he said that, but I can't remember the rest of it—something about the police—'They're thinking she did it, but of course she didn't.' I'm not sure about that part, because I was in a hurry to get to the telephone."

She could hardly have given herself away more completely. With Lila under the suspicion of murder, she had been able to devote only a fragmentary attention to the one person who protested her innocence. Her colour flamed. If Miss Silver hadn't known all about her before, she would certainly do so now. She might just as well have said straight out, "I was going to ring up Bill Waring, and I hadn't room in my head for anything else."

Miss Silver said, "I see—" Her gaze rested calmly on Ray's flushed face. "And was that all?"

"Oh, yes—I think so. He went away."

Miss Silver smiled very kindly indeed.

"And you rang up Mr. Waring at the Boar. You would naturally be in some concern for him."

The flush subsided. It didn't matter what Miss Silver knew. Ray said quite simply,

"Yes, I was. You see, he asked me to come down here—I told you about that—and I hadn't seen him. I wanted to see him dreadfully. I didn't know if he was being arrested or anything. That is why

I wasn't taking much notice of Frederick. Lila was here in the house, and I knew what was happening about her—I mean, I knew she wasn't being arrested or anything. But I didn't know about Bill. And I expect you know how it is, when people are out of sight you can't help thinking of all the things that might be happening to them."

There was a note of appeal in her voice, and before Miss Silver could make any reply she went on in a kind of soft rush.

"I keep thinking like that all the time. Sometimes I feel as if it's too dreadful to happen. And then I feel it must be going to happen just because it is too dreadful. I mean, I can't really see why they don't arrest him. He was there, and Lila was there, and I know that neither of them could have done it, but I can't see why the police should think so, or why they didn't arrest them straight away. And now I am afraid they are going to. You know, Mary Good lives next door to Inspector Newbury, and Mrs. Newbury is her cousin or something."

Miss Silver coughed.

"She has been talking?"

"Well, not really. She just said that some big man was coming down from Scotland Yard tomorrow—a Chief Detective Inspector, I think. And she kept looking at Lila in a hushed sort of way—you know how people do when they think something horrid is going to happen and they feel sorry for you. I think she is sorry for Lila. She has got rather fond of her, you know."

Miss Silver inclined her head.

258

"Let us now return to Frederick. He also is sorry for your cousin. I would like to know a little more about the attachment you mentioned. Is it to a local girl?"

"Oh, yes. Didn't I tell you? She is a sort of relation of Mary Good's. You know how it is in country places, they are all married to each other's relations or something. This girl's name is Gloria Good. Her stepfather married an aunt of Frederick's, and she isn't very happy at home. Frederick gets worried because he's afraid she will run away, and she isn't seventeen yet."

Miss Silver smiled benignly.

"He seems to have confided in you to a considerable extent."

"Oh, he's bursting with it, poor lad. Boys will always talk if you let them, and he saw I was interested. People *are* interesting—don't you think so? The way their minds work, and the odd kind of things they do."

Miss Silver had recourse to Alexander Pope for an apt quotation.

"The proper study of mankind is man."

Ray looked a little taken aback. She hadn't been studying Frederick—she had merely listened to him. She said so, and added,

"He was so worried, poor lamb, or he wouldn't have—"

Since she did not finish the sentence, Miss Silver prompted gently,

"He would not have?"

Ray's colour rose.

259

"Well, I was going to say something, but I think I had better not. It wasn't anything really—just the sort of thing boys do. I wouldn't like to get him into trouble."

Miss Silver coughed gently.

"He was so worried? He did something that might get him into trouble, but it wasn't anything serious?"

"Oh, no." Ray sounded distressed. "I oughtn't to have said anything. I thought I had stopped in time, but you're so quick."

Miss Silver looked at her gravely.

"I really think you had better tell me what you mean. If it has nothing to do with the case in which we are both so much interested, I will regard it as a confidence. If on the other hand it has to do with that case, you would be very unwise to withhold it, and you will not expect me to do so."

"Oh, but it isn't anything like that—it isn't really. I'd better tell you, or you will be imagining all sorts of things. It's only that Frederick slips out of the house sometimes after he has finished his work and goes down to see Gloria. I know he did it once when they had had a quarrel and he wanted to make it up, and another time when he thought she was going to run away. You won't say anything, will you? He really was dreadfully upset, because he said Gloria is only a kid and she wouldn't know how to look after herself. He says his aunt is quite kind, and the stepfather isn't a bad sort, but he and Gloria have rows, and then Frederick has to

260

soothe her down and stop her from doing anything silly."

Miss Silver gazed abstractedly at little Josephine's vest, which was now between four and five inches in length.

"You interest me extremely," she said. "Since Frederick has been so informative, may I ask whether he mentioned at what time he was in the habit of getting out of the house?"

Ray had a rueful expression.

"I expect it would be pretty late."

"After Marsham had made his rounds?"

"Well, I expect so."

"And Gloria—he could hardly expect to find her up at such an hour."

Ray coloured high.

"Oh, Miss Silver, I do feel such a beast, giving the poor child away like this. But I'm sure there wasn't anything wrong—I'm really sure there wasn't. He's just a boy, and frightfully romantic and very fond of her. And there's an apple tree— he gets into the crotch about a yard away from her window, and they talk. The aunt and the stepfather are the other side of the house, and anyhow nothing wakes them. But there's no harm in it—or he wouldn't have told me, would he?"

Miss Silver gave a thoughtful cough.

"Did Frederick happen to mention whether he was out of this house on the night of the murder?"

The question hit Ray like a blow. Afterwards she couldn't think why it had been left for Miss Silver to ask it. Her mind had been taken up with Bill, with Lila, with herself, and with the relation in which they stood to each other, and she to each of them. Frederick's artless tale had remained upon the very surface of her thought. She did not connect it with herself, with Bill, or with Lila. It was like something she had read in a book picked up to pass the time. And then all at once it was real, it linked up. She caught her breath and stammered,

"No—no—I never thought—he didn't say—"

Miss Silver's needles clicked.

"I was wondering if it was he who left the door to the terrace unfastened," she said.

Chapter 35

As soon as the first curve in the drive took her safely out of sight of the house Ray started the kind of broken run which can be kept up for quite a long time—three steps running and two walking. It gets you along very fast indeed, without making you too much out of breath. It wouldn't do Bill any harm to wait, as she had already reflected, but she didn't want to miss any of their time together. They were going to have coffee at the Boar. Mrs. Reed made marvellous coffee—at least Bill said she did. If it had been bilgewater, Ray wouldn't really have cared, only she wasn't going to arrive all out of breath and have Bill think she had been in a hurry.

262

He probably only wanted to talk about Lila any-how.

She came out of the drive and ran right into him. No car this time, just Bill on his own large feet. She really did run into him, because he stepped out suddenly from behind the gatepost and she couldn't help it. She had a bright colour and she was out of breath. He hadn't any business to lurk behind gateposts and catch her out, when they had agreed to meet at the Boar. If he had stayed put, she could have walked the last hundred yards or so and given a satisfactory performance of the girl who always keeps men waiting. And now all she could do after blundering into him was to give a gasp like a fish and say,

"Miss Silver kept me."

It was a lamentable business. Any girl of sixteen could have done better than that. At sixteen she could have done much better herself. What un-dermines you is caring, and at sixteen she didn't give a damn.

With all this going through her mind in rather a horrid flash, she was aware of Bill gripping her by the arm as if he was holding her off or up and frowning with a good deal of intensity. He gripped, he frowned, and said in a short, angry voice,

"You can't come to the Boar!"

"Why can't I?"

"That's why I walked up instead of waiting for you."

"What's the good of saying 'That's why,' as if you had told me something you haven't?"

263

"But I have. You can't come to the Boar. I told you so."

Ray stamped her foot on a bit of loose gravel. It hurt, but she had only herself to thank for it, which naturally made her feel angrier with Bill. It was extraordinary what a relief it was to be angry. It took away the frightened feeling which she had about him all the time now.

He was still holding her by the arm. But as the sound of a car came to them from the road, he swung her about and walked her quickly in at the gate and out of sight behind a large evergreen bush. She began to say, "What on earth—" when he dropped her arm and interrupted.

"You'd better not be seen with me—either here, or at the Boar, or anywhere else. If you had any sense you would have thought of that for yourself. You don't belong in this mess, and the sooner you get out of it the better. There's an afternoon train at about two-thirty—you had better catch it and clear out."

"I like that—when you asked me to come down!"

"I know I did, and I've been kicking myself ever since. I wasn't thinking about you, I was thinking about Lila."

All Ray's flame died down. She said in a quiet, careful voice,

"Lila is still here, you know. There's just as much reason for me to be with her as there was, isn't there?"

"If they arrest her, you won't be able to be with her, and you'd better clear out before it happens,

264

or you'll be getting mixed up with it."

She said, her voice dragging,

"Don't be a fool, Bill. Has anything happened?"

"Not yet, but it's going to. I don't know about Lila, but I'm pretty sure I am going to be arrested before the day is out. It's all over the village that there's a big man coming down from Scotland Yard, and that Abbott has had it put across him for not getting on with it and arresting us."

Ray felt as if she had come a long way and got nowhere. If they arrested Bill, there might be an endless way to go—a lonely, endless way. She had to force her voice to make it sound at all.

"How do you know?"

"I heard two girls talking. I was in my room, and they were down in the garden. One of them is a niece of Mrs. Reed's. She said it was ever so dreadful, wasn't it—and I didn't look like a murderer, but you couldn't always tell, could you? And the other one said the piece about a Chief Inspector coming down from Scotland Yard, and she knew that was right, because Lizzie Holden told her, and she had it from Mrs. Newbury, only she promised she wouldn't say a word, and she wasn't telling anyone but me, because she knew I was safe—and so forth and so on."

"Mrs. Newbury hasn't any business to talk."

"Of course she hasn't. And of course she does. If there is any way of stopping a leaky tongue, nobody has even found it yet."

"Well, whatever she says, I don't suppose she knows very much. And anyhow anything she did say would pile up like a snowball before it got half way round the village."

He nodded gloomily.

"That isn't all. There's been a mob of reporters milling round, wanting to know all about everything—Lila—me—you—what it feels like to be engaged to a girl and come back from America to find she's going to marry someone else next week—what it feels like to be a suspect—"

"They didn't ask you that!"

"Not quite. But they'd have liked to, and they got precious near it."

She thought, "It's the reporters who have really got under his skin."

He went on in an angry voice.

"If you had shown up at the Boar they'd have been on to you, and you'd have been torn to bits. I kept on saying, 'No statement,' in the best diplomatic manner, and Mrs. Reed helped me to give them the slip. I gather she's one of the people who think perhaps I didn't do it, or if I did, he was asking for it and only got what was coming to him. He doesn't seem to have managed to get himself liked very much down here, and they all seem to be sorry for Lila, but—Oh, Ray, it's a mess! And you had better clear out—you really had." He put his two hands on her shoulders and let them rest there heavily.

Standing like that and looking up at him, her face very clear and pale, she said,

"Oh, no, Bill. You didn't really think I would, did you?"

"I don't want you mixed up in it."

"If you are mixed up in it—and Lila—then I am too."

"I don't want you to be."

"You can't help it. I'm here. And I'm going to stay. And they haven't arrested you yet anyhow. You know what village gossip is—bits and scraps all well boiled up and passed along, with a new bit added every time anyone can think of something fresh to say. And tomorrow there'll be quite a new story all about somebody else. After all, Bill, you didn't kill Herbert Whitall, and somebody else did. Just hold on to that. Somebody killed him, and the police are going to find out who it was. Or if they don't, Miss Silver will."

The words came tumbling out. The dragging pain had gone. She was ready to fight again. Colour and courage came back. The face turned up to Bill's was so warm and glowing that if he had not let go of her and stepped back he would have kissed it. And if he were going to kiss Ray now, it would mean too much to both of them. The time was gone when he could give her a friendly hug and brush her cheek with casual lips. It had gone by. It wouldn't come again. Something ran between them, quick and strong. He stepped back and said,

"All right—we pin our faith on Miss Silver. But she'll have to be quick about it. I don't see the police working overtime to get me out of a hole. It looks as if they were all set in the opposite direction."

"Like us," said Ray firmly. "We're going down

to the Boar to get that coffee."

"Oh, no, we're not."

She stamped again, but this time it was on soft earth.

"Do you want me to go down there by myself? I will if you won't come with me!"

"The place is full of reporters."

"Do you suppose I care? I want that coffee, and I'm going down to the Boar to get it! And if you don't come with me, I'll talk to the reporters and say anything that comes into my head—anecdotes of your youth—how you made seventy-five not out in a village cricket match—how you jumped in off the pier at Brighton to save a child—"

"I never did such a thing in my life!"

She laughed.

"But I can say you did, and the more you say you didn't, the more they'll only think you are being modest. I can think up a lot more things like that, and I will if you don't take me down to the Boar and give me that coffee."

"Ray, don't be a fool! Don't you see, if we go down there together—"

She said lightly,

"Of course I see! They'll think I'm a girl friend, and they'll think perhaps it wasn't so awfully serious about Lila, and that will be all to the good."

"Oh, you're being a smoke-screen? I don't think I want one."

Ray began to be afraid she had gone too far. She hadn't meant to say all that—it just slipped out. She let her voice tremble.

"Oh, Bill—"

"Well, I don't."

"Bill, I'm sorry—I didn't mean it that way."

"And now you are trying to get round me."

"Of course I am. And I really do want that coffee. Oh, Bill, don't quarrel—I do hate it so!"

She slipped a hand inside his arm. There was an odd moment of emotion. So little time to quarrel in. Perhaps no time to make it up. He said in a forced, jerky voice,

"All right, let's come."

CHAPTER 36

Miss Silver remained in the Blue Room. She was considering what she would do next. An interview with Frederick? If she rang the bell in this room, he would answer it. But she would rather choose a more natural opportunity. She had no wish to startle him or to increase his obvious nervousness. Since this room appeared to be his charge, he would probably come in presently in order to attend to the fire. She decided to remain where she was and see what would happen.

It was a little later that the telephone bell rang. It was not, of course, her business to answer it, but since she was there on the spot, she did so. Frank Abbott's voice said, "Hullo!"

"Miss Silver speaking."

"I'm just off to meet the Chief. This is to let you know that I asked Newbury the question you suggested, and he says yes, the sister has a bicycle. He noticed it when he was there. That's all. Goodbye. Love to the Chief, I suppose?"

He had rung off before Miss Silver could reprove this impertinence. The whole encounter had passed so quickly that it was over by the time Marsham had reached the extension in his pantry and lifted the receiver.

With a look of satisfaction Miss Silver resumed her seat. She had felt quite sure that there would be a bicycle. She took up her knitting, and had made good progress when Frederick came in with a basket of logs. Drilled by Marsham always to shut a door behind him, he did so now, and knelt down before the hearth to make up the fire. Miss Silver was struck afresh by his pallor. Either the boy was ill, or he had something on his mind. The something on his mind might be Gloria Good, or it might not. It might be something a great deal more serious.

Sitting to one side of the hearth, she had a good view of Frederick's profile. Now, as she addressed him, he turned towards her.

"You have not been here very long, have you?"

"No, miss."

She coughed gently.

"This is a very disturbing and terrible thing to have happened in a house. It must have upset you very much."

270

The hand in which he was balancing a log of wood shook perceptibly. The log slipped and fell clattering upon the andirons. Since no other answer appeared to be necessary, Miss Silver continued.

"I can see that it has upset you. But you must not let it weigh upon you too much. All this will pass—for you. There are others who may be more sadly and more permanently affected. It will be a terrible thing if any suspicion should continue to rest upon Miss Lila Dryden."

A distressed flush came up into Frederick's face. The words which he had used to Ray Fortescue sprang to his lips.

"She never did it!"

The atmosphere of friendliness which emanated from Miss Silver had gained her many confidences in the past. It was neither calculated nor insincere, but the natural outcome of a deep interest in other people's problems and a warm desire to help them. She felt a true concern for Frederick. She said in her kindest voice,

"I do not think that anyone who knows her would believe her capable of violence."

"Oh, no, miss—they wouldn't! That's what I said to—to—somebody—only they didn't see it that way."

"You were talking about it to a friend?"

"Well, I was, miss. When a thing is weighing on you like, it seems as if you've got to talk about it to someone—only she didn't see it that way."

Miss Silver smiled.

"It was a girl then. Perhaps she did not know Miss Lila."

"Well, not to say no, miss. She seen her of course. We've been going together ever since we were kids. She works for Mrs. Considine, and what I say is, she did ought to stay on there till she's a bit older. She's only sixteen, and Mrs. Considine's learning her to cook lovely."

"And that will be so very useful when she has a home of her own."

"That's what I was thinking," said Frederick artlessly. "But Gloria wants to go into a shop in Emsworth, and I don't like it for her—not winter evenings, with that long road back in the dark, and you can't always get on a bus just when all the shops come out."

Miss Silver said in an indulgent tone,

"I should not say too much against it if I were you, Frederick. Girls like to have their own way, you know, and it is a pity for a discussion to become a quarrel."

He looked worried.

"That's right—we had ever such a quarrel about it Saturday."

Miss Silver continued to knit. She gazed with interest at Frederick and said,

"A quarrel should never be allowed to go on. I hope you were able to make it up without delay."

The colour rushed up under his pale skin. He turned his head away and fumbled with the wood.

"Oh, we made it up all right," he said.

"On the Saturday night?" said Miss Silver.

There was a horrid pause. She repeated her question.

"On Saturday night, Frederick?"

"Oh, miss!" The words came out with a gulp.

Miss Silver said with gentle authority,

"You slipped out of the house and went down to see her and make it up, did you not? When the house was quiet and you thought everyone had gone to bed? Pray do not be so much alarmed, my dear boy. You were breaking a rule, but I would not readily believe that you have done anything that is really wrong. I am sure that you only wanted to make it up with Gloria, but I think when you were coming, or going, that you may have seen or noticed something which is weighing upon you, and which you should not now keep to yourself."

Frederick stared with bolting eyes. Sweat broke out upon him. From his wet and sticky hands a log dropped unregarded upon the hearth-rug. Miss Silver's mild gaze appeared to him in the terrifying aspect of a searchlight. That stealthy passage from his room, the even more stealthy return, and all the horror that lay between, were most startlingly revealed by it. In a moment the thing which no one knew—that he hardly dared to think about—the thing that came walking into his dreams to wake him drenched with fear, would be trumpeted aloud. In the next moment, here in this room, he would have to hear the words against which he stopped his ears in the night, cramming the blankets over his head and cowering down in his bed, shaking with terror as he was shaking now.

Miss Silver laid down her knitting and leaned forward to put a hand on his arm.

"My poor boy! Pray do not be so much distressed. No one is going to harm you, and you can harm no one who is innocent."

The kindness which flowed from her completed the overthrow of Frederick's self-control. He broke into tears and stammered between sobs,

"That's Miss Lila—she never done it—she's the innocent one—she wouldn't harm anyone—not for the world she wouldn't. I did ought to have said so before—it didn't seem as if I could. It wasn't just getting into trouble with Mr. Marsham— though I'd have done that all right, sneaking out in the night, and he'd have thought worse about it than what it was. There wasn't any harm in it, miss—I'll take my Bible oath there wasn't—only to see Gloria and make it up."

The words came out between choking gulps. There were tears and rending sniffs, there was a hasty fumbling for a handkerchief which could not be found. Always equal to the occasion, Miss Silver produced a clean one of her own, neatly folded and of a most sensible size. Under its ministrations and her steadying air of calm the sobs lessened in violence and the words with which they were interspersed became more coherent.

When her experience informed her that a suitable moment had arrived she said briskly,

"And now suppose you tell me all about it."

CHAPTER 37

Chief Detective Inspector Lamb was in no mood to be trifled with. His second daughter, Violet—the flighty one—had been trying his temper to the utmost and upsetting her mother to a really serious extent by announcing that she proposed to become engaged to a South American dance-band leader. It was in vain that his other daughters, Lily, now a comfortable matron, and Myrtle, on the point of completing her training as a nurse, took every opportunity of pointing out to him that Violet was always getting engaged and it never came to anything, so why worry. As Lily said, "If she didn't go through with it when it was that nice Major Lee, or that very goodlooking Squadron Leader, or the young man whose uncle had a blacking factory, well, why shouldn't she break it off with Pedrillo?" The mere name sent the blood to Lamb's head in a most alarming manner. Foreigners existed, and a nice mess they made of things by all accounts. Look at Hitler—look at Mussolini—look at all those foreign Communists! Well, there they were, and they'd got to be put up with or got rid of, according as the case might be, and no doubt some of them were to be pitied and given a helping hand to. But to go bringing them into the family was just a bit of tomfool craziness. Violet and her "Hasn't he got lovely dark flashing eyes, Pop?"! She needn't think she could get round him with silly pet names. He was a Chapel member in good standing, but he'd never been nearer swearing in his life.

He was therefore in no mood for tolerance. Frank Abbott, encountering the slightly bulging eyes which had so often evoked an irreverent comparison with the larger kind of peppermint bullseye, was made duly aware that he had better mind his p's and q's. The slightest sign of uppishness, and one of the Chief's most formidable harangues would be forthcoming. Frank knew them all by heart, and had no desire to hear any of them again. He therefore trimmed his course with care, and having weathered the short passage from Emsworth Station to the office which the County Superintendent had placed at their disposal, was rewarded by a menacing glare and a rasp in the voice more suggestive of a lion than a lamb.

"Very mim and meek all of a sudden, aren't you? Makes me wonder what you've been getting up to. It's not natural, and when people don't act naturally, that's the time you've got to watch 'em. What have you been doing?"

Frank's left eyebrow rose almost imperceptibly. With a slight accentuation of his usual manner he replied,

"Nothing, sir."

The suggestion of an approaching storm was intensified. Lamb sat back in his chair, his big body filling it squarely, his face ruddy and lowering, his strong black hair asserting its vigour by something as near a curl as a drastic hair-cut would allow.

"Nothing?" he repeated. "Well, I suppose you think that's a recommendation. A man is murdered in his own house four or five days before his wedding, the girl he's going to marry is found with her hands all over blood, the dagger that stabbed him lying at her feet, and the man she was going to elope with—old lover chucked over for a richer man—actually in the room."

"Only one hand, sir."

"Only one!" The Chief Inspector drew in his breath and let it out again explosively. "It doesn't take more than one hand to stab a man, does it?"

"No, sir."

Lamb thumped his knee with a powerful fist.

"Well then, get on and arrest her—get on and arrest young Waring! It's as clear as daylight, isn't it? She was going to elope with him. Sir Herbert Whitall comes down and catches them, and one of them stabs him. Looks as if it was the girl. The dagger was lying there handy, and she grabbed it."

"Well, sir—"

He got no farther than that, because the storm broke.

"Too easy for you, I suppose! Not clever enough! No scope for showing off and making a splash! That's about the size of it, isn't it?"

"No, sir."

"Yes, sir—no, sir—well, sir! Might as well be a talking dummy and have done with it! Polite as pie and respectful as you please on top, and as insub-ordinate as the devil underneath! If there's one thing that riles me more than another, it's that, and you know it! If you've got anything to say—and I suppose you have—you'd better by half come out with it!''

Frank Abbott came out with it. The medical evidence—Adrian Grey's evidence—Marsham's evidence as to hearing voices in the study—the Professor's magnifying-glass—the Professor's statement—Miss Whitaker and her alibi—Mr. Haile's interest under the will, his dubious financial position—the very curious conversation between him and the butler as overheard by Miss Maud Silver—

A deep plum colour suffused the face of Chief Inspector Lamb.

"Miss Silver!"

"Maudie the Mascot. All present, and as usual superlatively correct. She has a new knitting-bag, I think. And it's vests this time, not stockings—pale pink, for a little girl of about three."

"Well, I'm—" Lamb made a commendable effort and checked himself. It was against his principles to swear, and he had already allowed himself to be goaded into mentioning the devil.

No one could have returned his glare more innocently than Inspector Abbott. He risked a "Yes, sir," and went on rather hastily.

"Lady Dryden got her down. And you know, sir, it really is extremely useful having her there in the house. I remember your saying what an advantage it was, her being there on the inside, seeing the people in a natural everyday sort of way."

"I don't remember saying anything of the sort!"

"It was over the Latter End case,* I think, sir. I remember thinking how well you put it."

"Soft-sawdering me now, are you? Well, there's something in it of course. We come in on a case—everyone's rattled, most of 'em have got something to hide. Remember that case I told you about? Woman looked as guilty as if she'd done seven murders instead of one, and all she was afraid of was her husband would find out she wore a wig. He was a bit younger, and it seems he'd always thought what pretty hair she had. That's the kind of thing that tangles up a case, and I won't say that Miss Silver doesn't come in handy here and there when it comes to that. No, I'll give her her due—she knows people, and she sees through 'em. If she'd lived a couple of hundred years ago she'd have been in the way of getting herself ducked for a witch. Pretty short way they had with them too—put 'em in the nearest pond. If the poor creature floated, they took her out and hanged her or burned her at the stake. If she sank, well, that proved she was innocent, so she only got drowned, and everyone went home happy. Nice times and nice doings! But I've often wondered about those old women, whether there wasn't something in it. Poison and suchlike," he added hastily.

*Latter Ends: A Miss Silver Mystery

There was a knock on the door followed by the appearance of a fresh-faced young constable.

"Beg pardon, sir, but there's a lady on the line—Miss Silver. Wants to speak to Inspector Abbott—says it's very important."

Inspector Abbott got up with an impassive face. Inwardly he allowed himself a rueful "That's torn it! And just when he's talked himself into a good temper!" His languid "I suppose I'd better see what it is, sir," did nothing to avert a frown.

He followed the young constable to the telephone, and heard Miss Silver say on an interrogative note,

"Inspector Abbott?"

"Speaking."

"I am sorry to disturb you, especially as I understand you are engaged with Chief Inspector Lamb, but there is some new evidence—very important evidence indeed—and I feel that there should be no delay at all in acquainting you with it and laying it before the Chief Inspector."

Frank whistled.

"How important is it? He doesn't particularly care about being deflected, you know."

"I said very important. I have a witness here whom you should see immediately. It is the young footman, Frederick. He was out of the house that night, and he saw something. I think that if you could bring the Chief Inspector here, and his evidence could be taken on the spot—"

There was a slight pause. Then he said,

"Well, I did suggest that you should pull a rabbit

out of the hat, so we are in it together—but we're not going to be popular. I'll go and tell him. Will you hold on?"

After a brief stormy passage he returned.

"Are you there? . . . All right, we're on our way. It had better be important, you know. There's a good deal of high explosive about. *Au revoir*."

It was unfortunate that the Chief Inspector should have overheard the last two words. Irrupting into the room rather after the manner of a tank, he was able to discharge one of his more vehement homilies—The Ample Provision afforded by the English Language for the Full Expression of all such Sentiments as it is Proper for a Police Officer to entertain.

"And if there are things that need wrapping up in a foreign language, it's either because someone's got wind in the head and wants to show off, or because he's got something to say he's ashamed of putting into decent English."

Frank, who had heard it all before, could only hope that his esteemed Chief would have got the last of it off his chest by the time they arrived at Vineyards.

CHAPTER 38

It being Frederick's duty to answer the front door bell at this hour of the day, it was he who presently admitted Inspector Abbott whom he knew, and the large man in a dark overcoat whom he guessed with a sinking heart to be "the High-up from Scotland Yard" whom everyone in the village was expecting to come down and arrest somebody. At the moment, Frederick felt that it might easily be himself. Irrational but quite vivid pictures of the dock, the condemned cell, and the gallows, passed in horrid procession before his shuddering eyes.

Miss Silver, coming up behind him, shook hands warmly with Chief Inspector Lamb. Her pleasure at this meeting with an old friend was so evident, her enquiries after Mrs. Lamb and his daughters so warm, that he found himself responding to it.

"And Lily's little boy and girl? Is Ernest still so much like you?"

"Well, they say so, poor little beggar. But Jenny is like her mother—just what Lily was at her age."

The cloud which appeared on his brow at the mention of Violet's name caused Miss Silver to pass tactfully to Myrtle, of whom there was never anything but good to be said.

"Only trouble with her is she's too unselfish—

always thinking about other people. Her mother worries and says she doesn't take proper care of herself."

They reached the study and passed into it. Frederick, his office done, and in hopes that he might now slip away, found himself under the big man's compelling eye.

"Is this the young man? . . . All right, come in and shut the door!"

As he obeyed with a feeling that the ground beneath him had suddenly become unsteady, he found Miss Silver's hand upon his arm.

"Now, Frederick, you have only to speak the truth. There is nothing to be afraid of."

The words appeared to bear no relation whatsoever to the horrid facts with which he was now confronted. They could not cause these formidable policemen to disappear—they could not put back the clock and untell the tale which he had stammered out less than an hour ago. He had got to go through with it, and when you have got to do a thing you have somehow to find enough courage to do it.

They gave him a chair. The big man sat at Sir Herbert's desk. Inspector Abbott got out his notebook. They were going to write everything down.

Miss Silver had taken a chair where he could see her. She met a wandering apprehensive glance, smiled reassuringly, and addressed Chief Inspector Lamb.

"This is Frederick Baines. He had a quarrel with a friend last Saturday, and he slipped out of the house to go down to the village and make it up with her. He is going to tell you what happened."

Lamb turned his large ruddy face upon the wretched Frederick. He didn't look like a town policeman at all, he looked like a farmer. He looked terribly like Mr. Long at Bullthorne who had once caught him and Jimmy Good stealing his plums at ten o'clock on a fine August night. He had walloped them well and threatened them with the police. And now here were the police, and he had got to talk to them. He found that he still had Miss Silver's handkerchief in the pocket of his grey linen house-coat. He fished it out and mopped a streaming brow.

The rather bulging brown eyes of the Chief Inspector regarded him without giving anything away. He said, with a homely touch of country accent in his words,

"Well, my lad—speak up. You slipped out of the house on the night of the murder to go and see a girl. Was that it?"

"Yes, sir."

"Had a quarrel with her and wanted to make it up?" The tone was not unkind. It even inclined to the indulgent. Thirty-five years ago a boy called Ernest Lamb had also slipped out at night to throw a pebble up at the window of the girl who was now Mrs. Lamb.

Encouraged by the fact that he was not immediately required to disclose the climax of his tale, Frederick produced a number of artless facts about himself and Gloria Good, his voice steadying as he went along and his recourse to the borrowed handkerchief becoming less frequent. Miss Silver was satisfied that he was making a good impression.

Lamb listened, put in an occasional question, and finished up by saying,

"So you made it up, and no harm done. Of course you oughtn't to have slipped out of the house that way—you know that without my telling you."

"Yes, sir."

"Now what time would it be when you slipped out?"

"A bit after eleven, sir. There was the gentleman with the autobike, Professor Richardson, he come round the house and got on his bike and off down the drive."

"Dark night, wasn't it? How did you know it was the Professor?"

"I was looking out, sir. My room looks to the front. He'd left his bike right down underneath where I was. He barked his shin against the pedal, and he swore. You can't mistake the Professor when he swears, sir."

"And what time was that? Have you a clock in your room?"

"Oh, yes—alarm clock, sir. It was between the ten and a quarter past eleven."

"What were you doing, looking out of the window?"

"I'd seen the Professor come, and I was waiting for him to go, sir."

"And then?"

"I thought Mr. Marsham would be doing his rounds. He'd have done all the back premises first and be well out of the way. I listened at the top of the back stairs and slipped down."

Lamb sat back in the writing-chair, a massive hand on either knee. Frank Abbott wrote in his quick, neat shorthand. He thought, as he had often thought before, "The Chief is good with people. He thinks this boy is honest, and he's giving him a chance to steady down and tell what he knows in his own way. If he bullied him he wouldn't get a word of sense."

Lamb nodded.

"How did you get out—by the back door?"

"No, sir. Mr. Marsham bolts it, and the bolts creak. There's—" he faltered a little—"there's a window in the housekeeper's room, sir."

Lamb regarded him fixedly.

"So you didn't go out by the study?"

There was horror in Frederick's tone.

"Oh, no, sir! Sir Herbert was there."

"How did you know that?"

"Because of the Professor, sir—he'd just gone. Sir Herbert always sits up late."

"You didn't go into the study at all?"

"N-no, sir."

"Sure?"

"Oh, yes, sir."

"All right—go on. You went out and saw your girl. What else did you see?"

Frederick lost colour.

"It was when I was coming back, sir."

"Well?"

"I was in the drive—near the top of it, close to the house—and I heard something behind me—it was a stick cracking. So I stood still, and she come up past me on her bicycle."

"Who did?"

"I didn't rightly know—not then, sir. She was riding without a light, and just after she passed me she got off and started wheeling the bike, so I thought I'd go after her and see who it was."

Frank Abbott lifted his head and looked across at Miss Silver. She nodded briefly.

Lamb said without hurry,

"And who was it?"

"I couldn't rightly see, sir. She put her bike against a tree a little way from the top of the drive, and she went along the path that goes through the shrubbery. It's all in amongst the bushes, and I thought, 'Well it's someone that knows the way.' But I kept after her, because it didn't seem right her leaving her bike like that. I mean, I couldn't think who it could be—because Miss Whitaker had gone to her sister's, and none of the maids sleep in."

Lamb said, "Go on."

"The path turns and comes out by the terrace. She went up the steps. I darsn't keep too near in case of her seeing me, because I began to think it was Miss Whitaker, and she'd have got me into trouble about my being out. She'd get anyone into trouble and like doing it—we all know that. So I kept well back."

"Yes?"

"I thought she'd gone in—by the study window. I thought that was funny, and I thought perhaps it wasn't Miss Whitaker and I'd better find out. So I went up on to the terrace, and there was a light in the study, and the glass door open."

"Go on."

"There's two steps, sir. I went up them, and I looked in." He used the handkerchief again with a shaking hand. "Oh, sir, it was 'orrible! Sir Herbert, he was lying there dead and that knife with the ivory handle sticking up out of his shirt front."

Frank Abbott looked up and said,

"The dagger was sticking in him? You're sure about that?"

"Oh, yes, sir—it was 'orrible."

Lamb drummed on his knee with clumsy fingers.

"What was the woman doing?"

"She was standing there looking down at him. It was Miss Whitaker, sir."

"Was she bending over the body?"

"No, sir—she just stood there. She was talking, sir."

"What did she say?"

"It made my blood run cold, sir. She said, 'You asked for it, and you've got it.' And I thought she was going to turn round and come away, when the other door opened." He pointed. "That one, sir. And Miss Lila come into the room."

"Miss Dryden?"

"Yes, sir—walking in her sleep, sir. My sister

288

that died, she used to, and the doctor said never to wake her sudden."

"You are quite sure she was walking in her sleep?"

"Oh, yes, sir—because of my sister—she looked just the same. She come into the room. Miss Whitaker could see how it was, the same as what I could. She laughed something horrid, sir, and she said quite quiet, 'This is where you come in, I think.' "

"Yes—go on. What did Miss Dryden do? Did she touch the body?"

"Oh, no, sir. She just come in about as far as the middle of the room and stood there. They don't know what they're doing when they're like that, and they don't remember nothing about it. Miss Whitaker, she goes over to Sir Herbert and she pulls out the knife with the ivory handle—"

"With her bare hand?"

"Oh, no, sir—she'd got her gloves on. She fetches it out, and she wipes the blood off it with the front of Miss Lila's dress and she puts it in Miss Lila's hand. Oh, sir, it was *'orrid!'*"

"You saw her do that?"

No one could have doubted that he had seen it. The boy's face twitched and worked. His pallor had taken on a greenish tinge. His eyes remembered. He drew a shuddering breath.

"Oh, sir, I seen it! I wish I never, but I did— Miss Lila's dress and that 'orrid stain—and the blood on her hand!"

"I thought you said she wiped the knife before

she put it in Miss Dryden's hand?"

Frederick stared.

"Yes, sir, she did. But she didn't wipe it clean—
it was all blood—and some of it stayed on Miss
Lila's hand."

"What did Miss Lila do?"

"She didn't do anything—she just stood there.
I was afraid she'd wake up—it's awful bad for them
to be waked sudden—but she didn't. She let go of
the knife, and it fell down on the floor."

"Can you show me the place?"

"Oh, yes, sir."

It was better now that he had got it out. The
worst part was over. He could show them where
the body was, and where Lila Dryden stood and
let the knife fall down.

"And Miss Whitaker?"

He could show them that too—where she was
when he looked between the curtains, and how
she straightened up with the knife in her hand and
went over to where Miss Lila was.

Frank Abbott scribbled on a bit of paper and
passed it to the Chief Inspector. Lamb glanced
down at it, read, "Positions O.K.," and turned
back to Frederick.

"All right, my lad, you can sit down again. . . .
Now go on and tell us what happened after that."

"She come away—Miss Whitaker. She says,
whispering like, 'You'll be for it, lovely Lila,' and
I see she was going to do a bunk, so I got down
off the step and behind the bush on the far side,
and she come out and down off the terrace as quick

as quick—didn't make a sound neither. I thought I had better get out of it—only I didn't like leaving Miss Lila like that."

Lamb said in his weighty voice,

"Why didn't you give the alarm? That's what you ought to have done, you know."

Frederick disclosed an unexpected vein of shrewdness.

"And have everyone thinking it was Miss Lila—and me making up a story against Miss Whitaker that no one liked in the house? I thought about it as well as I could, and I seen how it would look, and—I darsn't."

"Well, what did you do?"

"I stood there and thought, and I didn't know what to do. And then I heard someone coming along the path by the side of the house and up on to the terrace. It was Mr. Waring, sir. Miss Whitaker, she'd left the study door ajar when she come out, and as soon as he touched the handle it moved. I see him go in. At first he looks through the curtains, and then he pushes them and goes in. That's when I see it was Mr. Waring. I knew he was sweet on Miss Lila, because he give me a note for her the time he come up to the house and Lady Dryden sent him away. So I thought if he was there he'd look after her a lot better than what I could, and no need for me to get myself mixed up with it. And I come away."

"And then?"

"I got back through the window in the housekeeper's room and went up and got into my bed."

Lamb took a moment, tapping with his fingers on his knee. Then he said,

"Any idea what time it was when all this happened—Miss Whitaker coming up the drive on her bicycle—Mr. Waring coming along to the study?"

"Yes, sir—it was gone twelve."

"What do you fix that by?"

"The church clock, sir. You can hear it strike when the wind is that way."

"You heard it strike on Saturday night?"

"Yes, sir. Miss Whitaker, she had gone up on to the terrace, and I was waiting like I told you. That's when I heard it—just before I went up too."

Frank Abbott wrote that down. It fitted—it all fitted—the boy was telling the truth. Bill Waring had listened to the church clock striking twelve a little after he heard something move on the shrubbery path, and a little before he took his own way to the study.

The Chief Inspector bent a long, serious look upon Frederick.

"It's all true what you've been telling us?"

"Cross my heart, sir!"

"The truth, the whole truth, and nothing but the truth? You'll have to swear to it, you know. Are you prepared to do that?"

"Oh, yes, sir."

"All right then. Inspector Abbott has been taking down what you have said. It will be read over to you, and then you can sign it. Don't put your name to anything you're not quite sure about."

Frederick wiped the sweat of relief from his forehead. It was over—he had got through with it. The awful burden that he had carried since Saturday night was shifted to the broad shoulders of the police. He felt as if he had waked up from a nightmare.

CHAPTER 39

There was a knock on Miss Whitaker's bedroom door. She did not pause in her pacing up and down. She had risen early because bed had become intolerable during the endless hours of a wakeful night. The fire was dead, but a couple of half-burned logs sprawled on the still warm ash. She coaxed them until a smoulder of sparks quickened in the wood. She had paper to her hand. She had sat till past midnight reading old letters. Now she fed them to the springing flames, leaf by leaf and sheet by sheet. Sometimes a line would catch her eye, starting out in letters of fire before the page crumpled into ash like Herbert Whitall's promises. "You and the child—" that was one of the sentences. It came to her then with a deadly certainty that if the child had been strong and healthy she wouldn't have had to whistle for her ten thousand pounds. It was because he was frail, because he was delicate, because he needed so much care, that Herbert denied him the means of having these things. She would never, never, never forgive him for that. She fed the flames with his letters as she fed her anger with the thought of him lying dead, and of Lila Dryden with the blood on her hand and on her dress. Herbert was dead, and the girl would hang for it. She fed her anger.

When all the letters were burned, she fell to pacing the room. With brief intervals, she had been at it ever since, her door locked against the housemaid.

"It's your tea, miss."

"Put it down. I'll take it presently."

She had gulped the scalding tea, and only realized then how cold she was—through and through, and deep, deep down in spite of her anger and the blaze Herbert Whitall's letters had made.

Presently she dressed and fell to her pacing again. So many steps to the window, so many steps to the bed. Count the steps, and it stopped you thinking. Go on counting, or you'll start thinking again.

The knock came on her door for the second time. She jerked her head round and said,

"I don't want anything. Let me alone!"

It was Marsham's voice that answered her.

"Chief Inspector Lamb and Inspector Abbott are in the study, Miss Whitaker. They would be glad if you would come down."

She stood for a moment before she unlocked the door. She went over to the dressing-table, touched the ordered waves of her hair, used powderpuff and lipstick. She was wearing the black dress which looked like mourning, high to the neck and long to the wrists. She was thinner than when she had bought it. Her eyes burned against the pallor of her face. She walked past Marsham as if he wasn't there, and so down the stairs and along the passage to the study.

As she came in, three pairs of eyes were turned towards her, Frank Abbott murmured, "Medusa—" under his breath, the word being most unfortunately overheard by Lamb, who had never heard of the lady but was immediately convinced of her being foreign. The blank innocence of Inspector Abbott's regard did nothing to shake this conviction, but at the moment he had Miss Whitaker to deal with.

Having offered her a chair and seen her seat herself in what he would have described as a "tragedy queen kind of way," he cautioned her that anything she said would be taken down and might be used in evidence, and proceeded to unmask his guns.

"Miss Whitaker—in a statement made on Sunday morning you say—" Here he paused, received a paper from Frank Abbott, unfolded it with deliberation, and read:

" 'I received a telephone call from my sister, Mrs. West, at approximately nine p.m. on Saturday evening. She was not at all well, and I became very anxious about her being alone in the house with her little boy, who had been ill. I told Sir Herbert that I was going to spend the night with her, and I asked Mrs. Considine to give me a lift as far as the village so that I might catch the last bus into Emsworth. I took the bus, got off at Emsworth Station, and proceeded to 32 Station Road where my sister lives. I stayed the night with her, and returned to Vineyards by the ten o'clock bus next morning, when I learned of Sir Herbert Whitall's death.'

"Now, that's your statement. Anything you'd like to alter—or add to it?"

She sat up straight, her hands in her lap—white hands with blood-red nails—black dress—white face with blood-red lips, and the eyes with their smouldering fire. The lips opened and said,

"Nothing."

"Well, Miss Whitaker, it is due to you to tell you that I have here a statement from a witness who is prepared to swear that instead of staying at Emsworth all night with your sister you bicycled back to Vineyards, arriving there just before twelve o'clock. This witness says that you left your bicycle leaning against a tree near the top of the drive and proceeded through the shrubbery on foot. He followed you, and saw you go up on to the terrace. He waited a little, and then followed you. The glass door to the study was open. Looking between the curtains, he saw Sir Herbert Whitall lying dead on the floor with the ivory dagger still in the wound. He states that you were standing beside the body, and that he heard you use these words—'You asked for it, and you've got it.' After this—*after* this, Miss Whitaker, Miss Dryden came in by the door from the passage. She was walking in her

296

sleep. The witness is quite positive on this point. He had a sister who used to walk in her sleep, and he is quite positive that Miss Dryden was in that state and had no idea what was going on. I think you know what happened next. This witness saw you withdraw the dagger, wipe it on Miss Dryden's dress, and put it into her hand. He heard you say, 'You're for it, lovely Lila.' Miss Dryden let the dagger fall, but of course her fingerprints were afterwards found on it and her hand was stained."

Millicent Whitaker had not stirred or shown by even the slightest change in her expression that his words either reached or moved her. Her face presented a cold, lifeless surface which seemed as incapable of expression as a mask. Only the eyes were alive with a spark which might yet smoulder into flame.

After making a very decided pause Lamb said, "Is there anything you would like to say?"

She did make a movement then. The hands with the blood-red nails unclasped, and then clasped themselves again. The lips opened.

"You say you have a witness. Who is he?"

Lamb said, "The young footman, Frederick Baines. He was out on Saturday night—slipped out to see his girl. You passed him in the drive when he was coming back. He followed you."

"It's a lie." Voice and words were without expression.

"He is prepared to swear that he followed you to this room, saw you withdraw the dagger from the wound, and stain Miss Dryden's dress and hand. In view of this, I have no choice but to arrest you. I shall take you down to the station and charge you with the murder of Sir Herbert Whitall."

The mask broke up, colour rushed into her face. She threw up her head as if she were jerking something away.

"I tell you it's a lie! It's a damnable lie! He's making it up! He's crazy about that stupid girl Lila Dryden! He's making up a story to protect her, and to spite me! It's a lie from the beginning to end! I didn't pass anyone in the drive—there wasn't anyone to pass—" She checked on the last word, her hand to her mouth as if to push back the words which had come flooding out. But they had been spoken. The sound of them was still on the air. They couldn't be unsaid.

Lamb said gravely,

"Then you were in the drive a little before twelve on the night of the murder."

She looked at him, at Miss Silver, at Frank Abbott—three faces, all grave, one of them compassionate. The last chance in the world, the chance she could not have foreseen or guarded against, had tripped her. The whole plan, so carefully prepared, so efficiently carried out, had come to grief on a boy's fancy for a village girl. Passion died in her. She was too tired, too beaten to go on. She said in an exhausted voice,

"He's got it wrong—you've all got it wrong. I didn't kill him. I meant to. I took my sister's bicycle and came back. I meant to kill him. He wouldn't let me go. He didn't want me any more, but he

298

wouldn't let me go. I was to stay and see him with that girl Lila—I was to go on being the perfect secretary—"

Lamb said,

"You could have left."

She gave a curious little laugh.

"Could I? Look here, I'll tell you, and you will see what kind of a man he was. There was a cheque—for my salary. He was in America. The child was ill—his own child. I had to have enough money—I altered one of the figures. I told him as soon as he came back—I didn't try and hide it. It wasn't for me, it was for the child. And he said that was all right, and not to worry. But when I wanted to leave he said he had kept the cheque, and if I didn't stay he would use it to ruin me. So I was going to kill him."

Frank Abbott said sharply,

"You expected to come in for ten thousand if he died before he could sign the new will he was planning."

She lifted a hand and let it fall again.

"Oh, yes. He cheated about that—I might have known—"

Lamb said,

"This is a confession you are making, Miss Whitaker—before witnesses. I have cautioned you."

She stared at him.

"You mean—about the cheque? It was five years ago."

Lamb sat forward.

"I don't mean anything of the sort. I mean the murder."

She shook her head.

"Oh, no—I told you. You've got it wrong. I was going to kill him, but I didn't have to. I had a knife—I was going to use it. I knew he would be in the study—I had left the window unbolted—"

Frank Abbott said, "When?"

"After dinner, when they were all in the drawing-room. He had been reminding me about the cheque just before Mr. Haile arrived, so I was going to kill him. I thought it would be a good night to do it—because of there being so many people in the house. Mr. Haile was going to ask him for money, and Herbert always quarrelled with the Professor. So I unbolted the glass door, and asked Mrs. Considine to give me a lift to the bus to go to my sister at Emsworth. She really did telephone. The child hadn't been well—she was ringing me up every evening—so everything fitted. You mustn't think she knew anything—she didn't. I said I would go straight to bed. She didn't know I got out and took her bicycle. I had it all worked out. It was a very good alibi. But I needn't have bothered—a lot of people hated Herbert. He was dead when I got here. One of them had killed him."

She spoke with a kind of weary calm. The dreadful tension of the last few days was relaxed. This release was all that mattered. Fear, hope, passion, the poison of jealousy, even the will to survive, dissolved in it and were gone.

When Lamb asked her if she wished to make a

300

statement she agreed without interest. What Frank Abbott then took down differed by scarcely a word from what she had already said.

When the statement had been read over to her she signed it and asked if she could go to her room and lie down, because she thought that now she might be able to sleep.

Lamb let her go. With Mary Good in charge and a constable on the landing, it would be better to defer the arrest until her statement had been carefully checked over with that of Frederick Baines.

CHAPTER 40

When she had gone Lamb said,

"Well, that lets Miss Dryden and young Waring out. I thought that lad Frederick was speaking the truth, and she doesn't deny it. Only says she found Sir Herbert dead—didn't kill him herself. A pretty tall story!"

Miss Silver coughed.

"You do not consider that it might perhaps be true?"

He slewed round to train a frown upon her.

"Now, now, Miss Silver, don't you start making things difficult. Here you bring in this boy Frederick and his evidence—he would have had to come across with it sooner or later of course, but

I don't say you didn't do a good bit of work getting it out of him before there had been any arrest made—well, I say first you dig all this out of him, and then you start casting doubts on it."

Miss Silver imparted a gentle distance to her manner. She esteemed the Chief Inspector, but she sometimes found him a little too blunt. The tone of her reply informed Frank Abbott, if not Lamb himself, that this was one of these occasions.

"Oh, no, Chief Inspector, I have no intention of casting any doubt upon Frederick's evidence. I feel quite sure that he has spoken the truth. But I am certain that you will have noticed, as I do myself, that there is a very important time factor. Frederick says that he followed Miss Whitaker through the shrubbery, but remained at the foot of the steps when she went up on to the terrace and into the study. The question is, how long did he wait? Was there really time for the murder to have been committed by Miss Whitaker?"

Lamb said,

"It wouldn't take such a lot of time, you know. She admits that she came over here intending to kill him. She admits having left the glass door unbolted so that she could get in. Well, she comes in, and there he is, sitting at his table with the ivory dagger in front of him. As likely as not he was examining it with the Professor's magnifying-glass. Probably was—it would account for the glass dropping and rolling to where it was found. Well, Miss Whitaker comes in. He may have known she was there, or he may not—in any case he wouldn't disturb himself. She has only to come up behind him, lean over his shoulder to pick up the dagger, and stab him where he sits. Not likely he'd suspect a thing until it was too late. You don't have to allow much time if it was done that way."

Miss Silver inclined her head.

"I understand that the medical evidence supports the view that Sir Herbert was sitting at the writing-table when he was stabbed, that he pushed back his chair, rose to his feet, turned to confront his assailant, staggered back a step or two, and collapsed. Was there sufficient time for all this? Did no words pass between Sir Herbert and the person who murdered him? Was there no cry, or sound of a fall? All these things have to be considered, and you will naturally wish to question Frederick very closely. I have made no attempt to do so, as I felt it was due to you that you should have his evidence just as he gave it, and without its being prompted or coloured by any questioning of mine."

Lamb said gruffly,

"Very good of you, I'm sure—I appreciate that. It's easy enough to put ideas into a witness' head. You didn't question him at all?"

"I very carefully avoided doing so."

"All right then, we'll have the lad in. Ring the bell, Frank!"

Marsham took the message. He also took time enough to mend the fire and brush up the hearth. Since there appeared to be no need for either task, Frank Abbott suspected him of wishing, for some reason, to dally. Perhaps he wanted to have a look at the Chief Inspector—perhaps he wanted the Chief Inspector to have a look at him. Whichever of these purposes was in his mind, as it happened, both were served. When the door had closed behind his majestic presence, Lamb slapped his knee.

"Good enough for a stage play—isn't he? I didn't know they made his sort any more. Puts me in mind of the butler up at the Hall when I was a boy."

When Frederick came in it was obvious that this recall dismayed him. He sat awkwardly on the edge of the chair which he had been invited to take and wondered what they wanted with him now.

Lamb gave him quite a friendly nod.

"It's all right, my lad—don't get the wind up. You've made a statement, and we just want to go into the question of how long some of the things you have described would take. You say you were at the foot of the steps when you heard the church clock strike twelve."

"Yes, sir."

"You watched Miss Whitaker go up the steps and into the study, and you waited a bit before you followed her."

"Yes, sir."

"How long did you wait?"

"Only till I see her go in."

"You could see the door from where you were?"

"I come up a step or two, and I see the door move. There was a bit of light coming through the curtains—it made a shine on the glass when it moved. So I thought she'd gone in."

"And after the glass moved and you thought she had gone in—how long did you wait before you followed her?"

"I went right up, sir."

"Right up to the door?"

"Yes, sir. I didn't know it was Miss Whitaker till I see her in the room. I thought I did ought to see who it was."

Lamb nodded approvingly.

"You did quite right. Now—after the door moved and Miss Whitaker went in, did you hear anything?"

"Only Miss Whitaker."

"Sure you didn't hear Sir Herbert speak or cry out?"

"Oh, no, sir."

"No sound of a cry—of a chair being pushed back—a fall?"

"Oh, no, sir. There wasn't nothing—only Miss Whitaker talking."

Lamb said sharply,

"When did you hear that?"

"When I came up to the door like I told you, sir."

Lamb was frowning. He put a hand on the table and got to his feet.

"Look here, we'll try this out. Miss Silver, would you mind taking Miss Whitaker's part? Now, my lad, you go down those steps with her. She will come up them and in through this door the way you say Miss Whitaker did, and you follow her just

305

the way you did on Saturday night." He turned to Inspector Abbott. "Take the time, Frank!"

Miss Silver came up the steps and on to the terrace, then up the two steps to the glass door, which Lamb had left ajar. It swung open and she passed inside.

Twelve seconds later Frederick's fair head came into view over the edge of the terrace steps. He stood for a moment when he reached the top, then came slowly between the rosemary bushes to the glass door.

Frank Abbott had drawn the curtains. He and Lamb stood on the terrace and watched. They saw Frederick stoop, part the curtains, and look between them. Thirty seconds from start to finish.

They took him back into the room and shut the door. Lamb resumed his seat and his questioning.

"You didn't hear anything at all—you're sure about that?"

"Only Miss Whitaker."

"Oh, yes—you said you heard her talking. Where were you?"

"Coming up the two steps to the door, sir."

"That's not what you said before, my lad. You said you looked between the curtains and saw her standing by the body, and you heard her say, 'You asked for it, and you've got it.' "

"That's right, sir—that was afterwards."

"Oh, you heard her say something before that, did you? Why didn't you say so?"

"I didn't rightly know what she meant, sir."

"What did she say?"

"Something about saving the trouble."

"What!"

"Yes, sir—I thought it sounded funny. That was when I knew it was Miss Whitaker. I was just up on the top step, and I heard her say, 'Someone has saved me the trouble.' I couldn't think what she meant."

"And you can't now?"

"I don't know, sir—"

Lamb said heartily,

"Well, I wish I could say as much!"

CHAPTER 41

"Looks as if we were back where we started."

The Chief Inspector's tone was a gloomy one. Frederick had been dismissed. He spoke to Frank Abbott and Miss Silver, and his expression indicated that this unfortunate state of affairs could only have arisen through negligence on their part. He would not have put the accusation into words, but he was certainly in the mood in which a man feels that he has been let down, and casts about him for someone to take the blame.

Miss Silver, opening her work-bag and picking up her knitting, was perfectly aware of this. She observed a tactful silence, and left it to Frank Abbott to say,

"That's about the size of it."

Lamb thumped the table.

"First it looks like a cast-iron case against Miss Dryden and young Waring, and then you go and make a red herring out of the Professor and drag him across the trail. For all we know, he may have done it. I grant you there doesn't seem to be any adequate motive, but there have been murders done with less. It isn't always the motive—it's the state of a man's mind. If he's worked up to a certain pitch he loses control, lets go of himself, and hits out with anything that comes handy. Take this Professor. He and Sir Herbert have a kind of running quarrel—like to score each other off. Looks as if Sir Herbert had the money and the Professor had the brains. You can get a lot of jealousy and illfeeling out of a situation like that. Well, the Professor was here with Sir Herbert for about twenty minutes between a little before eleven and the quarter past. And we've only got his word for it that he left him alive. There's quite a case to be made out there, you know. If it hadn't been for things looking so black against Waring and Miss Dryden, I might have told you to go ahead with it. And now they're out, I think we had better come back to the Professor again."

Frank said,

"I don't think he did it, sir. As you say, the motive isn't much. Mr. Haile has a stronger one. Even Lady Dryden. There's no absolute evidence that he was blackmailing her into pushing her niece into marrying him, but I haven't the slightest doubt

308

that he was bringing some pressure to bear. Quite frankly, I think that Lila Dryden's money is gone, and that Lady Dryden knows where. We could check up on that, you know, and it would certainly provide her with a motive. As to opportunity, any one of the people in the house that night could have come down to the study and bumped Whitall off. The bother, as stated by Miss Whitaker, seems to be that there is quite an embarrassment of choice—so many people disliked him and were going to be the better for his death. Haile, I gather, is going to be the better for it to the tune of something like three-quarters of a million, even after the Chancellor has had his whack. Quite a lot of people have been put out of the way for a good deal less than that."

Lamb looked up with his lips pursed, as though to whistle.

"Three-quarters of a million? My word!"

"And Haile was up to his eyes in debt. According to Lady Dryden and Miss Whitaker he came here on Saturday night to ask for a loan, and Whitall was going to refuse him. He admits that he had hopes of a legacy from his cousin. That would be under the old will. But in three or four days' time there was going to be a new will. He may easily have supposed that his prospects were diminishing. There's a whale of a motive there."

Lamb nodded slowly.

"And not as much evidence as you could put on a threepenny bit—the old kind, before they took to making a cheap show of them with plants growing."

They went on talking—about Haile, about Lady Dryden, about the Professor. And what it came to in the end was that there wasn't enough evidence to make a case against any of them. Haile had a very strong motive if he knew what was in the first will, but there was no proof that he did. Lady Dryden had a motive if Herbert Whitall was blackmailing her into pushing on the marriage to Lila, but there was no proof that there was any blackmailing going on. The world is full of women who will push a girl into a marriage they consider advantageous. Professor Richardson could hardly be said to have a motive at all. On the other hand, he admitted to something like a quarrel, and he was certainly one of the last people to see Herbert Whitall alive. He left Vineyards at a quarter past eleven, according to his own statement and the evidence of Frederick. Either Haile or Lady Dryden could have come down and stabbed Sir Herbert after that. Or Adrian Grey, or Marsham, or Mrs. Marsham, or Frederick. So far as opportunity went, they all had it and could have availed themselves of it. And there wasn't any evidence to show that any one of them did.

Miss Silver had been knitting in a thoughtful silence. She now gave a gentle cough.

"If I may make a suggestion—"

Lamb turned to look at her.

"Think you've got something?"

"I would not go so far as to say that. It was just a suggestion."

She smiled disarmingly.

"Well?"

"The time that is so important is from a quarter past eleven, when Professor Richardson is known to have left, and twelve o'clock, when according to her own evidence and that of Frederick it seems probable that Miss Whitaker found Sir Herbert dead. The medical evidence also supports this probability. We have, therefore, rather less than three-quarters of an hour during which anyone in the house could have come to the study and stabbed Sir Herbert. Since you have seen Professor Richardson's statement, you will remember that he says he heard Sir Herbert bolt the door behind him, yet Miss Whitaker found it open. Sir Herbert may have admitted someone from outside, in which case we are left without any clue to his identity, or, the crime having been committed by someone in the house, the door may have been unbolted by the murderer in order to make it appear that some person had come in from outside."

The Chief Inspector nodded.

"Very nicely put and all that. But it doesn't get us anywhere, does it?"

Miss Silver's look held some slight reproof.

"I believe it might do so. What I was about to say is this. During the critical period which we have to consider, we know for certain that one of the people in the house was actually moving stealthily about in it. I refer, of course, to Frederick. He came down the back stairs, satisfied himself that Marsham was nowhere in the back premises, and finally left the house by the housekeeper's room. I think it might be advantageous to press him closely as to why he was so sure that Marsham was in the front of the house. You will have noticed that whilst he answers any question that is put to him, he does not readily volunteer anything."

"Well, we can press him on that point. I don't suppose we shall get very much."

Miss Silver continued to knit.

"From the conversation which I overheard between Mr. Haile and Marsham it appears to me that there is some implication that the former had been seen by the latter in circumstances which he was not willing to have disclosed. This may, or may not, refer to the night of the murder, but I am inclined to believe that it does. Finally, I think that Mr. Adrian Grey should be questioned very closely as to his movements on Saturday night. His story that he heard Miss Dryden come out of her room and followed her to the study is disproved by what Miss Whitaker and Frederick have told us. He could not have been immediately behind Lila Dryden, or he would have seen Miss Whitaker and heard what she said, in which case he would certainly have intervened and given the alarm. I think he should now be pressed to correct his statement." She paused, smiled in an encouraging manner, and concluded, "Those are the suggestions which I thought might be productive of something which you would admit to be evidence."

Lamb frowned, drummed on his knee, and finally nodded.

"All right, we'll have Mr. Grey. I can't say I think it's any use, but we'll see what he says."

CHAPTER 42

Adrian Grey was his unhurried and quiet self. In a gently disarming manner he acquiesced in the suggestion that he had not been perfectly frank when he made his original statement. He had followed Lila Dryden down, but he had not followed her immediately.

"You see, I was thinking—I may even have been a little drowsy—I don't know. I heard her door open just as I said, but for the moment I didn't connect the sound with her, or with anything. As I say, I was thinking about something else. Later on—"

Lamb interrupted him.

"How much later on?"

"A minute or two—I don't know. I came back to what I had heard, and I got up and looked out. Lila's door was open. I went to the head of the stairs and saw her in the hall. She was going in the direction of the study. I went back to my room and put on my dressing-gown and slippers, then I went across the landing and closed her door just in case anyone should be about. It wasn't till after that I went down and followed her to the study."

The Chief Inspector's solid bulk was facing him, the Chief Inspector's whole solid personality registered the most uncompromising disapproval.

"In fact, Mr. Grey, your original statement to Inspector Abbott was deliberately misleading."

"That is rather a harsh way of putting it. I knew that Miss Dryden was quite incapable of stabbing anyone, but I could not help seeing that she was in a very dangerous position, and I naturally wished to protect her."

Lamb's rather prominent brown eyes gazed imperturbably at him. A very composed gentleman considering he had just been found out in a lie and been obliged to admit it. Sweet on the girl of course—that stuck out a mile. Too much relieved to hear she was out of the wood to bother about anything else. A very quiet, pleasant gentleman. He recalled the proverb, "Still waters run deep." All very pleasant on the surface, Mr. Adrian Grey—but he got five thousand pounds out of the will, didn't he? He began to wonder just how deep the waters might be. He said,

"When someone admits that part of a statement is false, it makes you wonder about the rest of it— doesn't it, Mr. Grey?"

Adrian smiled faintly.

"Oh, naturally. But there isn't much more of mine that could be false, is there? I did come into the study just when I said, you know, because Bill Waring saw me, and he and I were on either side

314

of the sofa looking at Lila Dryden who had fainted, when Haile came into the room a minute or two later. So all the rest of my statement is corroborated."

Lamb nodded.

"And just as well," he said in a tone of heavy reproof. "I suppose you don't need me to tell you that it's a very serious thing to try and mislead the police in the execution of their duty. If people would stop thinking about their own private affairs, hedging here and trying to cover up there, it would be a whole heap easier to clear things up. Now, Mr. Grey, I take it you'll agree that it's up to you to make what amends you can. I want you to go over in your own mind every minute of the time between eleven o'clock and a quarter past twelve—every single minute of it. You were awake?"

"Yes. I may have been a little drowsy towards the end, but I wasn't asleep."

"It was eleven o'clock when you saw Mr. Haile in his room with the door open as you came back from the bathroom?"

"Yes."

"He was in his pyjamas?"

"Oh, yes."

"Anything odd about him—anything noticeable—anything unusual in his manner?"

"No." There was just the faintest shade of hesitation about the way the word came out.

Lamb said,

"You don't seem to feel quite sure about that."

Adrian looked unhappy.

"It's nothing of course—I just wondered why his door was open—that's all."

"It was wide open?"

"Yes."

"And where was he? What was he doing?"

"He was over by the bed. He wasn't doing anything. He was just standing there looking in the direction of the door."

"As if he was waiting for you to come along and see him?"

"Well—I don't think that's quite fair—"

Lamb said,

"He might have wanted you to say you had seen him ready for bed at eleven o'clock that night?"

Adrian shook his head.

"You don't really expect me to answer that, do you, Chief Inspector?"

"Well, well—what about the rest of the time?"

"I am afraid there isn't anything to say. I just went into my room and stayed there till after I heard Miss Dryden open her door."

Lamb pressed him a little more—took him in detail through the time, and finally let him go.

"Not much there," he said when the door was closed behind Adrian Grey. "We'll have Haile in next."

Eric Haile, in the chair so lately vacated by Adrian, was as complete a contrast as could be. Ruddy and vigorous, with his air of having always done himself and been done extremely well, he sat there, the genial host, only too anxious to assist the law and be of any service that he could.

"I am sure you will appreciate, Chief Inspector, how very glad I shall be to have this painful matter cleared up. If there is anything I can do—"

Lamb retained his stolid reserve.

"Naturally, Mr. Haile. We are anxious to cover the time between eleven o'clock and a quarter past twelve on Saturday night. If you would tell us anything you did, or saw, or noticed—"

"But I'm afraid I can't. After having a last drink with my cousin just after half past ten I went upstairs and had a bath. I was in bed by just after eleven."

Lamb nodded.

"Yes—Mr. Grey passed your room at eleven o'clock and saw you in your pyjamas. Your door was open. Do you mind telling us why?"

Haile burst out laughing.

"Because I hadn't shut it! Come, Chief Inspector, that's a little too much like 'Why did the chicken cross the road?' "

Lamb was not amused. He stared and said,

"And why hadn't you shut it?"

"I really don't know."

"It wasn't because you heard Mr. Grey coming along the passage?"

Haile gave a careless nod.

"I expect so, now you mention it. Rude to shut the door in anyone's face."

"You might have wished him to see that you were ready for bed."

Haile's laugh came easily.

"Not a very good alibi, Chief Inspector. I expect I could have done better than that if I had thought I was really going to need one." Then, after a pause and in the face of Lamb's portentous stare, "You are not by any chance serious, are you?"

"Perfectly serious, Mr. Haile."

"Good lord, man—what possible motive could I have had for wishing my cousin out of the way?"

Frank Abbott's light, cool gaze rested on him appreciatively. Nothing could have had a more natural ring.

Lamb's face remained as wooden as the figurehead of a ship. He said with as little expression in his voice,

"Some people might consider three-quarters of a million or thereabouts quite a sizable motive."

Haile made a face of almost comic protest.

"But, my good sir, I hadn't the remotest idea that I was going to get it. A small legacy perhaps— it would just depend on what mood he was in when he made that will. But residuary legatee, and all that money! I give you my word I never dreamed of such a thing. Just look at it from my point of view. I'm a careless chap about money—have been all my life—one of the diminishing class who live happily on an overdraft. When my bank manager became too pressing I could generally touch my cousin for a loan. Hang it all, I've been doing it for the last twenty years! He used to be fairly rude about it, but he generally paid up. It was as good as having a second overdraft. Now, family feeling and a natural disinclination for bloodshed apart,

318

wouldn't I have been a damned fool to cut off the supply by killing my cousin on the off chance that he might have done something handsome for me in his will? And mind you, like everyone else, I knew he was making a new will in anticipation of his marriage, and I had no idea at all whether he had already signed it or not. He wasn't a man who talked about his affairs—anyone will tell you that. He certainly didn't talk about them to me. If the new will had been made in time, the off chance I spoke of would be practically no chance at all. That is my position, and I think it is a reasonable one."

Lamb said, "Very reasonable." He turned to the table, moved the papers that were lying there, and picked up one of them, then swung round again. "I believe you had a conversation with the butler, Marsham, last night."

Haile's eyebrows rose.

"One does, you know, with one's butler. He comes along and says, 'Anything I can get for you, sir?' and you say, 'Yes,' or 'No,' or whatever the occasion calls for."

"It was a rather longer conversation than that, Mr. Haile. And it was overheard."

"Indeed? How very interesting! May I ask what your eavesdropper made of it?"

"Oh, yes—I was going to tell you. Marsham began by enquiring what you were going to do about keeping on the staff. You proceeded to let him know that you were in possession of some damaging facts about himself. He had been fleecing your cousin, and Sir Herbert was about to discharge him without a character. After asserting that he had merely been taking a commission on wine and cigars, which had been his custom under a previous employer, Marsham denied that he was being dismissed and said that it was quite the other way about—he was anxious to leave, and Sir Herbert was using the threat of prosecution in order to compel him to stay. There then follow some very curious passages which I will read out to you from this transcript."

He proceeded to do so in his best official voice, and having read, he summarized.

"Up to this point you appear to have had, as it were, the upper hand—Marsham has put himself on the wrong side of the law, and you are letting him know it. But now he puts what he calls a hypothetical case. He says 'Everyone has some private affairs which he would not like to have intruded upon. Let us take the question of last Saturday night, or of any other night, sir. There are always a number of persons in a house any one of whom could be about his private business at an hour or in a place which might be considered compromising. By the police for instance. Their profession induces a very suspicious habit of mind. If I may say so, sir, it would be most unwise to import them into the matter under discussion.' "

He paused for long enough to mark the end of the quotation, and then continued weightily.

"On this you immediately take up the attitude that he is attempting to blackmail you. He comes out with what he calls a vulgar proverb about letting sleeping dogs lie, and you ask how long they are going to lie and whether they don't come back to be fed again and again and again. Marsham comes out with a piece about the subject being a painful one and the less said about it the better, and suggests that if you accept his notice and give him and his wife a testimonial, it will be satisfactory to all concerned. Upon which you burst out laughing, tell him he's a thundering hypocrite, and agree that there are things which are better forgotten. Well, Mr. Haile?"

Eric Haile had maintained his smile of amusement. He laughed right out now.

"My dear sir—what a lot of cooked-up nonsense! I don't know who your informant was, but—well, there used to be a game called Russian Scandal. Something was whispered from one to another, and you have no idea what it would come out like by the time even a few people had had the handling of it. All this rubbish is a case in point. I saw Marsham, I told him I knew he had been peculating, and he came back with the suggestion that he knew things about me which perhaps I would not care to have repeated. Well, so he did—and as I don't choose to be suspected of murder I'm going to tell you what they were. We're all human, and the last time I stayed here Marsham happened to run into me in circumstances which would have compromised a lady. I'm sure you won't expect me to take you any further into my confidence than that."

Lamb consulted the paper which he still held, and read from it.

"'Let us take the question of last Saturday night—'"

Haile finished the sentence: "'—or of any other night,' Chief Inspector. It wasn't Saturday night he was hinting at so far as I was concerned, and whether your eavesdropper thought it was or not is neither here nor there. And you know perfectly well that all this hearsay stuff isn't evidence and you can't use it. Marsham is a magnificent butler and a magnificent rogue. He gave me a good laugh, and I didn't want to be hard on him. Hang it all, man, even your eavesdropper admits I burst out laughing. Do you really suppose I'd have done that if I had thought he was hinting that I'd had a hand in my cousin's death?" He got up, still smiling, still genial. "I have a great deal of business to see to, so you must excuse me now. If you have any more posers for me, I'll do my best to answer them later on."

Lamb sat where he was.

"Just a minute, Mr. Haile. There is something I would like to ask you now."

"I am all attention."

"You were ready for bed at eleven o'clock, but at a quarter past twelve or so you were downstairs at the study door listening to a conversation between Mr. Waring and Mr. Grey."

"What about it?" Haile's tone had a shade of impatience.

"You came in very pat, didn't you? I should like to know what brought you down to the study."

"Do you always go off to sleep as soon as you

put out the light? I don't. I think I said as much in my statement. I didn't go to sleep. I thought I heard something in the shrubbery—went and looked out of the window for a bit. Then I thought I could do with a nightcap. My cousin might have gone to bed, or he might not—anyhow the whisky would be there. So I went down. Simplicity itself!"

"I think you said in your statement that you weren't satisfied about the noise you had heard and came down to investigate."

Haile laughed.

"It was a bit of this and a bit of that, I expect. Perhaps I didn't want to confess to the nightcap! You may have it any way you like. And if that is really all—"

"For the present, Mr. Haile."

CHAPTER 43

The opening door disclosed Frederick with a basketful of logs to replenish the wood-box. He stepped back with a murmured apology. Haile waved him on.

"That's all right—you can go in. You don't mind, Chief Inspector? . . . All right, Frederick—carry on."

Never was anyone more easily at home—he might have been the master of Vineyards for twenty years. He passed out of sight down the passage.

Frederick, having disposed of his logs, picked up the empty basket and turned to go.

Miss Silver leaned towards the Chief Inspector and said something in a low voice at which he first frowned and then nodded, turning finally to say,

"Just a moment, Frederick—shut that door and come here. Miss Silver wants to ask you something."

Encouraged by the fact that it was not the police who now wished to question him, Frederick approached, the big open basket dangling from his hand.

"Yes, miss?"

She brought a bright attentive look to bear upon him.

"It is just this, Frederick. You say you came out of your room after you had seen Professor Richardson go away at a quarter past eleven—"

"Yes, miss."

"Marsham had not come upstairs to his room?"

"Oh, no, miss."

"You would have heard him?"

"Oh, yes, miss."

"How did you know that you would not meet him on the stairs?"

"I listened very carefully, miss. I reckoned I'd hear him if he was anywhere about. I reckoned he'd be through the other side of the house. He'd always do the back premises first. I reckoned I'd hear the baize door if he come through and have time to slip into one of the rooms."

Miss Silver's hands were folded upon her knitting. She said kindly but firmly,

"And did you hear the baize door?"

"N-no, miss—" But his voice wavered.

"I think you did hear something—or see something."

"N-no, miss—only—"

Frank Abbott had looked up. Lamb, who had appeared to give a very scant attention to the first questions and answers, now turned in his chair, frowning and aware.

Miss Silver continued without any change of manner.

"Only what, Frederick?"

"There wasn't nothing, miss—only I thought I'd get along to the baize door and just have a look to see the coast was clear. I mean, I wouldn't want Mr. Marsham to catch me getting out of a window."

"Of course you would not. So you opened the baize door?"

"Just the least creak—not so anyone would notice."

"And was there anyone to notice, Frederick?"

"Well, miss, there was and there wasn't, in a manner of speaking."

"Do you mean that you saw someone, but he did not see you?"

"That's right, miss."

Frank Abbott took a sharp breath. Lamb sat like a rock.

Miss Silver said equably,

"Whom did you see?"

"Only Mr. Marsham—going into the study, miss. Lucky I wasn't only half a minute sooner, or he might have seen me move the door."

"He did not see you? You are sure about that?"

"Oh, no, miss. He was half way in—he wasn't looking my way."

"You are sure that it was Marsham you saw? Going into the study at about twenty minutes past eleven on Saturday night?"

"Oh, yes, miss."

Lamb's big hand lifted, and came down with a resounding slap on his knee.

"Then why didn't you say so before?"

"I—sir—" Frederick turned an alarmed and bewildered look upon the Chief Inspector.

"Why—didn't—you—say—so—before?"

"It was only Mr. Marsham, sir, going his rounds."

Absorbing as was the sight of a purple-faced Chief Inspector and a young man who appeared to be about to burst into tears, it was at this moment that Miss Silver and Frank Abbott found their attention irresistibly diverted by the appearance—the very rapid and energetic appearance—of Professor Richardson who, having come up the terrace steps two at a time, was now rattling the handle of the glass door with one hand whilst knocking loudly with the other.

Frederick turned, Lamb turned, they all turned. Frank Abbott got up with a slight shrug and opened the door. The Professor bounded in, his square form enveloped in tweeds of a prehistoric cut, his red hair standing up wildly about the bald patch on his crown.

"Ah," he said—"That's better! I thought the damned thing had stuck. What do you want to go locking doors for in the daytime? Never lock mine—insult to one's neighbours. If a burglar wants to get in he will. And what are the police for anyhow? Haven't arrested anyone yet, have you?"

Frank Abbott, his voice at its coolest, performed an introduction.

"This is Professor Richardson, sir."

The Professor was unwinding a large mustard-coloured scarf.

"You keep this place too hot. Always told Whitall he kept it too hot. No living-room should have a temperature of over sixty Fahrenheit. Have you arrested anyone yet? Because if you have, you're probably making a mistake—and if you were thinking of arresting me, you would be making a bigger one. So I've come here to tell you something."

At the Professor's entrance Frederick had removed himself as far as he dared. He was now kneeling on the hearth and making believe to be very busy over the fire.

The Professor came round the table, flung his scarf on the ground, and thumped down into the just vacated chair.

"Now you just listen to me!" he said in his most sonorous tones. He appeared to be unaware of the

Chief Inspector's dominating stare. He had come there to say something, and he was going to say it. "I made a statement yesterday to that young fellow-me-lad. All correct, and I'm standing by every word. But I've got something to add to it." He addressed Lamb. "I take it you're the Lord High Something-or-other from Scotland Yard—and that you know what's been going on."

Frank Abbott raised an eyebrow.

"The Chief Inspector has seen all the statements." He dipped into the case before him and passed some typewritten sheets to his Chief.

"All right—that's what I wanted to know. Now we can get going!" He directed himself to Lamb again. "If you'll turn to the end of my statement you'll see I said I went away at getting on for a quarter past eleven. I'd pretty well flattened Whitall out—he wouldn't admit it of course, but he knew it all right—and there wasn't anything to stay for. So I went out by that door to the terrace, and he fairly banged it after me and drove down the bolt. A grown man should have more control over his temper. Well, then I went round the house, picked up my autocycle—I'm not one of your plutocrats, I don't run to a car—and went off down the drive. I hadn't got far along the road when I remembered I had left my magnifying-glass— Whitall had it in his hand, and I hadn't got it back from him. It was a good glass, and I wasn't going to lose it. The temper he was in, he might have chucked it in the fire, or out of the window, or anything. So I went back."

Everyone in the room held their breath. Lamb said,

"If this is a confession, I must warn you—"

The Professor said, "Pchah!" in a loud explosive manner.

"I must warn you—"

"You don't have to! I'm not confessing anything! Do you suppose I'd be such a fool? I'm engaged on some very serious research work, and I couldn't possibly spare the time to be arrested. Anyhow I haven't got anything to confess, and if you'll listen to me instead of interrupting, I can prove it. What do you suppose I'm here for? Now listen!"

Lamb nodded.

"All right—what do you want to say?"

"That's more like it! Well, I came back, pushed my bike up against a tree at the top of the drive, and came round the house to the terrace. I got to the steps, and I thought, 'That's queer.' Because I told you Whitall had banged and locked the door behind me, and it was open—or, I should say, it was opening. The curtains didn't meet, because there was a man standing between them and he was opening the door. I was two-thirds of the way up the steps by this time, but I didn't go any farther. I thought it was damned queer. I was wondering why on earth Whitall should be opening the door at that time of night."

"You say it was Sir Herbert Whitall who was opening the door?"

"I don't say anything of the sort! I thought I told you not to interrupt! I only thought it was Whitall

329

just long enough to get the feeling that it was queer. And then I saw it was only the butler going round making sure everything was shut up for the night—though why he should have wanted to open that damned door passes me. Didn't trust anyone to do it properly except himself, I suppose. Always did think the man had wind in the head. So you see, you've only got to ask the fellow, and he can tell you he was in the study after I left, and Whitall—" he stopped suddenly, the blood rushing to his face, and said in a voice like an explosion, "Oh, good lord!"

If he wished to strike everyone dumb, he achieved this object.

The Chief Inspector was the first to recover. He said in his most authoritative manner,

"You say that you saw Marsham come to that glass door and open it?"

"Don't any of you understand plain English? Of course I saw him—that's what I came here to tell you! Because I thought he could clear me—and, believe it or not, it wasn't until I had the words on my tongue that I saw it could mean that the fellow had done it himself." He pulled a loud bandanna from his pocket, rubbed his face vigorously with it, and thrust it back again. "My word, it's stinking hot in here!"

Lamb rapped on the table.

"This is a very serious statement, Professor Richardson."

The Professor exploded again.

"Serious? Of course it's serious! I'm a serious person—I've no time to waste over trivialities!"

Lamb rapped again.

"You say you saw Marsham opening this door at—what time would it be?"

"Might have been five and twenty past eleven— mightn't have been as much—I don't go about looking at my watch."

"Could it have been later than that?"

"Might have been—by a minute or two—not more."

"You came to recover your magnifying-glass, but you went back without attempting to do so. Why?"

"I don't know. I thought Whitall had gone off to bed and the man was shutting up. I just thought I'd ring up in the morning—well, if you really want to know, I thought it would look a bit queer, my looming up out of the dark like that. Never really cottoned to the man—didn't feel like putting up with any of his superior airs."

He looked so like a rueful schoolboy that Frank Abbott's hand came up to cover his mouth. It is as true today as in Shakespeare's time that one touch of nature makes the whole world kin. Even Lamb could remember to have quailed before a butler. It was a long time ago—when he was very young— but he remembered it now.

"So I went home," said the Professor in a diminished voice.

Lamb looked across to where Frederick still knelt before the fire, his ears flapping, his mind in a turmoil of terror and dismay.

"Here, you, Frederick Baines—you can let that fire look after itself. Come here!"

Frederick came, a streak of black on one pale cheek.

"Yes, sir?"

Lamb addressed him sternly.

"You say you saw Marsham enter this room a few minutes after Professor Richardson had left?"

"Yes, sir."

"How many minutes after?"

"Three or four, sir."

"Not more than that?"

"No, sir."

"And then you got out of the window in the housekeeper's room and went down to the village. Did you see or hear the Professor on his autobike?"

The Professor burst in.

"He didn't, because I wasn't riding it when he passed me. I had remembered my magnifying-glass, and I was going through my pockets just to make sure. I was off the road on the grass verge, when something long and thin ran past me. Going quite a pace he was."

"That correct, Frederick?"

"I was in a hurry, sir."

The Professor burst out laughing.

"Girl in the case, eh? Well, I said you were running, and you say you were running. How's that, Chief Inspector?"

"It'll do. Then Frederick sees Marsham come into this room at, say, twenty past eleven. You, Professor, see him opening the door on to the terrace somewhere between that time and the half hour. He had five, six, seven, eight minutes. Long enough—and it wouldn't take so long. Sir Herbert was there at the table. The ivory dagger was there. Marsham crosses behind him to go to the window—no one takes any notice of a manservant doing his job. He leans over, picks up the dagger, and stabs. That's how it would be. Then he opens the window to make it look like an outside job. He had been feathering his own nest, and Sir Herbert had found him out—he was under the threat of exposure. He's a proud man, and there were plenty of others most likely to be suspected. That would be it—he took a chance."

Lamb had spoken almost as if he were thinking aloud, manner abstracted, voice subdued. He roused now and said sharply,

"Who answers the bell in this room?"

Miss Silver coughed.

"Marsham, I believe."

Lamb turned to Frederick.

"Go over and push the button, my lad!"

They sat and waited for Marsham to come in.

CHAPTER 44

Ray Fortescue came back to a disorganized house and the news of Marsham's arrest. It was Mary Good who poured it all out to her in Lila's room, with a good deal of "Who would ever thought it!" and "It only shows you can't ever tell."

"And I'm sure I don't know how we're going to carry on—not with the house full the way it is now. I suppose that won't only be till after the inquest, but Frederick, he don't seem to know whether he's coming or going—you'd think he'd never as much as laid a table. And those two girls carrying on and saying they wouldn't have come in to oblige if they had known they were going to get mixed up with a murderer! I'm sure the only one going on as if nothing had happened is Mrs. Marsham. It don't seem natural, but there she is, beating up eggs for a soufflé and planning to make an orange cake with those tangerines that come in. And when I said to her, 'You take and have a lay-down, and I'll make you a good strong cup of tea,' all she has to say is, 'Thank you, Mary.' She's a very well-spoken person, I'll say that for her. 'Thank you,' she says, 'but there's no need, and I've got the lunch to do.' Always very set on her cooking, Mrs. Marsham, but it don't seem natural to me. They say Marsham was quite out of himself when the Chief Inspector told him he was going to be charged with the murder—took up a chair and threw it clean across the room. Frederick says it took the three of them and Professor Richardson to master him. Strong as a bull, Frederick says he was, and roaring like anyone crazy."

There was a good deal more on the same lines, but in the end Mary Good remembered that Frederick must be superintended and went away in a hurry.

Ray felt rather as if the sea had been breaking over her. If it was really all over, if Bill was clear, if the nightmare had broken, why, then anything was possible. She must let Bill know—she must go down to the Blue Room and ring him up at once. But as she turned to the door, Lila caught at her—a pale, wide-eyed Lila with soft trembling lips.

"Ray—"

"What is it? Don't keep me. I must let Bill know."

"No, Ray, wait! Please, *please* wait! I don't want him to come—I don't really. It's no good his being angry, or anyone being angry."

Ray subdued her throbbing impatience. It was no good being impatient with Lila, it only muddled her. She said quite gently,

"I promise you he won't be angry."

Tears had brimmed up in the blue eyes.

"He will when I say I don't want to marry him. It always makes them angry when I say that."

Ray took her by the shoulders.

"Look here, let's get this perfectly clear. You

don't want to marry Bill?"

Lila shook her head. Two large, beautiful tears overflowed and ran down. "Oh, no!"

"You don't want Bill Waring—you're quite sure about that?"

Lila gave a big childish sob.

"I don't want anyone—*anyone*—except Adrian."

Ray laughed, shook her a little, and kissed the wet patch on her left cheek.

"All right, darling, don't worry. You shall have Adrian if you want him. I rather think I'm taking Bill myself. 'Jack shall have Jill, Nought shall go ill. The man shall have his mare again, And all shall be well!' "

She ran out of the room, leaving Lila confused but comforted.

On her way across the hall Ray encountered Adrian Grey. Impulse having the upper hand, she caught him by the arm.

"Look here—is this all true about Marsham?"

"I'm afraid so."

"Mary Good was telling me. I'm ringing up Bill. If you've got five minutes to spare, would you like to go up to Lila and do a bit of soothing? She's in a flap. She seems to think someone is going to try and make her marry Bill. See if you can get her to believe that Bill doesn't want to marry her any more than she wants to marry him."

"Why doesn't he?" Adrian's tone was a little indignant.

A very beautiful colour came up in Ray's cheeks. Her dark eyes sparkled.

"I think he sees it was a mistake."

The indignation faded. He said,

"Lila doesn't want him?"

Ray shook the arm she was holding.

"Of course she doesn't want him—she never did! She only wanted to get away from Lady Dryden. There's only one person she wants. And if you don't know who it is you had better go and find out."

She let go of him and ran on to the Blue Room. When she looked back at the door Adrian was already half way up the stairs.

CHAPTER 45

Miss Silver entertained Frank Abbott to tea and muffins in her flat. Frank, at his third muffin, was very much at his ease. He might in these moments of privacy have been a favourite nephew. In return for a good deal of indulgence on Miss Silver's part he regarded her with a respect affectionately tempered with impudence. Having just been addressed as "Esteemed Preceptress," she reproved him with a somewhat serious smile.

"I do not feel that I contributed greatly to the solution, my dear Frank. Frederick would probably have spoken in any case."

Frank shook his head.

"You know, I doubt it. Single track affair, the village mind. He was so accustomed to the fellow going his rounds that I doubt if it would ever have occurred to him that Marsham going into the study wasn't the butler on his lawful occasions, but a murderer going in to bump his victim off. You know, if you see a man doing a job every day of his life, you are apt to associate him with that job and nothing else. It's true Marsham wasn't in the habit of waiting up for Sir Herbert, but if Sir Herbert had gone to bed, he would probably go in and give the place the once-over, so there would be nothing in that. It's more than likely that Frederick would never have said a word if you hadn't got it all out of him."

Miss Silver poured herself out a second cup of tea, rinsing the cup carefully and putting in the milk first. She then observed that simple people can be very secretive.

Frank helped himself to a fourth muffin.

"That's because they are like children. I'd back a child to keep a secret against all the grown-ups in the world. Remember that yarn about the two little girls who found what they thought was a string of black beads in a ditch? They were five and six years old—cottage children—and they never said a word to a soul, because last time they found something their mother took it away from them. So they put the beads in an old soap-box and played with them secretly. One little girl died, and the other grew up. And when she was grown up she went to a dance with her young man who was a jeweller's assistant, and she wore the beads. She didn't admire them very much, but she hadn't anything else. As soon as her young man saw them he got all het up and wanted to know how she came by them. He said they were Lady Baldry's famous black pearls, and every jeweller in the trade had a description of them. They and some valuable emeralds had been stolen. The thief was disturbed, and arrested after a cross-country chase. He had the emeralds on him, but he must have thrown away the pearls as he ran. And all those years there they were, knocking about in a dirty old soap-box and being played with by a couple of children."

"What happened?" said Miss Silver with interest.

"Oh, they rang up the Baldrys, and the young man took his girl round with the pearls and her story. There was a five hundred pound reward, and they got married on the strength of it. And the moral of that is, Frederick might quite easily have held his tongue until he was old enough to babble to his great-grandchildren—and a lot of use that would be to whoever got hanged instead of Marsham."

"My dear Frank!"

He said seriously,

"Quite frightening, you know, to think how easy it would have been to build up a case against Lila Dryden either with or without Bill Waring, or against Bill Waring either with or without the lovely Lila. Juries don't give a lot for an alibi which turns on a doctor's opinion that a man had been dead for an hour instead of twenty-five minutes or so, and I have quite an idea that a defence based on sleep-walking might fail to touch a chord. Then there's the Professor. He might have told his tale to some very unbelieving ears if Frederick hadn't prepared the way. No, the bouquet is rightfully yours—'The laurel and the violet and the rose—Fame, modesty, and sweet affection's flower,' as Lord Tennyson so appositely remarks."

Miss Silver regarded him with indulgent reproof.

"I do not recall the passage."

Since Frank Abbott had just evolved it out of his inner consciousness, this did not surprise him. He murmured something about "one of the lesser known poems," and was in some haste to change the subject.

"What I could bear is to know something more about the activities of our Mr. Haile. I've got an idea there may be an eel under that rock, as they say in France, or a nigger in the woodpile, if you prefer the American version. We don't seem to have one of our own, which may be due to (a) our native honesty, or (b) our beautiful unsuspicious natures. If you plump for (b), I fail to qualify. I nourish a fairly strong suspicion that Haile knows more than he will ever give away. There may have been a compromised lady, or there may not, but I don't believe that was what Marsham was hinting at. What do you think?"

He passed up his cup as he spoke. Miss Silver attended in thoughtful silence to its replenishing.

It was not until she had handed it back that she said,

"I think there is something—not very much perhaps, but still something—that would account for Marsham's words. There is of course no proof, but it is my belief that Mr. Haile intended to make a further appeal to his cousin that night. It is possible that he intended something more. We shall never know. I think he left his room after Mr. Grey saw him there, and I believe he was seen by Marsham. We do not know whether he actually entered the study and found his cousin dead. If he did so, he would, I think, have acted as we may suppose he did act. He would not wish to be the one who discovered the body. He may have known that he would benefit largely under Sir Herbert's will. He may have suspected that there would be people in the house who knew that he had come to ask his cousin for a loan, and that it had been refused. He would certainly be aware that his financial position would not bear scrutiny. He had, therefore, very good reasons for not immediately giving the alarm. I think he would return to his room and remain there until he either heard Lila Dryden open her door, or, more probably, Mr. Adrian Grey come out upon the landing. It would be of the highest importance for him to know what was going on, but it would not do for him to risk being seen, which would account for some slight delay in his following Mr. Grey. This would bring him on the scene at the time when, as we know, he entered the study. After that he had every opportunity to

341

display his zeal, his family feeling, and his presence of mind."

Frank nodded.

"If it was an act, it was a very good one."

Miss Silver sipped her tea.

"It would not need to be, as you put it, an act. Mr. Haile has certain qualities. He displayed them. I do not wish to imply that he had any guilty knowledge to conceal. I think he may genuinely have suspected Lila Dryden for a time. Later he must have had his suspicions about Marsham. I do not think it would be fair to put it more strongly than that. Human nature is a strange mixture. As Lord Tennyson so truly says, 'How many among us at this very hour Do forge a lifelong trouble for ourselves By taking true for false, or false for true!' In Mr. Haile, I think, we may be particularly aware of this mixture. He is not a very scrupulous man. I fear that his morals are lax. He has an equable temper, and some kind impulses. He is, for example, settling an extremely generous sum of money upon Miss Whitaker and her child."

"And pray how do you come to know that?"

Miss Silver coughed in a deprecating manner.

"I ventured to approach him on her behalf. She has acted very wrongly. She came very near the commission of a terrible crime—'Jealousy is cruel as the grave.' But Sir Herbert had not treated her rightly. He had forced her into a position which any woman might find intolerable, and it was certainly his duty to have provided for his child."

"And Haile played up?"

"He responded in a most gratifying manner," said Miss Silver demurely. "He is also caring for Mrs. Marsham. She will, I understand, remain with him."

Frank Abbott burst out laughing.

"He may have a kind heart, but sticking to Mrs. Marsham seems rather to suggest an appreciative palate! I'm told that her cooking has to be tasted to be believed—one of those beautiful dreams that have almost vanished from a utilitarian world. Yes, I think the palate has it—with perhaps a strong dash of self-interest. He might want to give Marsham an inducement to hold his tongue. The poor devil is for it anyway, and he knows it, so he has nothing to gain by spattering Haile, and he may have something to lose—if Haile is going to look after his wife. Not very much in it, but 'The little more, and how much it is! And the little less, and what worlds away!' as Browning has it."

Miss Silver set down her cup.

"Yes—there is that mixture of motives. It is pleasanter to turn to others. Lila Dryden will be safe and happy with Mr. Grey. I suspect that her money is all gone, but he has a modest competence, and country life will be good for her."

There was a sarcastic gleam in Frank Abbott's eye.

"I don't envy Grey the job. Perpetual nursemaid to a perpetual child!"

Miss Silver smiled.

"It is not a role for which you are suited, but Mr.

Grey will be happy in it. As for Miss Fortescue and Mr. Waring—"

"Oh—are they to be happy too?"

"I hope so. They have invited me to their wedding. It will be very quiet indeed. Just a few intimate friends."

"I shall fish for an invitation. Why, I almost arrested him. A unique and unforgettable bond! I suppose he wouldn't like me to be best man on the strength of it? And do you give the bride away? As fairy godmother I think you should."

Miss Silver shook her head reprovingly, but she smiled.

"My dear Frank, you really do talk great nonsense," she said.

THE END